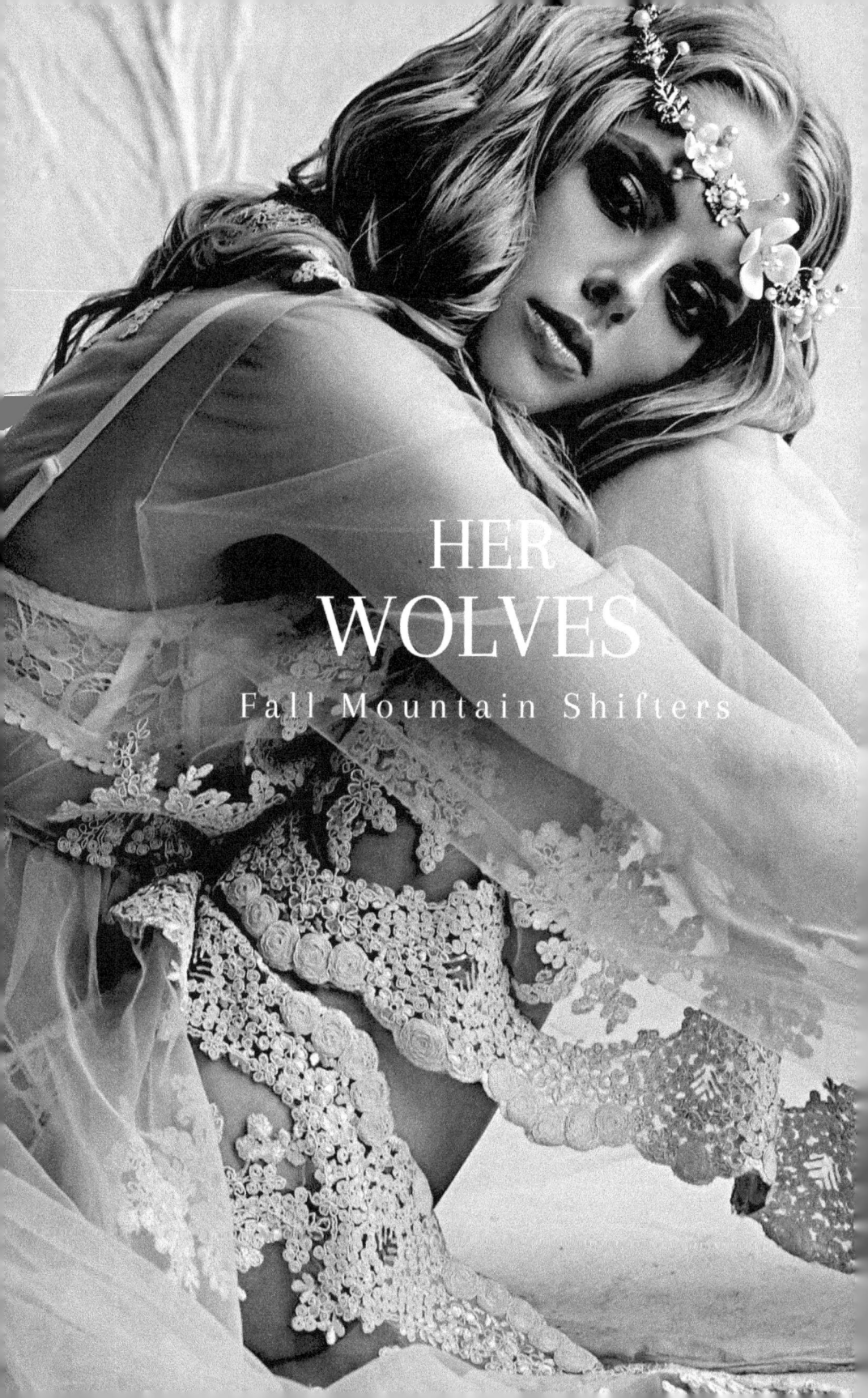

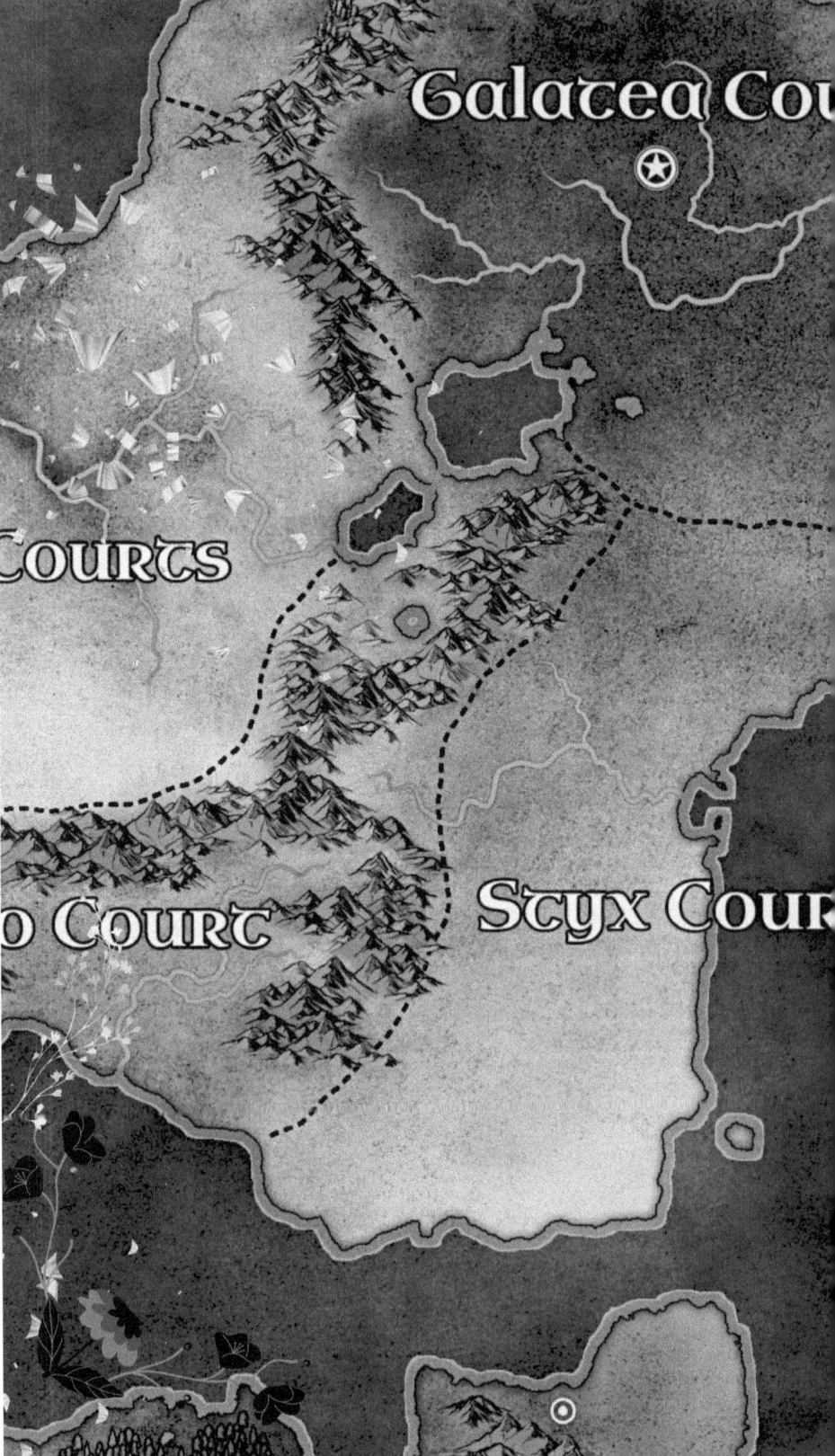

Her Guardians Series

Her Fate Series

Protected By Dragons Series

Lost Time Academy Series

The Demon Academy Series

Dark Angel Academy Series

Shadowborn Academy Series

Dark Fae Paranormal Prison Series

Saved By Pirates Series

The Marked Series

Holly Oak Academy Series

The Alpha Brothers Series

A Demon's Fall Series

The Familiar Empire Series

From The Stars Series

The Forest Pack Series

The Secret Gods Prison Series

The Rejected Mate Series

Fall Mountain Shifters Series

Royal Reapers Academy Series

The Everlasting Curse Series

Her Wolves © 2021 G. Bailey
All Rights Reserved.

This is a work of fiction. Names, characters, places, and incidents either are the products of the author's imagination or are used fictitiously. Any resemblance to actual persons, living or dead, businesses, companies, events, or locales is entirely coincidental and formed by this author's imagination. No part of this book may be reproduced or used in any manner without the express written permission of the publisher except for the use of brief quotations in a book review.
Cover Design by Rebecca Frank
Edited by Polished Perfection
Artwork by MageonDuty

✼ Created with Vellum

*Some people are born with a million stories in their minds.
This is one of mine.*

Contents

Description   xvii

CHAPTER 1   1
CHAPTER 2   10
CHAPTER 3   18
CHAPTER 4   25
CHAPTER 5   30
CHAPTER 6   36

CHAPTER 7   45
Ragnar Fall   45

CHAPTER 8   50
CHAPTER 9   62
CHAPTER 10   68
CHAPTER 11   78

CHAPTER 12   95
Silas Fall   95

CHAPTER 13   99
CHAPTER 14   111

CHAPTER 15   124
Ragnar Fall   124

CHAPTER 16   129
CHAPTER 17   144
CHAPTER 18   149
CHAPTER 19   168
CHAPTER 20   179
CHAPTER 21   189
CHAPTER 22   196
CHAPTER 23   206

CHAPTER 24	212
Author's Note:	219
Other Books by G. Bailey	221
About the Author	223

Part I

Description	271
1. BONUS READ OF ALPHA HELL… *Lilith Thornblood*	273
CHAPTER 2 *Lilith Thornblood*	285
Lilith Thornblood	285
CHAPTER 3 *Lilith Thornblood*	291
Lilith Thornblood	291
CHAPTER 4 *Lilith Thornblood*	300
Lilith Thornblood	300
CHAPTER 5 *Lilith Thornblood*	312
Lilith Thornblood	312
Description	319

I knew nothing about mates until the alpha rejected me...
Growing up in one of the biggest packs in the world, I have my life planned out for me from the second I turn eighteen and find my true mate in the moon ceremony.
Finding your true mate gives you the power to share the shifter energy they have, given to the males of the pack by the moon goddess herself. The power to shift into a wolf.
But for the first time in the history of our pack, the new alpha is mated with a nobody. A foster kid living in the pack's orphanage with no ancestors or power to claim.
Me.
After being brutally rejected by my alpha mate, publicly humiliated and thrown away into the sea, the dark wolves of the Fall Mountain Pack find me.
They save me. The four alphas. The ones the world fears because of the darkness they live in.
In their world? Being rejected is the only way to join their pack. The only way their lost and forbidden god gives them the power to shift without a mate.

I spent my life worshipping the moon goddess, when it turns out my life always belonged to another...

This is a full-length reverse harem romance novel full of sexy alpha males, steamy scenes, a strong heroine and a lot of sarcasm. Intended for 17+ readers. This is a trilogy.

Chapter One

"Don't hide from us, little pup. Don't you want to play with the wolves?"

Beta Valeriu's voice rings out around me as I duck under the staircase of the empty house, dodging a few cobwebs that get trapped in my long blonde hair. Breathlessly, I sink to the floor and wrap my arms around my legs, trying not to breathe in the thick scent of damp and dust. Closing my eyes, I pray to the moon goddess that they will get bored with chasing me, but I know better. No goddess is going to save my ass tonight. Not when I'm being hunted by literal wolves.

I made a mistake. A big mistake. I went to a party in the pack, like all my other classmates at the beta's house, to celebrate the end of our schooling and, personally for me, turning eighteen. For some tiny reason, I thought I could be normal for one night. Be like them.

And not just one of the foster kids the pack keeps alive because of the laws put in place by a goddess no one has seen in hundreds of years. I should have known the betas in training would get drunk and decide chasing me for another one of their "fun" beatings would be a good way to prove themselves.

Wiping the blood from my bottom lip where one of them caught me in the forest with his fist, I stare at my blood-tipped fingers in a beam of moonlight shining through the broken panelled wall behind me.

I don't know why I think anyone is going to save me. I'm nothing to them, the pack, or to the moon goddess I pray to every night like everyone in this pack does.

The moon goddess hasn't saved me from shit.

Heavy footsteps echo closer, changing from crunching leaves to hitting concrete floor, and I know they are in the house now. A rat runs past my leg, and I nearly scream as I jolt backwards into a loose metal panel that vibrates, the metal smacking against another piece and revealing my location to the wolves hunting me.

Crap.

My hands shake as I climb to my feet and slowly step out into the middle of the room as Beta Valeriu comes in with his two sidekicks, who stumble to his side. I glance around the room, seeing the staircase is broken and there is an enormous gap on the second floor. It looks burnt out from a fire, but there is no other exit. I'm well and truly in trouble now. They stop in an intimidating line, all three of them muscular and jacked up enough to knock a car over. Their black hair is all the same shade, likely because they are all cousins, I'm sure, and they have deeply tanned skin that doesn't match how pale my skin is. Considering I'm a foster kid, I could have at least gotten the same looks as them, but oh no, the moon goddess gave me bright blonde hair that never stops growing fast and freckly pale skin to stand out. I look like the moon comparing itself to the beauty of the sun with everyone in my pack.

Beta Valeriu takes a long sip of his drink, his eyes flashing green, his wolf making it clear he likes the hunt. Valeriu is the newest beta, taking over from his father, who recently retired at two hundred years of age and gave the role to his son willingly. But Valeriu is a dick. Simple as. He might be good-looking, like most of the five betas are, but each one of them lacks a certain amount of brain cells. The thing is, wolves don't need to be smart to be betas, they just need the right bloodline and to kill when the alpha clicks his fingers.

All wolves like to hunt and kill. And damn, I'm always the hunted in this pack.

"You know better than to run from us, little Mairin. Little Mary the lamb who runs from the wolf," he sing songs the last part, taking a slow step forward, his shoe grating across the dirt under his feet. Always the height jokes with this tool. He might be over six foot, and sure, my five foot three height isn't intimidating, but has no one heard the phrase *small but deadly*?

Even if I'm not even a little deadly. "Who invited you to my party?"

"The entire class in our pack was invited," I bite out.

He laughs, the crisp sound echoing around me like a wave of frost. "We both know you might be in this pack, but that's only because of the law about killing female children. Otherwise, our alpha would have ripped you apart a long time ago."

Yeah, I know the law. The law that states female children cannot be killed because of the lack of female wolves born into the pack. There is roughly one female to five wolves in the pack, and it's been that way for a long time for who knows what reason. So, when they found me in the forest at twelve, with no memories and nearly dead, they had to take me in and save my life.

A life, they have reminded me daily, has only been given to me because of that law. The law doesn't stop the alpha from treating me like crap under his shoe or beating me close to death for shits and giggles. Only me, though. The other foster kid I live with is male, so he doesn't get the "special" attention I do. Thankfully.

"We both know you can't kill me or beat me bad enough to attract attention without the alpha here. So why don't you just walk away and find some poor dumbass girl to keep you busy at the party?" I blurt out, tired of all this. Tired of never saying what I want to these idiots and fearing the alpha all the time. A bitter laugh escapes Valeriu's mouth as his eyes fully glow this time. So do his friends', as I realise I just crossed a line with my smart-ass mouth.

My foster carer always said my mouth would get me into trouble.

Seems he is right once again.

A threatening growl explodes from Beta Valeriu's chest, making all the hairs on my arms stand up as I take a step back just as he shifts. I've seen it a million times, but it's always amazing and terrifying at the same time. Shifter energy, pure dark forest green magic, explodes around his body as he changes shape. The only sound in the room is his clicking bones and my heavy, panicked breathing as I search for a way out of here once again, even though I know it's pointless.

I've just wound up a wolf. A beta wolf, one of the most powerful in our pack.

Great job, Irin. Way to stay alive.

The shifter magic disappears, leaving a big white wolf in the space where Valeriu was. The wolf towers over me, like most of them do, and its head is huge enough to eat me with one bite. Just as he steps forward to jump, and I brace myself for something painful, a shadow of a man jumps down from the broken slats above me, landing with a thump. Dressed in a white cloak over jeans and a shirt, my foster carer completely blocks me from Valeriu's view, and I sigh in relief.

"I suggest you leave before I teach you what an experienced, albeit retired, beta wolf can do to a young pup like yourself. Trust me, it will hurt, and our alpha will look the other way."

The threat hangs in the air, spoken with an authority that Valeriu could never dream of having in his voice at eighteen years old. The room goes silent, filled with thick tension for a long time before I hear the wolf running off, followed by two pairs of footsteps moving quickly. My badass foster carer slowly turns around, lowering his hood and brushing his long grey hair back from his face. Smothered in wrinkles, Mike is ancient, and to this day, I have no clue why he offered to work with the foster kids of the pack. His blue eyes remind me of the pale sea I saw once when I was twelve. He always dresses like a Jedi from the human movies, in long cloaks and swords clipped to his hips that look like lightsabres as they glow with magic, and he tells me this is his personal style.

His name is even more human than most of the pack names that get regularly overused. My name, which is the only thing I know about my past thanks to a note in my hand, is as uncommon as it gets. According to an old book on names, it means Their Rebellion, which makes no sense. Mike is apparently a normal human name, and from the little interaction I've had with humans through their technology, his name couldn't be more common.

"You are extremely lucky my back was playing up and I went for a walk, Irin," he sternly comments, and I sigh.

"I'm sorry," I reply, knowing there isn't much else I can say at this point. "The mating ceremony is tomorrow, and I wanted one night of being normal. I shouldn't have snuck out of the foster house."

"No, you should not have when your freedom is so close," he counters and reaches up, gently pinching my chin with his fingers and turning my head to the side. "Your lip is cut, and there is considerable bruising to your cheek. Do you like being beaten by those pups?"

"No, of course not," I say, tugging my face away, still tasting my blood in my mouth. "I wanted to be normal! Why is that so much to ask?"

"Normal is for humans and not shifters. It is why they gave us the United Kingdom and Ireland and then made walls around the islands to stop us from getting out. They want normal, and we need nothing more than what is here: our pack," he begins, telling me what I already know. They agreed three hundred years ago we would take this part of earth as our own, and the humans had the rest. No one wanted interbreeding, and this was the best way to keep peace. So the United Kingdom's lands were separated into four packs. One in England, one in Wales, one in Scotland and one in Ireland. Now there are just two packs, thanks to the shifter wars: the Ravensword Pack that is my home, who worship the moon goddess, and then the Fall Mountain Pack, who owns Ireland, a pack we are always at war with. Whoever they worship, it isn't our goddess, and everything I know about them suggests they are brutal. Unfeeling. Cruel.

Which is exactly why I've never tried to leave my pack to go there. It might be shit here, but at least it's kind of safe and I have a future. Of sorts.

"Do you think it will be better for me when I find my mate tomorrow?" I question…not that I want a mate who will control me with his shifter energy. But it means I will shift into a wolf, like every female can when they are mated, and I've always wanted that.

Plus, a tiny part of me wants to know who the moon goddess herself has chosen for me. The other half of my soul. My true mate. Someone who won't see me as the foster kid who has no family, and will just want me.

Mike looks down at me, and something unreadable crosses his eyes. He turns away and starts walking out of the abandoned house, and I jog to catch up with him. Snowflakes drop into my blonde hair as we head through the forest, back to the foster home, the place I will finally leave one way or another tomorrow. I pull my leather jacket around my chest, over my brown T-shirt for warmth. My torn and worn out jeans are soaked with snow after a few minutes of walking, the snow becoming thicker with every minute. Mike is silent as we walk past the rocks that mark the small pathway until we get to the top of the hill that overlooks the main pack city of Ravensword.

Towering buildings line the River Thames that flows through the middle of the city. The bright lights make it look like a reflection of the stars in the sky, and the sight is beautiful. It might be a messed up place, but I can't help but admire it. I remember the first time I saw the city from here, a few days after I was found and healed. I remember thinking I had woken up from hell to see heaven, but soon I learnt heaven was too nice of a word for this place. The night is silent up here, missing the usual noise of the people in the city, and I silently stare down wondering why we have stopped.

"What do you see when you look at the city, Irin?"

I blow out a long breath. "Somewhere I need to escape."

I don't see his disappointment, but I easily feel it.

"I see my home, a place with darkness in its corners but so much light. I see a place even a foster wolf with no family or ancestors to call on can find happiness tomorrow," he responds. "Stop looking at the stars for your escape, Irin, because tomorrow you will find your home in the city you are trying so hard to see nothing but darkness in."

He carries on walking, and I follow behind him, trying to do what he has asked, but within seconds my eyes drift up to the stars once again.

Because Mike is right, I am always looking for my way to escape, and I always will. I wasn't born in this pack, and I came from outside the walls that have been up for hundreds of years. That's the only explanation for how they found me in a forest with nothing more than a small glass bottle in my hand and a note with my name on it. No one knows how that is possible, least of all me, but somehow I'm going to figure it out. I have to.

CHAPTER TWO

"Wake up. You have a book on your face."

Blinking my eyes open, I see nothing but blurry lines until I lift the book I was reading off my face and rub my nose. Damn, I must have fallen asleep reading again. I close the human-written romance book about demons at an academy and turn my gaze to where my foster brother is holding the door open. Jesper Perdita has dark brown, overgrown hair that falls around his face and shoulders, and his clothes are all a little too big for him and torn in places because they are hand-me-downs. But he smiles every single damn day, and for that alone, I love him. At just eight, he acts the same age as me thanks to losing his family a year ago and having no relatives offer to take him in. I don't care that we aren't blood-related, somehow I'm always going to be here for him, because he hasn't had a childhood any more than I have. We are foster kids in a pack that hates our very existence, and they make damn sure we know about it.

The fact they keep him alive is just because one day he might have a powerful wolf when he turns sixteen. If he doesn't, he won't have any family to save him from what happens next. I'm a little luckier in the sense I will find a mate, every female always does at the mating ceremony in the year they turn eighteen, and my mate will have no choice but to keep me alive. Even if he hates who I am, our fate is linked from the second the bond is shown.

"What time is it, Scrubs?" I ask, needing to pull my thoughts from the ceremony to anything else before I freak out. He twitches his nose at my nickname. That came from how many times he needed to scrub his face of dirt and mud every single day. He is the messiest kid I've ever seen, and it's awesome. I want a different future for him, one where he could have the same last name as everyone in the pack other than the foster kids. We are given the last name Perdita, which means *lost* in Latin, because we are lost in every sense of the word.

Everyone else in the pack shares the same last name as the pack alpha. Ravensword.

"Six in the morning. We have to leave for the ceremony in an hour, and Mike said you need to bathe and wear the dress in the bathroom," he answers. He looks down, nervously kicking his foot. "Mike said something about brushing your hair so it doesn't look like a bat's nest."

I snort and run my hand through my blonde hair. Sure...I might not have brushed it a lot, but the unruly waves don't want to be tamed.

"I won't go, get a mate and never come back. You know that, right?" I ask him, sliding myself out of my warm bed and into the much colder room. Snowflakes line my bedroom window that is slightly cracked open, and I walk over, pushing it shut before looking back at Jesper. He meets my gaze with his bright blue eyes, but he says nothing.

"Whoever finds out you're their mate is going to want you to start fresh. Without this place and me following you around. I might be eight, but I'm not stupid," he replies. Floorboards creak under my feet as I walk over to him and pull him in for a hug, resting my head on top of his. The truth is, I can't promise him much. The males in mating have control over the females, and to resist that control is painful, so I'm told. That's why the moon goddess is the only one who can choose a mate for us, because if it went wrong, it would be a disaster for all involved.

"If my mate does, then I will figure out a way to get him to let me see you. The moon goddess will not give me a mate I am going to hate. All mates love each other," I tell him what I've heard.

"I don't like goodbyes," he replies, pulling away from me. "So I won't come with you today. I won't."

"I get it, kid," I say as he walks to the stairs. He never looks back, and I'm proud of him, even if it hurts to watch him make another choice that only adults should have to make. I head back into my small bedroom, which has a single bed with white sheets and a squeaky mattress, and one chest of drawers. I grab my towels and head down the stairs to the only bathroom in the old, very quirky house. The bathroom is through the first door in the corridor, and I shut the door behind me, not bothering to switch the light on as it is bright enough in here from the light pouring through the thin windows at the top of the room. Peeling dolphin-covered wallpaper lines every wall, and the porcelain claw-foot bathtub is right in the middle of the room. A cream toilet and a row of worn white cabinets line the other side, with a sink in the middle of them. Hanging on the back of the door is the dress I have dreaded to see and yet wanted to because it's the nicest thing I am likely ever going to wear.

The mating dress is a custom-made dress for every woman in the pack, paid for by the alpha to celebrate the joy-filled day, and each is made to worship the moon goddess herself. Mine is no different. My dress is pure silk and softer than I could have imagined as I run my fingers over it. The hem of the dress is lined with sparkling white crystals, and the top part of the dress is tight around the chest and stomach. The bottom half falls like a ballgown, heavier than the top and filled with dozens of silk layers that shimmer as I move them.

As I stare at the dress, the urge to run away fills me. The urge to run to the sea and swim to the wall to see if there is any way to get out. Any way to escape the choices I have been given in life.

Mike was right, I can't see the light in the pack, because the darkness smothers too much. It takes too much.

I step away until the back of my legs hit the cold bathtub, and I sink down to the floor, wrapping my arms around my legs and resting my head on top of my knees.

One way or another, the mating ceremony is going to change everything for me.

"Do hurry, Irin. We have a four-hour drive, and this is not a day you should be late like every other day of your life!" Mike shouts through the door, banging on it twice.

"On it!" I shout back, crawling to my feet and pushing

all thoughts of trying to escape to the back of my mind. It was a stupid idea, anyway. The pack lands are heavily guarded, and they would scent me a mile off. After a quick bath to wipe the dirt off me and wash my hair, I brush my wavy hair until it falls to my waist in bouncy locks, even when I know the wind will whip them up into a storm as soon as I'm outside. The dress is easy to slip on, and I wipe the mirror of the steam to look at myself after pulling my boots on.

My green eyes, the colour of moss mixed with specks of silver, look brighter this morning against my pale skin, framed by blonde, almost golden, hair. I look as terrified as I feel about today, but this is what the moon goddess wants, and she is our ancestor. The first wolf to howl at the moon and receive the power to shift.

She will not let me down today.

I nod at myself, like a total loser, and walk out of the bathroom to find Mike and my other foster brother waiting for me. Mike huffs and walks away, mumbling something about a lamb to the slaughter under his breath, and I look at Daniel instead. His brown eyes are wide as he looks at me from head to toe, likely realising for the first time the best friend he has is actually a girl. He is used to me in jeans or baggy clothes, following him through the muddy forest and not giving a crap if every single one of my nails is broken by the end.

And I never wear dresses. Not like this. Daniel runs his hand through his muddy-brown hair that needs a cut before he smiles.

"Shit, you look different, Irin," he comments with a thick

voice. Daniel is one year older than me, and when he was tested for his power last year, he was found to be an extremely powerful wolf. He is next in line to be a beta if anyone dies, which would be a big thing for a foster kid to be a beta. Either way, he is free of this place, and who knows, he might even be my mate. A small part of me hopes so because Daniel is my best friend, and it would be so easy to spend my life with him. I don't know about romance, as I have never seen him like that. He is good-looking in a rugged way, so I guess we could figure it out.

"Nervous about today?" I ask him, as this is his second mating ceremony, and it's likely he might find a mate. It's usually the second or third ceremony where males find their mates, but for females, it's always the first.

He clears his throat and meets my eyes. "Yeah, but who wouldn't be?"

"Me. I'm totally cool with it," I sarcastically reply. He laughs and walks over, pulling me into a tight hug like he always does. This time, I hear his wolf rumble in his chest, the vibrations shaking down my arms.

"If you're mated to a tool, I'll help you kill him and hide the body. Got it?" he tells me, and I laugh at his joke until he leans back, placing his hands on my shoulder. He moves one of his hands and tips my chin up so I'm looking at him. "I'm not joking, Irin. I don't care who it is, they aren't fucking around with you."

"Mates are always a perfect match," I reply, twitching my nose. "Why would you think—"

He lowers his voice as he cuts me off. "You don't live in the city like I do, and I can tell you now, mates are not a perfect match. Not even close. The moon goddess...well, I don't know what she is doing, but you need to be cautious. Very cautious because of your background."

"Why didn't you tell me this before?" I demand.

He shrugs. "Guess I didn't want you to overthink it and try to run. I can't save you from what they'd do if you ran, but I can protect you from a shitty mate. I.e., threaten to break every bone in his body if he hurts you."

"Daniel—" I'm cut off as Mike comes back into the corridor and clears his throat.

"Get in the car, now. It looks bad on me when we are late!" he huffs, holding the front door open. Daniel uses his charming smile to make Mike's lips twitch in laughter as I hurry to the front door and step out into the freezing cold snow. It sinks into my dress and shoes, but I welcome the icy stillness to the air, forcing me to stop over worrying for a second.

"Always daydreaming, this one," Mike mutters as he passes me, talking to Daniel at his side. "Her eyes are going to get stuck looking up in the clouds one day."

"At least I'd be seeing a pretty view for the rest of my life," I call after Mike as I hurry after them down the path to the old car waiting by the road. We don't use cars often, only today and travelling to funerals is permitted, mostly because the cars are old junk that make a lot of noise and take up fuel. Daniel pulls the yellow rusty door to the car open, and I slide inside to the opposite seat before doing up my seatbelt as Daniel and Mike get in the car. Mike drives and Daniel sits next to me rather than shotgun.

About ten minutes into the drive, I realise why Daniel sits

next to me as my hands shake and he covers my hand with his.

Please, moon goddess, choose Daniel or someone decent. I don't want to become a mate murderer in my first year as a wolf.

CHAPTER THREE

Flickering, multicoloured lights drift across my eyes as I wake up, finding my head lying on Daniel's broad shoulder, his arm wrapped around my waist, and it's so unexpected, I jolt up, almost hitting my head against Daniel's chin. He moves super fast, with reflexes his wolf gives him, and just misses my head. I slide out of Daniel's arm, and he clears his throat, straightening up on his seat and running a hand through his thick hair. Rather than talk about that awkward moment, I turn and look out the window, frost stuck to its edges, to see we are driving down by a cliff that overlooks the glittering sea between Wales and Ireland. I've been to this place once when I was fifteen on a school trip to see where a mating ceremony is held and what we should expect for our future.

If anywhere in this world made me believe in magic, it was this place. A place that has been in my dreams for so many years. For most wolves, this is the place they will meet their wolves and start their new life. For me, it's a way of escaping my past and finally finding out what the moon goddess wants for me. It can't be this life I have, the torture at the hands of pack leaders, the pain of being an outcast with no family.

I catch Mike's eyes in the middle mirror and see a little sadness in them like always, because he has heard and seen all the horrors the pack has forced on me throughout the years. Protecting me was something he has struggled to do, because, at the end of the day, he couldn't be everywhere.

"Nearly here, aren't we?" Daniel interrupts my thoughts, and I'm thankful for it. That's a dark memory lane to go down. "They should let you wear a coat over the dress, it's freezing."

"I've never cared about the cold," I remind him, gazing back out of the window as we pull up in the gravelled area by the cliff. Several groups of people are standing around or walking down the stone cliff pathway to the beach that is marked with fire lanterns on wooden poles every few metres, making the walk look eerie and frightening.

"You can do this, Irin. You've been brave ever since you were found in the woods, half-starved, dirty and alone. Look at you now," Mike tells me as he turns the car off, meeting my line of sight through the mirror. "You are a woman this pack will be honoured to have. Now hold your head high, put the past away and show them. Show them who you are, Irin."

My cheeks feel red and hot as I wipe a few tears away and force my hands to stop shaking as I grab the handle of the door. I can't tell him, not without my voice catching, that I will miss Mike and his words of wisdom. His kindness and general attitude towards life, the ways he has shown me how to be strong even at my lowest points. Pulling the door handle open, I step out onto the lightly snow-covered ground, and the cold, brittle sea air slams into me, making me shiver from head to toe. I can taste the salt in the air and smell the water of the sea and hear it crashing against the sand below us. The wind whips my hair around my face as Daniel walks past me, looking back once before he walks down the path to join the other men at the beach where they have to stand. Mike moves to my side, and we simply wait as all the men leave for the path down to the beach, while the women, us, wait at the top for our time to descend.

Some parents linger for a while before they walk to the edge of the cliff in the distance where there's a massive crowd of spectators waiting to watch the magic of the mating ceremony. Mike leaves eventually to join them, never glancing back at me. The girls all gather, pretending I don't exist like they always have done since I turned up at their school. A small, tiny part of me hurts that not a single one of the forty-two girls in my class who have known me six years even looks my way.

I'm invisible to them, to my pack, to everyone.

Rubbing my chest, I gulp when the bell rings. A single, beautiful bell ring fills the air to start the beginning of the mating ceremony, and tension rings through the air as everyone goes silent. Like ducks in a row, the women all line up, and of course I move right to the back, behind Lacey Ravensword, someone who has never even looked my way, even though she is considered a low potential mate because of her father trying to run away from the pack, and he was killed when she was a toddler. Even she, with her family basically betrayers to the alpha himself, is higher ranked than I am. She flicks her dark brown hair over her shoulder, glancing back at me and sneering once with her beautiful face before turning away.

The cold seeps into my bones by the time the line moves enough for me to walk, and my legs feel stiff with every step, the nerves making me feel so close to passing out right here and now. Every single step off the cliff and down the path feels torturous until I see the beach.

Then everything fades into nothing but pure magic. In the centre of the sandy yellow beach is a massive archway, sculpted into two wolves with their noses touching where they meet in the middle. The wolves are so high the tips of their ears touch the heavy clouds above us, and icicles line the grooves of the fur on their snow-tipped backs. In the centre of the archway, one of the first females steps into the pool of water under the archway, sinking all the way under completely before rising and swimming slowly through the archway. The water suddenly glows green, lit up with magic from the moon goddess herself.

The young lady with long black hair climbs out of the pool on the other side, her entire body glowing green with magic, and the magic slowly slips from her skin, turning itself into a swirling ball of energy and shooting away from her. It flies into the crowd of wolf shifter men waiting on the other side, all of them too hard to really see from here, and there are cheers when the mate or mates are no doubt found. I can't see who the female goes to as the cliff winds around, but I hope she is happy with her new mates. Daniel's warnings about mates not always being happy fills my mind, making me more nervous than ever before, because what if he is right? What if I end up with a mate who I hate and he hates me?

I trip on a small rock, slamming down onto the path and hissing as my hand is cut. I look up as Lacey turns back, and then she just laughs, leaving me on my knees on the path as she carries on behind the queue. Tears fill my eyes that I refuse to let fall, and I stand up, seeing my dress is now dirty with sand and mud, and I lift my hand to see blood dripping down my palm to my wrist from a long cut. Sighing, I close my palm and let my blood drop against the wet sand as I know I have to carry on down this path.

What feels like forever later, I get to the beach and look across to see Lacey waiting behind three other classmates, just as one of them steps into the water. Four left before my fate is decided. I'm tempted to slip my shoes off, to enjoy the feel of the cold sand under my bare feet, but I keep my boots on. I don't want to lose them. I walk over the beach, feeling so many eyes watching and judging me. I refuse to look at the men on the other side, knowing the new alpha will be there, and seeing him brings up so many dark memories. He was just the alpha's son back then, back when we were fifteen and he tricked me by pretending to be my friend.

Now he is the alpha, at only eighteen, after he ripped his father to pieces four months ago. The pack is scared of him, but me?

He terrifies me.

Keeping my eyes down, I only look up to see Lacey step into the water with perfect poise and elegance I could never master in my wildest dreams. She sinks under the water, and it glows bright green, and this close, I can feel the magic like it's pulling me towards it. The water is enchanting, and I can't take my eyes off it until the glow fades, and I glance up to see the magic surrounding Lacey as she stands on the other side of the pool. The magic leaves her body and gathers in a ball, before slamming left and straight into the chest of one of the men near the front.

Not just any man.

Daniel.

He stands in pure shock, looking at the green magic bouncing around his skin before he looks up at Lacey, and then he turns to me. Our eyes meet, and silently I try to tell him it's okay.

Even when it feels like a storm has just started in my chest and that storm is going to take every bit of hope from me.

Daniel doesn't move for a long time, and Lacey follows his gaze back to me, her eyes narrowing as I quickly look away and back to the water. Out of the corner of my eye, I see Lacey walk to Daniel, and he places his hand on her back, leading her away from the crowd and towards the pathway to the crowds of people waiting at the top of the cliff to celebrate with them. To cheer about their mating.

And now it's my turn.

Everything is silent, even the violent sea and snow-filled sky seem to still for this moment as I take a step forward and my foot sinks into the warm water. It instantly glows green, so bright it hurts my eyes, and pulls me in, my body almost betraying my fear-filled mind as I sink into the water until my head falls under. The green light becomes blinding as I float in the water, seeing nothing but light, until a voice fills my mind.

"You are my chosen, Irin. My chosen."

Something appears in my hand as I'm pushed up to the surface, and I gasp as I rise out of the water on the other side, almost stumbling to my feet on the sand, seeing the green magic swirling around my body in thick waves. It bounces, almost violently, in swirls and waves before pulling away from me into a giant ball of green magic, much bigger than anyone else's.

Why the hell do I have to stand out in this of all things? With so many people watching? I can't bear to look or hear anyone as I watch the sphere of magic spin in the air before shooting across the sand right into the man in the middle of the pack.

A man of my nightmares.

A man who took my innocence, crushed it, and made me fear him.

The alpha of my pack.

CHAPTER FOUR

The silence is damning. Damning and hollow as I stare into the unfeeling hazel eyes of the wolf shifter who is apparently my fated mate. An alpha doesn't share his mate, so this is the only man in the entire world who the moon goddess believes I should be with. And he is a monster. The alpha doesn't move as green magic crackles around his body, picking up his fur cloak that hangs off his large shoulders. Thick black hair falls to his shoulders in a straight line, not a strand out of place, and his stern face is stoic as he looks at me. Water drips down my dress, my wet hair sticking to my shoulders, and all the warmth from the water is gone now. The magic is gone, replaced only with fear for what happens next.

"No."

His single word rings out across the beach to me, the few yards that are between us are like nothing. No. No to the mating? No, it being me the moon goddess chose as the alpha's mate?

I agree with him...hell no. Mating with this excuse of an alpha, a man with no soul and a scar on his chin I caused when

I was fifteen, is a life I would rather not live. Only once have I ever thought about giving up on my life, once on a wintry day like this, caused by the same man I'm looking at right now. This is the second time I have wanted to give up completely.

Whispers and gasps from the crowd of wolves behind him and from the crowds on the cliff finally reach my ears, and I try to block out what they are saying even when some of their words are perfectly heard.

"Her? The alpha's mate? Disgusting!"

"Maybe the moon goddess made a terrible mistake."

"He should kill her and be done with it."

The whispers never stop, and the same thing is chanted as the alpha's eyes bleed from hazel to green, his wolf taking over. Then he takes one step forward towards me, and I itch to run, to turn and leave as fast as I can, but something tells me not to.

Maybe that bit of stubborn pride I have left. Mike always said pride is a bigger killer than any man. I can see his point as my legs refuse to move and I stay still as a deer caught in a wolf's gaze. The alpha walks right up to me, his closeness making me feel sick to my stomach as he grabs my throat and lifts me slightly off the ground. Not enough to strangle me or cut my airways off, but enough to make me gasp, to make me want to struggle. I claw at his arm to get him off, but I'm nothing but a fly buzzing around a cake to him. I can see it in his eyes, his eyes owned by his wolf.

"How did you trick the moon goddess herself into believing a rat like you could ever be an alpha's mate?" he demands, and when I don't answer, he shakes me harshly, tightening his grip for a second. A second enough for me to scream and gasp, coughing on air when he loosens his grip. He shakes his head, his eyes bleeding from green back to hazel. To think I once trusted those hazel eyes, I dreamt about them, I thought he was my real friend.

"I asked you a question, Irin."

"My name is Mairin to you, not Irin. M-my friends call me Irin, Alpha Sylvester Ravensword. Kill me if you're going to do it. I have feared you for so long that you killing me is nothing more than the goddess giving me my wish."

The lie falls from my tongue easily, even if his name does not. The moon goddess never gave me my real wish, my wish I begged her for once, to kill him, the alpha's son, Sylvester Ravensword. Instead, in some twisted version of fate, she made him alpha and me his mate he has waited for. His eyes stay hazel, but in the corners I see the green struggling to take over. He slowly tightens his grip around my neck, and I close my eyes, wanting to see nothing in these last moments. I gasp as I struggle to breathe, instinctively smacking and scratching at his one hand holding me up by the neck. Fear and panic take over, making my eyes pop open just as I'm thrown across the sand. With a slam, I hit the hard sand on my side, and a cracking noise in my arm is followed by incredible pain as I scream.

"Irin!" I hear Daniel shout in the distance, a wolfy and deep noise just before a foot slams into my stomach once. Then twice, then again and again. The pain almost becomes numb when my voice gives out, and the kicks finally stop as I roll onto my back, looking up at Alpha Sylvester as he angrily kicks me one more time before stepping back, rubbing his hands over his face repeatedly.

"No one follows us. If anyone does, I will rip them to shreds," I hear Alpha Sylvester demand, and the noise of wolves fighting nearby mixes with the sound of the waves. A hand digs into my hair and pulls me up as I taste blood in my mouth. Everything is blurry as someone drags me by my hair and arm over sharp rocks that cut into my back and catch on my dress, but part of me detaches from my body, drifting into a world of no pain as I fade in and out of consciousness. Eventually I'm dropped onto grass, and I blink my eyes a few times, coughing on the blood in my mouth and turning my head to the side, every inch of my body hurting so badly the pain threatens to knock me out with every breath. A hand wraps around my throat once more, and I'm lifted into the air, my feet hanging as I struggle to breathe.

"Open your eyes," Alpha Sylvester demands, his fiery breath blowing across my face.

Opening my eyes is harder than I thought it would be, and when I do, I see he is right in front of me.

"I can't kill you, because my wolf will not allow it." He shakes me once. "Die in the sea for your fated mate, Irin. Die like you should have so many years ago, because if the sea does not take you, I will know. I will know, and I will never stop sending wolves to kill you. I have rejected you as my mate, you are not worthy of me, and you never could be. You are nothing."

"Then why does the moon goddess think otherwise?" I whisper back with all the strength I have. I should plead for my life, I should beg and cry, but I just stare at him as his eyes flash with pure anger, and he roars as he lets me go. The wind cannot catch my body as I fly off the cliff, well aware the sea is going to take my life in seconds.

And in those seconds I fall, I still pray to the moon goddess for someone to catch me.

CHAPTER FIVE

"Get the healer ready!" a deep voice demands, nothing more than a groggy sound to my sore ears as I struggle to wake up. Coldness like I've never known controls my body from head to toe, and it's not just cold, I'm soaking wet too. Every inch of my body hurts. Even my eyelids ache as I pull them open to see rocks in front of me. Smooth white rocks. Waves crash in the distance, and I can smell nothing but damp water. Lifting my head, which takes more strength than I thought it would, I see I'm still in my mating ceremony dress, but it's ripped around my stomach, and a large cut snakes down my ribs, hidden under the ripped fabric of my dress. My bare feet are stuck in the wet sand, and I'm curled up in a space between a group of rocks like the sea threw me here.

Flashes of memories attack me quickly. The sea. The mating ceremony. The alpha who was meant to be my mate but instead tried to kill me... How am I alive?

Scuffling of heavy booted feet reminds me I'm not alone, and I jump away from the noise behind me, pivoting to see a man standing on the rock. His silhouette blocks out the light, making all around him glow as I drift my eyes up his body. Thick black trousers cover large thighs, and he has a black shirt tucked into them. The shirt stretches across his large shoulders, large enough to make him a champ at a rugby match if he chose it. Following my eyes up over his golden skin, I suck in a deep breath when I see his face.

He is beautiful in a way men shouldn't be allowed to be. Strong jawline, high cheekbones, perfectly shaped lips and thick black eyelashes that surround clear blue eyes that remind me of a lake—still, in an eerie way that makes you wonder if there is any life below the waters. Black locks of hair that are a little too long, falling just over his eyes when the wind blows, look softer than the silk dress I'm wearing.

No one in my pack ever looked like him. I would have noticed.

The more I stare, the longer I realise he is staring right back at me, like he has seen a ghost. Like I'm familiar to him. Considering where I came from, he might have done. Not that I have a clue where we are. I lean up on my one arm, but I can't see out of the rocks or anything around the man standing over me.

Correction: the wolf. He is watching me like a wolf, that I am certain of. He is too direct, too inhuman like, and all that I need to see now is his eyes glow.

"Do you know me?" I ask, my voice throaty, and I clear it, tasting nothing but thick salt left over from the sea.

The man tilts his head to the side. "Why are you here?"

"I-I was..." I pause because I have no idea where I am, and telling this wolf I'm the alpha's rejected mate might not be the best idea if I'm still in Ravensword lands. He will drag me back to the alpha, who will try to kill me again. No, I can't do that.

"Answer me."

The man's command is clear, ringing with power and frustration. I look up, meeting his eyes once more even when I can't think straight or of a single word to say. Whatever I say is going to get me killed, and I can't help but think I've been given a second chance at life. I should never have survived falling into the sea, not with the injuries I have, not when I passed out, but here I am. Alive.

It's clear the moon goddess has much more planned for me than I know.

When I don't say a word for a long time, he moves. The man moves so quickly, and within seconds he is in my face, leaning over me on the rocks. His nose gently touches mine, my body a mix with fear and curiosity.

"Tell me," he commands once more. "Tell me why you are on the shores of the Fall Mountain Pack, or you will die this very second."

Fall Mountain Pack?

Oh my god... How am I alive and on this island? I know people usually die who try to swim between the islands, but for me to have gotten here unconscious is nothing short of magic. I'm yet to decide what kind of magic, considering all I know about the Fall Mountain Pack is that they are cruel and vicious. That they live in ways most wolves would never do or even think about. They don't trade with the Ravensword Pack, and every attempt at peace has been met with death. We are told they are monsters, and now I'm on their lands.

But truthfully, I'm dead either way. If they send me back, the alpha will kill me, and if I stay here, it's likely they will kill me.

I have nothing to lose by telling this man the truth.

"My name is Mairin Perdita, and I am a rejected mate of the Ravensword Pack," I announce, leaning back against the rocks and curling my legs underneath myself, needing space from his man. His eyes widen, but he doesn't say a word. "The mating ceremony named me as the alpha's mate, and because I am a foster child with no family or worth, he rejected me. After hurting me in anger, he tried to kill me by throwing me off a cliff. How I'm here, alive, is a mystery to me, but I guess I am asking for your help. I'm asking for a damn miracle, because my life has been anything but one."

"I would wager surviving your rejection is a miracle. The sea is a cruel mistress at the best of times, and last night was one of the worst storms seen in years," he finally replies, leaning back, his voice less hostile than it was. "I can always tell when someone is lying to me, and you are not, Mairin Perdita. My name is Alpha Henderson Fall, and I am going to help you."

"You're the alpha?" I whisper in shock and a little fear. It shouldn't surprise me he is so high in rank, just because of how commanding and powerful he comes across as, but it does.

"One of the four," he answers and moves closer. "You are weak, my wolf senses it, and I must carry you. Will you allow me? It is a twenty-minute walk to the lighthouse where there is a healer."

The part of me that hates being touched, especially by

men, makes me want to say no and stubbornly try to climb out of these rocks myself. But I know I can't. Every inch of me hurts, my stomach is bleeding, and my ankle looks swollen. Somehow I have survived the sea, but without help, I will not survive much longer. I nod once, unable to actually agree, and I'm sure my hesitancy shines in my eyes as he comes closer and wraps his arms underneath me before effortlessly picking me up. In order to steady myself, my hands go out around his neck, brushing against a necklace there that is tucked into his shirt. Henderson jumps out of the rocks, and I look around me to see a tall mountain right in front of us, and a small forest lies between the beach and the mountain. The mountain is topped with snow, and several caves look like they have lights inside from this distance. The beach is long with rocky sand and harsh waves that crash against everything they hit, and in the distance, I see a faded blue lighthouse with its bright light turning in circles. Henderson is silent as he jumps off the rocks into the sand and eats up the space between us and the lighthouse with his enormous steps. After a few minutes, I relax my shoulders a little.

"Is it just luck you found me, or do you live around here?" I question.

Henderson looks down at me, his blue eyes hard to read. "What do you know of my pack, Mairin?"

"That you are monsters," I tell him, remembering well how he said he could sense if I was lying.

His lips tilt up into a dazzling smile. "Lies are so easily told to those who live in fear, and your alpha lied, Mairin. We were never the monsters, but our life differs greatly from where you have come from. Here we don't have fated mates, we only mate with who we fall in love with. Wolves are free to date, to explore, to do whatever they want, and the only new wolves we accept into the pack are rejected or lost. We respect loyalty, and we take in those who are nothing to others."

"There have been other rejected mates?" I ask.

His smile falls. "I collect over one wolf a week from this shore. All of them rejected and thrown into the sea because their mate could not convince their wolf to kill them."

"I had no idea," I whisper.

"To answer your question," Henderson states, shifting me a little in his arms, "I do not live here, but I am called to the lighthouse every day to check out who has arrived. If you had lied to me, or if you were someone who just escaped the pack, then I am tasked with ending your life. We do not take in those who desert their pack and family. We want only those who will be loyal."

My heart beats fast in my chest, hearing the sincerity of his voice. He would have killed me. "So you kill for loyalty?"

"No, I kill for my pack," he answers, his tone clarifying that is the last of our conversation, and I rest back, watching the sea and the very outline of the land in the distance, hidden by clouds. All I can think of is Daniel and Jesper, and even Mike. I have to hope they look after each other, because I can't ever go back.

The Ravensword alpha is my mate, and he will do worse than reject me next time, he will have someone kill me.

So I have to make the Fall Mountain Pack my new home, whatever it takes.

Chapter Six

By the time we get to the lighthouse, I'm half falling asleep on Henderson's shoulder while I struggle to keep warm enough to actually sleep. Henderson smells like the strong whiskey drinks Mike always has every Saturday night, mixed in with smoky wood-like scent. His scent is really nice and comforting. It shouldn't be, as I don't know this man from Adam, but a part of me feels like I can trust him.

Or I hit my head in the sea, and I'm going crazy. It's one of the two things.

The light shines through the lighthouse door as Henderson climbs up the dozens of steps towards it, and someone opens it when he is near the top. A skinny little boy with blond hair and blue eyes, about eleven if I'm guessing right, holds the door open for us, and the warmth of the room makes me shiver in a little shock. Four cream fabric sofas make a square in the middle of the room, and a round oak wood coffee table sits in the middle of them with some seashells in a glass vase. One side of the wall is a big open fireplace with a wide oak mantel stretched across the top of it, and the fire is lit, making the room lovely and warm. Resting on the mantel are lots of little jars in a row, filled with white labels. Above them is a clock on the wall, showing its early morning, and there isn't much else in the room.

"What's your name then, dear?" an older-sounding woman asks as she walks down the stairs that curl around the top of the room and end by the door. The woman is dressed in all black, black high-waisted jeans and a black long-sleeved top tucked into them, but she is barefoot, which is odd. Her grey hair is shaped into a neat bun gathered low on the back of her head, and glasses are tucked into her hair, but she pulls them down over her brown eyes. "Place her on the sofa for me, Henderson."

Henderson nods, looking down at me once before carrying me over and gently laying me down. I stay still, nervous and more than a little frightened as she kneels down at the side of the sofa and looks at my stomach before picking up my wrist and pressing her fingers down on the middle of it.

"My name is Healer Saffron Fall, and I promise I'm here to help you, nothing more or less. So, your pulse is weak, you look like your ribs are broken, and you've lost some blood with that wound on your stomach. I need to stitch it as you've clearly never shifted, and it won't heal," she states, tutting once. "Anything else hurt you need me to look at, dear?"

"My name is Mairin, but my friends call me Irin. Thank you for helping me...and my right ankle hurts."

"Hi, Irin!" the little boy exclaims, popping up at the side of Henderson. He grins at me, and I can't help but give him a brief smile back as Saffron looks at my ankle. "My name is Trey Fall!"

"Hello, Trey," I whisper back, and then I cough. Saffron helps me sit up as I can't stop coughing, and hands me a tissue that I cough into for a long time. Blood coats the tissue as I rest back breathless, knowing things are worse than I thought when Saffron looks at me in concern before turning to Henderson. They both walk over to the stairs and start talking in hushed voices, but Trey stays with me, looking awkward and sweet at the same time. He reminds me of Jesper so much.

"It will be okay. Henderson is the nice alpha, and he looks after everyone who needs help," Trey tells me, patting my arm. "You don't have to be scared."

"You're kind, Trey," I reply in a strained voice. "It's nice to meet you."

"We are going to be friends when you're better," he tells me and lowers his voice. "The forbidden god told me."

I furrow my brow, wondering who the hell he is talking about, but I don't have time to ask as Henderson and Saffron come back over to me. Henderson nods at Saffron, and she wraps an arm around Trey, forcing him to the stairs and up to them.

"I'm sick, aren't I? Am I going to die?" I ask Henderson. If he is as nice as Trey claims, then he might tell me the truth.

Henderson shakes his head and rolls the sleeves on his arms up, revealing tattoos. Moons, starting with a full moon, a half-moon and then a crescent moon, are in lines on his inner arms, exactly the same on each side. He closes his eyes, his face strained for a second, and then the tattoos on his arms glow with magic, pure red magic. Nothing like the green magic of the mating pool, the moon goddess magic. This is different but just as amazing and addictive to look at. When Henderson opens his eyes, they aren't glowing green; they are glowing red, and it's almost terrifying to look at. His deep voice comes out as a grumble, almost growl like. "Do you want to live, Mairin?"

"At what cost?" I whisper back, black spots drifting in and out of my vision.

"The only cost for this is becoming your true self and being bound to my pack, to my forbidden god and no one else. You will become ours and heal," he replies, his voice like the devil, luring me into a world I shouldn't cross over into, but I want to.

The forbidden god?

I don't remember saying yes as pain slams into my chest, and I scream, but then Henderson picks me up, placing his hand on the back of my neck, and I feel nothing but magic pour into me. This is nothing like the mating ceremony pool, nothing as kind and relaxing. This magic is powerful and enticing.

I feel each of the markings on my back appear, one by one, until there are four of them from my neck to the middle of my back.

I just know, without looking, they are the moon marks that Henderson has.

"What the fuck are you doing?" a new voice roars, followed by the sound of a door slamming against a wall and cracking.

The magic instantly drops away, and Henderson lets me fall back on the sofa as I gasp, struggling for air. I quickly realise I'm not hurt anymore...in fact, nothing hurts at all. I look down to see the cut on my stomach is gone, the only blood left is what's marking my dress. I crawl back into the corner of the sofa, letting Henderson stand in front of me as I take in the three new wolves in the room. Each of them looks down at me with a mixture of shock and caution, which switches into pure anger from the man in the middle.

The four alphas of the Fall Mountain Pack bleed power and dominance.

It's intimidating and overwhelming.

And familiar in a way I don't understand.

The alpha in the middle is a big man, taller than all four of them, and I would guess over six foot five. His shoulders look big enough for two people to sit on, and his muscular arms stretch the short-sleeved white T-shirt he has on. He has the moon markings around his neck, starting with the full moon at the front, the others I can see going all the way around. His jeans are tight and ripped, and his boots are dripping mud and sand onto the floor. The alpha catches my gaze with his winter grey eyes that remind me of the first-day snow falls and the colour of it. The purest and brightest snow. His short blond hair is a similar colour to mine, just lighter, and it shocks me because I've seen no one with hair like mine before.

"Do I need to repeat myself, brother?" he asks, his deep voice gravelly and downright scary.

Henderson crosses his arms and doesn't say a word, just staring his brother down. Which is a dangerous thing to do.

A straightforward way to get killed is to stare down a wolf and imply a challenge, which it looks like he is doing.

One of the other alphas, who looks just like Henderson but with much shorter black hair, steps in the middle of them. "You know what he did, Silas. Let's take this outside, because the lighthouse doesn't need to be fucked up by your wolves."

Silas turns and walks right out, and Henderson follows right after him. The alpha who interrupted looks back at me and runs a hand through his hair. His eyes have infinite hues of blue, swirled together, and it really is something beautiful. Of course, the beautiful alpha had a just-as-beautiful twin brother.

There was no way they aren't twins, they look the same in every other sense.

"My name is Alpha Ragnar Fall, nice to meet you. You're safe, this isn't your fault," he tells me, holding his hands in the air. "But I need to sort them out. Stay here, all right?"

I flicker my eyes to the only alpha who has said nothing as he leans against the wall, the shadows hiding most of him from me.

Ragnar sighs and runs out of the door. The sound of wolves snarling, growling and scuffling fills the silent room as I stare at the shadow of an alpha by the wall. Eventually, he sighs and walks into the light, lifting a bottle of whiskey and drinking a long sip, drops of it falling down his brown beard. I can't see much of him through the beard, the long messy brown hair that hasn't been brushed in a long time. His clothes are torn all over, bits of his golden skin peeking out of his toned chest. He is a muscular alpha, and he must be commanding, or he wouldn't be an alpha.

He walks right over to me, and I move as far back as I can, wrapping my arms around my legs as he drops on the sofa next to me.

"Whoever you are, trouble, I'm no threat. Neither are any of those idiots fighting outside," he announces. "The name's Valentine."

"Like Valentine's Day?"

"Yup. It was the day I was born," he replies, taking another long sip. "What's your name?"

"Mairin," I whisper.

"I like it," he replies. "Tell those jackasses you have my blessing and permission to join the pack and shift, when they're done. I'm going back to bed."

Just like that, Valentine takes another long sip of his drink and then shifts there on the sofa. Instead of green magic, red shifter energy, or whatever it is, smothers him, and then there is a pure black wolf on the sofa. The wolf looks back at me, its eyes red and downright scary, before jumping off the sofa and running at the window. He jumps through it, smashing it to pieces, and I stare speechless at the ripped clothes and whiskey bottle left on the sofa.

The alphas of this pack are strange, and whatever god they worship, it isn't the moon goddess. Slowly I place my hand on the back of my neck, feeling the raised marks in the shapes of moons starting from the middle of my neck and going down.

Maybe I don't belong to the moon goddess anymore either.

Ragnar appears in the doorway, blood marking his bare sculpted chest and jeans almost all done up. He buttons up the top button on his jeans as he comes into the room and pauses as I lower my hand. Around his heart are the moon markings, and I stare at them for a second too long.

"The markings are from the forbidden god who protects us. Wearing them is the only way to enter this pack, and usually, you need to have every alpha's permission. The argument Silas and Henderson had is that you hadn't been given permission by any of us. We make all our choices together," he explains to me. "Henderson has explained you were dying. It was an unusual circumstance, but welcome. You have my permission and Henderson's."

"And Valentine's," I say, clearing my sore throat and forcing myself to sit up a little straighter.

Ragnar raises his eyebrows. "He spoke to you?" I nod. "Right, it's been a weird day. Silas will come around, and then you can shift."

"I can't shift without a mate. Everyone knows that," I reply.

He smiles and widens his arms. "Welcome to the Fall Mountain Pack, where you don't need a mate to shift. Our god doesn't force us to mate in order to shift. You only need the alphas' permission."

My eyes widen and I'm speechless. I could shift? I could have everything I've wanted without being shackled with a mate I don't want?

Why would the moon goddess force us into matings if she could give us the power as this forbidden god does?

"I believe Miss Irin needs a shower, food and rest, in that

order. I will look after her if you will allow it, Alpha Ragnar," Saffron asks, walking down the stairs with Trey following behind her.

Ragnar nods at her and turns back to me. "Rest, and I will return tonight to take you to your new home."

He walks out the door, shutting it behind him, and Saffron walks across the room as Trey sits on the sofa next to me. "Do you want a hot chocolate? Saffron is making us one, but if you don't like it, I can drink it for you."

I smile at him, still feeling very on edge. "A hot chocolate sounds lovely."

"I will get the cookies she hides," Trey says, jumping off the sofa and running across the room to a door behind the stairs where Saffron went. She comes out after he goes in, and brings over a steamy cup of hot chocolate in a white handmade mug.

"Thank you," I say, accepting it off her. She nods and goes to leave before pausing.

She looks to the door and then back down to me. "Be careful with the alphas. They came to this pack not too long ago, destroyed the old alpha and brought us into the protection of a new god. They will destroy whatever they want to win. Be careful."

I nod, understanding her perfectly, but what she doesn't realise is that I was broken on a beach, seconds after the moon goddess let me down.

The alphas can't destroy what is already broken.

CHAPTER SEVEN

Ragnar Fall

"She doesn't remember us."

Henderson's statement lingers in the air, turning our internal thoughts into a spoken thing too quickly. Too painfully. But it's been painful from the second Henderson found her, from the second she looked at us like we are strangers and we didn't grow up together. Mairin looks so different from when I last saw her, when she was shy of twelve years old and was my biggest crush since I realised girls were interesting at all. It was the same for all of us...until she was gone.

Then we all realised we had everything with her, and without her, we are nothing.

And she doesn't remember.

In my mind's eye, I see her on the sofa in the lighthouse, wearing some silk dress that's ripped, dotted with her blood and soaking wet from the sea. Blood and saltwater couldn't hide her scent from me, nor could how broken she looked hide how beautiful she is. Her long blonde hair, her bright green eyes that remind me of the dark green trees of our old home, and her long legs caught my attention right away.

She is stunning in every sense.

"Why would that poor excuse of an alpha reject her? Is he fucking blind?" Silas grumbles out, wiping a line of blood from his cut lip, which is healing already. Henderson, who did that, smirks at him.

"Shame your wolf is slow because of how big he is. You might have missed that hit otherwise," Henderson replies.

I stand up, drawing their attention. "Enough. You two have already scared Mairin with your fighting. Can we not get along for five minutes to discuss what we are going to say to her?"

Henderson looks away and walks to the window, detaching himself from any serious conversation like he always does, and Silas grumbles something I can't make out but nods. I glance at Valentine's room upstairs, wondering if he is listening at all as he drinks himself into a slumber.

"Ragnar, not to be a dick, but we should tell her everything. Rip off the Band-Aid, so to speak," Silas suggests.

"As usual, you always come up with the most dickish move out there. No, we can't." I pause as Henderson looks back. "She is broken, fucked up and doesn't trust us. If we tell her everything, she is going to jump back in that sea and disappear. Considering we have spent over six years looking for her, can we come up with a better plan?"

"Fine," Silas replies. "Our pack lifestyle is going to be a

shock, and either way, we get her back. I'm not letting her go. I will fight any pack for her."

"You're not alone in that feeling, brother," Henderson adds.

"Then she moves in here with us, and we ask questions. Figure out how she ended up in that pack and how they kept her hidden for so long. None of our spies said a word," I say, rubbing my chin.

"Maybe we need new spies," Silas remarks with a bloody grin.

"I doubt Mairin has been trained since she left us, we should take turns training her so she is up to speed in case they attack," I suggest.

"I will train her. You all know I am the only one who will do what is needed," Silas says.

"Do you plan on giving her your permission to shift?"

"Not until she is trained," Silas replies, and I growl at him.

He lifts his hands in the air. "Henderson shouldn't have fucking linked her to our god without explaining it to her or the consequences. She was brought up in the mind-control pack who worship a fake goddess, and she has no idea what she has signed up for. Don't look at me like that because I won't force her into shifting and making that final commitment."

"She was dying, and I would never let that happen. The alpha beat her, or someone did, and then she was thrown into the sea—"

All three of us growl. When I get my hands on that alpha, he is dead.

"I don't know how she survived, or how any of the rejected do, but she was in awful shape. I could hear her heartbeat fading...so I did what I had to," he finishes off. "If she hates me, at least she is alive."

"The mating ceremony, even uncompleted, leaves a bond. He will sense she is alive and send wolves to hunt her. Until she is dead, he cannot take another mate," I remind them.

"Let him send them. She is living with us, and I will enjoy ripping them apart," Silas replies, his calm voice downright murderous in its intent. Considering I've seen him rip wolves apart for breaking pack laws, and enjoy it, I know he isn't joking. It will be a bloodbath.

"So we agree she moves in, we train her, and we protect her until she remembers, or we tell her when she is settled?" I ask.

"Agreed," both Silas and Henderson state. All three of us look to Valentine's door, and I sigh, knowing it will be me who has to make sure he is all right with Mairin moving in with us. If Silas tries, it will cause a fight, Henderson will get pissed off by Valentine's lack of interest in talking to him, and I can stay calm.

Mostly.

"Good luck!" Silas calls out as I get to the stairs. "I'm going to find something to eat."

I hear both Silas and Henderson shifting behind me as I make my way to the top of the stairs and knock the first door before opening it. I duck straight away as a bottle flies over my head, over the banister and smashes into the middle of the living room floor.

Valentine, the broken asshole, shifts before I can ask him anything, and his wolf is left sitting in the middle of the room. His wolf shoves past me and runs out.

"I will take that as a yes!" I shout after him. Asshole.

CHAPTER EIGHT

"You can't catch me!" a young boy shouts, followed by children's laughter. I can't see who they are as I run through the forest, thick trees everywhere around me hiding the shadows of children I'm chasing.

"The trees only hide you in the dark!" I shout back, but my voice sounds so much younger. I pause when I get to a pond and look down, seeing my reflection as a young girl of about six just before everything fades.

"Morning...well, it's sundown, but I was told to wake you up," Trey mumbles out as I blink my eyes open in the dimly lit room, everything that happened before I fell asleep on the sofa coming back in a rush. I suck in a deep and nervous breath, unsure if I should start panicking or not. A thick yellow blanket falls down my body as I sit up, and Trey flashes me a toothy grin as he sits on the coffee table in the same clothes he was in earlier.

A shuffling of feet on the stairs catches my attention, and

I look up to see Saffron heading down the stairs in a yellow buttoned blouse and jeans, with her hair in the same style as when we met. "You slept for twenty hours, Miss Irin. Are you feeling better?"

Twenty hours? What the hell was in the hot chocolate she gave me? "Erm, yes. I think so."

"It's normal for the newly marked to sleep for so long. Do not look so worried," she replies. "Now gather that blanket and come upstairs. I've run you a bath and left out clothes. Time to clean you up before one of the alphas comes back again."

I scurry to gather the blanket and flash a smile to Trey before following Saffron up the stairs. Halfway up, I ask the question burning in my mind. "How does having four alphas work? Don't they kill each other for dominance?"

That's the only way I've ever seen it. There is one alpha, and he kills anyone for the alpha position.

Her kind eyes fall back on me as she opens a door on the first clearing on the staircase. She heads inside, and I follow her into a massive bathroom. A wooden bathtub is in the middle of the white-tiled room, filled with bubbling water in a rose pink colour. A toilet and row of cabinets with a sink line the one side of the wall, and on the other are hooks with towels hanging. "Anyone can challenge anyone in this pack, just like the pack you are from, but no one has survived challenging any of the alphas. And they do not challenge each other. From what I have gathered, they grew up together, and that is unheard of. Alpha pups are always kept away from each other to avoid fights, but not in their case. They may argue and fight, but when it comes down to it, they are a family of alphas who grew up together, and may the forbidden god help anyone who gets in their way. Clean up, and I will meet you downstairs."

"Saffron..." I hesitate. "What am I expected to do with the alphas? Why did they save my life? In my experience, alphas don't do good deeds for nothing."

She sighs and steps back, slowly closing the door. "Trey was a baby who was washed up on this shore in a basket with only a note in a glass bottle claiming he was a rejected baby because he wasn't born in a mating. The alphas took Trey in, loved him, made him one of them in every sense of the word, and that boy down there never once thinks of himself as rejected. They never treat him—and they will not treat you—any differently." She pauses. "Being rejected is a death sentence anywhere else, but here? Here, it is a new beginning. Be born again on that beach and hold your head high. You have a chance for something amazing here, Irin, and they won't ask for anything."

She opens the door again, but I have to blurt out one more question.

"Will the forbidden god I'm now bound to because he saved my life ask for something?"

She looks back. "The price is simple. You belong to the pack until your last breath."

Saffron leaves me with more questions than answers, but somehow making me feel a little better about what the alphas want with me. They don't scare me half as much as the idea of going back to the Ravensword Pack, that's for sure, and the alphas can't be that evil if they took in Trey. I can see he is a cheerful kid, even if he reminds me of Jesper and how I can't ever see him again.

Pushing the sadness aside, I walk to the edge of the bathtub and drift my fingers over the hot water before pushing off what is left of my dress and leaving it in a pile with the yellow blanket. The bathtub is high, so I have to push myself up to climb into it and sink into the relaxing hot water. I duck my head underneath it and come back up with a gasp, smiling to myself about the small luxuries of hot bathwater. Sometimes at the foster house, the boiling water and electricity would go out for weeks at a time, and this bath reminds of those first few days they were back on. How it's perfect. Finding a soap bar on the side of the bath, I wash myself and my hair until the water is brown instead of pink.

I don't stay in long before getting out and wrapping myself in a towel and going to the mirror. Somehow I bend myself to the side in an awkward angle to see the moon marks on my neck and upper back, but the sight of them shocks me. The full moon is on my neck, followed by a half-moon, a crescent moon, and then back to a full moon once more. The markings, very much like tattoos I've seen wolves in the pack get, are made with black ink and slightly risen. Suddenly Alpha Sylvester Ravensword's last words to me come back like a haunting dream.

"Die like you should have so many years ago, because if the sea does not take you, I will know. I will know, and I will never stop sending wolves to kill you."

I drop my hair back down and turn away from the mirror, trying to control my shaking hands and looking around for a distraction from my thoughts about the alpha of my old pack. I have to believe he can't know I'm alive and he won't send anyone after me...or this is all pointless. I might as well have died in the sea.

My eyes catch on a pile of clothes, and I walk over, picking the pile up. A soft white T-shirt, plain cotton underwear, a bra, and jeans with socks. I pull all the clothes on, finding the jeans are a little too tight and the top is too big, hanging down to my thighs. I pull it up and tuck it in the jeans before pulling the socks on. After running my fingers through my hair and drying it the best I can with a towel, I leave the bathroom and go down the stairs to see Saffron sitting on the sofa with Alpha Ragnar on her other side, but Trey is nowhere to be seen. Ragnar looks up when one of the stair boards creaks, and I hurry down to the bottom step. Saffron nods at me, and I smile at her.

"Thank you for the clothes and for looking after me. Is there anything I can do for you in return?" I question, and it makes her smile. She shakes her head.

"You're kind, but no. See the pack, I'm sure you will like it," she answers and turns to Ragnar. "I will bring Trey back home in a few hours."

"You're brilliant, Saffron," Ragnar tells her with a big smile and pats her shoulder. She nods to him before he walks over to me, picking up a familiar pair of boots. "I found these on the beach a few miles away from where Henderson said he found you."

"Thank you!" I say, happily taking them. "How did you know they were mine?"

"My wolf scented them," he answers. "They smell like you, of course."

I chuckle as I pull my boots on and notice they have been cleaned and polished. Not a bit of sand is in them, and they aren't wet. Someone has even replaced the worn laces I used to have on here. "Thank you for finding them and fixing them."

"No problem," he replies, rubbing the back of his neck. "Are you ready?"

"Yes," I answer, feeling more than a little nervous but excited to see the pack lands. There were never photos in books or anything to show us what the pack lands look like over here in what used to be Ireland, and I've only ever seen the island in the distance from the shores of Wales. A bigger part of me is nothing but nervous about what changes there will be to pack life, where I will live and how I will be treated. I'm pretty used to being the outcast of the pack, the one no one wants, I know how to handle that.

Just not anything else.

Ragnar walks down the steps with me at his side, but his enormous feet take the steps two at a time, and he reaches the bottom much quicker than I could. At the bottom of the steps, on the sand, is a strange sort of car. It has gigantic wheels, a white frame attached to it, but no doors at all, just glass panels at the front and back of the two seats. The frame is white and shiny, and clearly it's well looked after. I've seen things like these in human movies, but it's not the same, therefore I have no clue what to call it.

"I made it myself. I call her Daisy," Ragnar tells me, and I might not know him at all, but I sense the pride in his voice.

"I've always loved to tinker with humans' car machines and make new things. Daisy is my more reliable invention."

"Why is she called Daisy? Like the flowers?" I ask.

"Daisies are technically a weed that looks like flowers, and my Daisy is technically a lot of broken parts pieced together to make something amazing," he replies, patting the shell of the car thing. "Ready for a ride?"

I nod and step up, realising a little too late it's pretty high. I stumble back, but instead of falling on my ass, Ragnar's hands go to my waist, catching me, and burning heat spreads through my skin where his hands touch. My cheeks burn as he helps me into the passenger seat, and I tuck my hair behind my ears as I look away. He says nothing as he effortlessly jumps into the seat next to me, his arm brushing against mine, and the same burst of heat makes me shiver from the small contact. He makes me feel…alive? I'm not sure what to think about how he makes me feel. It's not something I've ever really felt before.

Ragnar looks down at me, everything about him expressing warmth and reminding me of the heat of a fire when you're too close. "Welcome to the Fall Mountain Pack, Mai. You're finally home."

"SLIEVE DONARD IS the old name of this mountain, and most still call it that, but mostly it is referred to as Slieve City because of the city we have built inside of the mountain and around it," Ragnar explains to me as we drive through thick forest, on roads that are nothing more than dirt lined with logs to mark the path. The only light trickles down through the bulky leaves, and the oddly grown branches cast so many shadows across the forest floor. I can smell nothing but pine and how Ragnar smells like bacon, which I assume he had for breakfast, and a subtle spicy scent with a woodsy sexy mix to it that I know is all him. And he smells too good. Carefully, I tilt my head away from the forest to take in Ragnar, looking him over from head to toe. His firm hands grip the steering wheel in a relaxed way, but his muscles are still tense in his arms. Most of the guys in my old pack were muscular, and I never once found it as attractive as I do right in this moment. Damn, the alphas of Fall Mountain Pack are hot.

"Mai, are you still listening to me?" he asks, taking his eyes off the road for a second to look at me. His blue eyes remind me of the colour of midnight.

"Sorry, I checked out. What did you say?"

He gives me a knowing smile, but he doesn't comment on my staring. "I said that there is only one city on the island and four other large towns. We live in the mountain, and we would like for you to live with us. If you agree, of course."

"Why do I get the feeling it really isn't a choice?"

He sighs, slowing down a little bit. "It is a choice. We won't force you into living with us, but you must know pack law. Anyone could challenge you and kill you for being different and not being able to shift yet. Henderson is working on Silas so he will give you permission and you can shift. That will deal with half the problem. The other half is the fact that here there are two types of challenges. One is a weapon challenge."

"We don't have that in my—"

"Your old pack," he growls out, interrupting me.

I shake my head, pulling myself away from him a little, and he swears under his breath. "Shit, I didn't mean to scare you."

"I'm used to alpha wolves being dickheads. Don't worry about it," I snap.

"No, my anger was directed at your old pack and not at you. If I had my way, we would announce war and challenge your old alpha for his pack. And take it," he tells me, turning to look at me once more. I see the apology in his eyes, and it makes me hesitant to be mad at him for long. I can understand his point of view; he has seen so many rejected apparently and hears what happened to them. He must know what happened to me at my mating ceremony.

"Okay," I say, deciding to leave this subject for now. "I was saying I don't know what a weapon challenge is."

"You get one weapon, and you aren't allowed to shift. The challenge takes place on circled areas where you can't shift due to the magic in them," he tells me. "Therefore, you need training before we let you go into the pack."

"Does every rejected get training?"

"If they're old enough, yes, but usually with a beta," he honestly replies.

"Then why can't I live with one of your betas?"

"They are all busy," he replies quickly. Too quickly. I want to call him out on it, but I realise what is the point? I would be safer at the alphas' house for a short amount of time so I can train and then find my place.

"It will only be for a short amount of time," I counter.

He nods. "Whatever you want, Mai."

"No one has ever called me that nickname before…I kinda like it," I tell him, looking at his short black hair and how it almost has a dark blue shine to it in the beams of light that escape through the trees. Ragnar looks over at me, and I get the impression he wants to say something, but it's gone too quickly, and he turns away. I lean back in my seat just as we come around a corner and straight into the city that was just here and gone in a second.

The city is picturesque in a way I didn't expect.

Tall cherry blossom trees line the light brown stone high street with dozens of five-story wooden houses with slate roofs on either side. In the middle of them are low gated gardens with children and wolves in them, their laughs echoing around in the wind that blows pink cherry blossom petals in the air. Wolves run down the street pathways, dodging through people who turn to look at us, and they all look so similarly dressed to my pack, a mixture of cloaks and jeans, T-shirts and some posh dresses here and there. But there are so many hair colours, not all of them are black-haired or brown-haired, there are some redheads and blonde-haired people walking around.

I will not stand out anymore. I turn back to see the road go up into a massive cavern opening with a border made of gold. Warm light shines from inside the cavern as Ragnar drives up the road and over the hill onto the flat surface right outside of the cavern, and we head inside where the view takes my breath away.

All the way from the base of the mountain to the tip are levels of houses built into the inside of the cliff with bridges in the middle that connect all the layers, and stairs in the middle that are made of stone, in one massive twirling staircase that could easily fit twenty people in a row to walk up together.

"I hate to say, this bit is bumpy. Hold on," Ragnar warns me as he drives right to the staircase, people moving out of the way for him and waving like it is normal for him to drive so quickly and treat people like bowling pins that need to move for him. I grab the sides of the seat as Ragnar drives the car up the staircase, and the car bounces up and down as we go up fast, people just moving to the sides. We pass five different exits on the stairs, but he never turns off them.

"D-do you do this o-often?" I blurt out, and in return I only get a laugh for a moment. A really sexy, deep laugh that makes all of me seem to burst to life.

His dark blue eyes meet mine for a single second. "Live a little, Mai!"

I smile and that turns into a chuckle as we keep going round and round until we finally come up to hefty gold metal gates at the top of the staircase, which slowly open. The tips of the gates are trees, so many of them it looks like a mini forest, and when the gates fully open, I see there are more actual trees inside of the mountain. The top level of the mountain is one big area with a massive Georgian style house in the middle and a forest of trees, gardens of grass and flower borders, and a big stone path right down the middle of it, diverging off to the sides and the main house.

I spot two small buildings in the trees, one of which looks like an enormous garage. Ragnar drives Daisy down the stone driveway. The crunching of the stones under the tires is all I hear, and I look back to see the gates slowly shutting behind me. I'm here now, and I might as well make the most of what life has given to me. I have zero plans for the future, mostly because I thought I wouldn't get one after the mating ceremony, and now I can actually make plans. A part of me knows I can actually have some kind of life once I know how to defend myself and shift into my wolf.

Ragnar pulls Daisy up in front of the house, and I undo my seatbelt and climb out, which is easier than climbing in. I look up at the big intimidating house in front of me and take a deep breath.

Everything is going to be okay if I can survive the next few weeks with the crazy alpha four.

The door slams open, and the sweetest looking woman I've seen walks out.

"I thought you only brought bitches back here on the full moon for one night? Have the rules changed?"

CHAPTER NINE

The sweet woman, wolf, doesn't match the not so friendly way she just called me a bitch, and I'm a little taken back by her. She has light red curly hair that is in two plaits that fall to her stomach, with tiny red silver wolf clips holding them together. She has a short black top on, black leather pants that are very tight, and she really does have a sweet face. On her back are two daggers, but I can only see the sharp tips on either side of her head. The woman arches her eyebrow at me, her green eyes showing me she is not sweet, not even one little bit. This is exactly why I was told never to judge a book by its cover.

"Mai, this is Seraphim Fall, our lead beta wolf, and I would say she isn't so rude, but she is," Ragnar introduces us.

"What kind of name is Mai?" she asks, cocking her head to the side and placing her hands on her hips. "In fact, who is she and why is she here?"

"Since when do I have to tell you shit?"

"Since the fact none of you lot could cope without me, that's why," she counters with a smile, which ends with them both laughing. I, on the other hand, am just confused.

"Women can't be betas. That's never happened before," I blurt out.

Seraphim sighs. "I get it, she is a reject."

"Mai is now in our pack, and I expect you to treat her as such. She is living with us," Ragnar firmly replies, his eyes narrowed at Seraphim. He didn't like her calling me a reject. A small part of me warms at being defended, because there are only a handful of people that have ever defended me before. Seraphim opens her mouth to say something, but Ragnar interrupts. "And"—Ragnar looks down at me—"we allow anyone who proves they are the best fighters, both in wolf and human form, to be beta. Seraphim is a deadly fighter, and her wolf is stronger than half the males in our pack. It may not be an accepted way in the Ravensword Pack, but here, we respect true strength, and Seraphim has earned her place. Just like any wolf could, even you."

"I respect that," I answer and turn to Seraphim. "It's nice to meet you, Beta Seraphim. Maybe if the Ravensword Pack had more females in charge, it wouldn't be so bad there."

She flashes me a smile full of malice. "I know how Ravensword works. I used to live there until I was rejected for loving someone who wasn't chosen for me. A girl, to be exact. Ravensword and the moon goddess don't let you love openly, and they threw me away, never checking how strong I would be."

I meet her eyes. "I'm sorry."

"As I am for whatever the messed up pack put you through. Trust me, it's better here. More than better. You can breathe now," she suggests and walks right up to me. "I'll be around." She looks to Ragnar. "Eleline is here, in the living room. Good luck with that."

Ragnar mutters under his breath and walks to the house, looking back to me when I haven't moved. "Are you coming?"

"Who is Eleline?" I question, moving to his side.

"An ex-girlfriend who keeps turning up," he admits, shrugging his shoulders.

"So you don't just bring women back on the full moon for sex?"

He jolts in the doorway and looks down at me. He tilts his head to the side. "And what would you know about that? Ravensword doesn't let females have sex before mating."

I gulp, the pressure a little too much under his gaze. "I know too much."

His eyes search mine, and I try to hide the turmoil going on inside, but I think he sees it. I think he sees me for a brief second. A stranger figuring out my secrets, figuring out everything that has broken me in my life.

"Who is she?" A high-pitched voice makes me jump away from Ragnar, but he doesn't move for a second, and I realise right away he is angry. His entire body shakes with it, and he closes his eyes for a few seconds as I turn to the woman. Eleline, I am guessing. She is staring at me, her hands on her small bare waist right above the tiny red skirt she has on. Nothing but a strap of fabric is wrapped around her breasts, and her blonde hair is darker than mine but cut short under her chin. Her eyes are a light brown but currently narrowed on me like I'm evil.

Then she growls. A possessive growl that I don't like.

Some part of me forces my eyes to meet hers, and I stare her down. Something I've never done before, but I can't stop myself. Soon I feel my hands shaking, and a strange deep wolf-like sound is escaping my lips.

Ragnar steps in front of me, placing his hands on my shoulders, and like a light switching off, I startle where I'm standing. He smiles kindly at me, but I see the tension in his eyes. "I will deal with Eleline. Your room is the third on the left when you go up the staircase. Meet you there?"

"What was that?" I quietly question.

"Your wolf is coming out, with or without Silas's permission. Seems you are stronger than anyone thought, Mai," he gently says and lowers his hands. "Now, see you upstairs."

"Okay," I shakily answer. I walk around him and past Eleline, who turns to look at me, but I refuse to meet her gaze for a second time, even when my body itches to do so. She growls at me as I pass, her growl nothing short of a threat. Making enemies on my first actual day in the pack isn't the best idea I've had, but I've done it now. She hasn't challenged me, which she could have done, so I have some luck.

My hands shake with the need to turn back, to do something insane and very wolf-like to someone my wolf clearly sees as a danger. I force my shaky body up the staircase, barely even taking a second to take in the wooden staircase below my feet. I take a left down a cream-carpeted corridor and find the third door, which is slightly ajar, and I push it with my hand until it swings open with a long creak. The bedroom is round with a square glass ceiling through which I can see tree leaves and the rock top of the mountain above.

The double bed is made of light wood with pillars in each corner, and a thick mattress on top. Three pillows and a thin blanket are in the middle of the bed, all of them a light purple colour and look like they're made of silk. The room is carpeted and it's soft, I discover as I walk further into the room and wrap my hand around one of the wooden pillars of the bed. The room has nothing else in it, and a part of me misses the small room I had at my foster home. It might not be as grand as this place is or have a double bed, but it was personal. It was my home, filled with drawings I did of Jesper and Daniel and anything I found to draw. It had the stones I collected from the river, all of them different colours, and some of them I painted over the years. This room is for a guest, but I will find a way wherever I go next to make it like home.

"Sorry about that," Ragnar's voice nearly makes me jump. He moves silently, I didn't hear even a footstep. I turn around as he steps through the doorway with a plate full of meats, cheeses and bread. "I thought you might be hungry, so I grabbed some quick food." He places the plate on the bed for me. "I'm moving a wardrobe in here for you in a moment, as this is just a spare room we had. We only have two bathrooms, and there is one next door. Valentine and Trey share it with you on this side of the corridor, so make sure to lock the door."

"Thanks," I say, rubbing my hands together. "For everything so far. You've been too kind."

His eyes search mine for a second. "Mai...it's no problem."

I tilt my head to the side. "You sounded like you wanted to say something else."

"Just that we are happy to have you here."

"Why would you be happy? You don't know me at all," I ask him, watching as he takes several steps back towards the door. The wolf would run for it to escape this question.

"Why wouldn't we be happy to have a beautiful woman living with us?" he counters, but I think it's a lie, even if his compliment makes me smile. "I won't have to look at Valentine's ugly mug over the table every morning and night."

I chuckle as he walks to the door and looks back over his shoulder. "Silas will be here in an hour for your first training session, and dinner is later on. Good luck."

"Thanks," I reply as he leaves my room, pulling my door shut for me. I sit down on the bed and lie back, staring up at the unmoving tree hanging over the glass window and the beams of light I can see through the holes in the stone.

The alphas of Fall Mountain Pack have welcomed me into their home…but why does it feel like I've just walked into the dragon's den and I'm not escaping as easily as I planned?

CHAPTER TEN

The house, despite having five people live in here, not including me, is quiet as I wander down the stairs and have a look around. I didn't notice before, but the banisters of the staircases are literal wolves carved out of wood, their bodies pouncing down ready to attack. I run my hand down the middle of the banister, the wolves' backs, until I get to the head of the wolves, which I can only just reach the sharp teeth that are the size of my hand.

"Careful, he bites."

I jump as I spin towards Henderson, who's filling the doorway to the left, his body taking up all the space with his wide shoulders. Henderson's hair looks damp like he must have taken a shower, and I don't know why, but I imagine myself brushing it.

"How the hell do you all move so silently?" I question, placing my hand on my racing heart.

"Habit born from training as a kid to be silent," he answers, running his hand through his hair, just like I was thinking about doing a moment ago. "I'm sure moving silently will be easier for you when you've shifted for the first time. Wolf senses make it easier."

"I'm still not used to the idea I can shift without a mate controlling when I can. I was taught—"

"Taught wrong," he interrupts. "Apparently, you almost showed a little wolf with Eleline earlier. That's a good sign."

Something in me bristles at the mention of her name from him. I furrow my brow, looking away.

"I felt...well, more. More angry, more possessive, more feral. Is that what it's always like?"

"Only when you're protecting what is yours. Wolves are possessive and stubborn bastards about anything they consider theirs," he answers me, but that doesn't make much sense. I wasn't protecting anyone, and I definitely don't think Ragnar is mine. He is a stranger. Deciding to drop the subject because these answers are just making me go in circles, I ask something else.

"Any chance you're free for a tour?"

He smirks as he walks over to me. "Sure, Mai."

"So you've picked up the nickname from Ragnar?" I ask as he leads me towards an archway door on the right side of the staircase. He holds it open for me, and I step through, my arm brushing against his hip, and nothing but pure heat burns through my skin from the touch.

He chuckles, a deep chuckle that sends more chills through me. The good kind of chills. "I can call you Irin or your full name if you wish."

"No, Hens," I tease back, using a shortened name for him that I don't know where it came from. He stills for a second, looking at me strangely before he blinks and looks away.

"This is the primary room. We play pool, watch movies, drink at the bar. It's where everyone can usually be found," he tells me, his voice warmer than I've heard him before. The main area is vast; at least half of the house is in this one room, and I don't know where to look first. Right in the middle are five sofas and two chairs, all the same, deep blue fabric with a few brown fur blankets resting on the backs of them. In the middle of them is a massive wool rug with a wolf design in brown with the rest of the rug a deep blue that matches the sofas. On the wall is a big television, much bigger and flatter than the ones we had back in my old pack. A pool table is further down the room, and on the other side is an area with five massive bookcases, one large deep wooden desk and an old armchair all fitted into the corner, making it look cosy and dark. Two big fireplaces are lit on the other side of the room, casting warm light across the space, mixing with the light coming from the seven large windows, which are designed to catch the light beams in the mountains.

"Did you design this house?" I question. "It's beautiful."

"The old alpha of this pack was a monster who treated the wolves in his pack like nothing more than toys to amuse himself, but he designed this house. The pack built it though, and it's their blood soaked into the walls of this entire mountain. We claimed it when we took this pack," he explains to me, passion and anger leaking through his voice. "This pack embraced our forbidden god, us as their alphas, and we know they are better for it. They are thriving now."

"Where did you live before?"

His eyes take on a strange look, but before he can answer, Silas walks into the room and clicks his fingers at me. "Time for training. If you pass out, I am just waiting for you to wake up before we continue. Think on that."

He turns and walks out of the room, and Henderson sighs.

"He is joking...I think."

I give Henderson a nervous smile before jogging after Silas, having a sinking suspicion he isn't joking one bit. Silas moves so quickly that I only just see the back door behind the stairs swing shut by the time I get across the entrance hall. I jog to the door and push it open to a massive empty room that reminds me of the gym from my old pack school. The floors are made with soft yellow tiles, and the walls are white with thin windows lining the top of the room. There is a door on the one side that has three big padlocks on it, and there isn't much else to see in here.

Silas is standing dead centre in the middle of the room. His muscular arms are tightly crossed, and he looks angry at the entire world, like they have done something personal to offend him. Although he looks so angry, I walk all the way across the massive open room that echoes every single footstep that I make until I'm standing right in front of him.

He looks down at me like I'm a little bug under his shoe that he would like to squash. I'm used to strong asshole men like this, dominating me with a stare. The betas of Ravensword had fun doing it to me because they knew I could never fight back. I could never give the alpha a reason to kill me. But apparently, things are better in this pack, not that I have seen much of it so far.

"Have you ever had any training before?" His coldly spoken question makes me almost smile. Does he know I was a foster kid? Can he see that I'm a woman, and women don't fight in Ravensword? They certainly aren't trained. I arch an eyebrow for a response, and he glowers at me. "Have they ever taught you how to fight at all? How to defend yourself? How to even be a wolf in the first place?" I look up nervously, knowing that I've had pretty much no training. I lived with Mike my entire life, who couldn't train me, and that wasn't his fault. The alpha would never have let him train me, but I saw him occasionally pick up a sword in the yard and swing it around expertly. The only reason Mike stepped down as a beta was because his wolf refused to fight anymore, a normal thing that happens to wolves of a certain age. Mike would have still been a beta if he had his way.

Eventually, I gather the courage to actually reply to Silas, knowing I need his help with training and he is unlikely to hurt me. If these alphas wanted me dead...I would be. "No, I have had no training, but I know how to defend myself or at least how to run fast when people are coming at me."

I chuckle a little, but it dies off when I realise he does not smile at my joke. In fact, if anything, he just looks more disinterested in me than when we both came in here. We've got a long way to go before he gives me permission to be a wolf, to be who I'm actually meant to be. He stares down at me, and then he finally looks away. Silas moves quickly; with loud footsteps, he stomps across the room towards the locked doors on the other side, and I jog to keep up with him, questioning what exactly he is doing now.

Part of me expected to get my ass kicked in here from the beginning, if I'm being entirely honest with myself. I was not expecting to feel this much disgust from him. The annoyance rolls off him like the way he smells like the forest and a deeply masculine scent that lures me closer to him. I want to push off his distaste for me, but it reminds me too much of Ravensword, of the place I have just survived. The alpha who just tried to kill me for being his mate.

Silas's shoulders are tense, and I admire his muscular back in the black T-shirt he has on, tucked into loose joggers that outline the rest of his body way too well. I wonder if he knows he looks good? Or are these alphas so sure of themselves that they don't care? It's clear they aren't lacking in attention from females, judging by Eleline, and I don't know why I care so much. I don't even know them. Not really.

Silas unlocks the padlocks one by one until they fall to the floor with a massive clunk, and he kicks them out of the way with his foot before pulling the massive doors open that look heavy and possibly made of metal as they scrape across the floor. He flicks on a light switch by the door, and the room is flooded with the small beams of light reflecting everything. Silver and gold swords, daggers and everything else that looks sharp and deadly line the small room. Every kind of weapon you could possibly imagine is in this tight little room, strapped to the walls or in boxes and barrels on the floor, and they are littered absolutely everywhere.

The most concerning of all is that some of them are left with blood, as they clearly have never been cleaned, and the smell coming up from them is metallic enough to make my senses twitch in disgust. God knows what it's doing to his wolf senses. Silas walks right to the other side where the dirtiest of weapons are and pushes them aside. The loud clatter of them on the ground makes me jump once until he picks up two long thin swords at the back. He grabs both of them by the handles and walks back to me, gently slapping one into my chest, not caring if I drop it as I struggle to grab it from him. The sword, though smaller than his, is a lot heavier than it looks like it is. But it's clean of blood. Small bonus. Silas storms out, not waiting for me or looking back once.

I grab hold of the sword and carry it straight out into the main training room that he has gone back into. Silas goes back to the middle of the room where he pauses and waits for me, curling his hand to call me over. The whole movement is overly sarcastic, and I ponder whether he's going to kill me now with these mini swords, because I don't get this guy. It would make more sense for Henderson or Ragnar to train me, they actually seem to like me. Not with Silas.

This sword is not quite mini. I dragged mine across the floor, lifting up just so it doesn't scrape across the floor to make an awful noise. Eventually, I get to him with the heavy sword and glance at it. The sword is quite plain. The silver handle is cold metal with no grip, and I glance at Silas's sword, which has a leather handle, no doubt making it easier to hold. I wonder if he purposely gave me the crap one that, quite honestly, looks broken and is hard to use. I wouldn't be that surprised.

"So what do we do?" I ask.

He sighs. "Hit me."

"With the sword?" I ask, double-checking. Everything about the idea of hitting an alpha with a sword feels so wrong... I have been trained for so long in pack laws, and attacking the alpha is a law I wouldn't ever think of breaking. But now everything is different.

"Yes, with the sword," he replies. "Imagine I'm that prick of an alpha. You know the one you're meant to be mated with?"

"The moon goddess was wrong," I counter, lifting the sword up. "You don't know anything."

"I know he was fucking insane," he replies, swinging his sword around in his one hand.

I blush at the compliment, not expecting it from Silas. "What if I hurt you?"

"Tell you what, Mai, if you manage to draw blood, I will give you permission to shift. Actually, I will help you shift," he replies with a smirk, because we both know I'm a long way off that.

I meet his eyes. "I accept your deal, Silas."

"I knew you would," he replies with a tilt of his lips that could be confused with a smile. "You don't seem like the type to back down. I'm going to teach you to fight, and you can grow out of the messed up lifestyle the Ravensword Pack taught you. Learn to be yourself here, and then you tell me if your old alpha deserves to breathe."

"I already know that answer," I reply.

He nods and waves his hand. "So do I. Fight me, Mai. Try it."

I suck in a deep breath and use all the strength I have to

slam the sword at him. He blocks my sword with his own, the smack of our swords vibrating down my sword, and I nearly fall over from the impact. I stumble back, and Silas rubs his chin.

"Decent move. I can work with this."

"You can?" I ask. "I kinda got the impression you don't like me or want me here."

"I don't like anyone, Mai, don't take it personally. As for wanting you here?" he pauses and lifts his sword up. "Well, I don't mind that all that much."

Then he swings at me. I just about jump out of the way and look at him in horror, but he is already moving to swing his sword again. This one, I block by lifting my sword up. He hits my sword so hard that the force knocks me straight onto my back on the floor, my sword slipping from my hand across the floor. Silas's sword is under my chin within seconds.

"Now you're dead."

I stare up at him, breathing hard with a mixture of anger and frustration. His eyes flash with something, and he moves his sword away just seconds before the door opens and Henderson walks into the room. I climb to my feet as Henderson rests his back against the wall by the door and has a stare-down with Silas.

"You aren't needed."

"I'm here to observe, nothing more," he responds with a too-friendly smile. "Carry on."

Silas growls, and I hurry to pick up my sword right before he swings at me one more time. This time, I barely dodge out of the way. He hits at me again and again, and each time, I dodge until I get brave enough to meet his sword with my own.

"Lift your elbow with the hit and aim to meet the middle of my sword," Silas instructs. I nod and do as he asks, finding that the slam of our swords is easier for me to hold onto this time. Silas stops, glancing over my shoulder once at Henderson before looking at me. "You're too weak. Every morning, I want you running two miles with me before doing core exercises like sit-ups for half an hour. Right now we can do a run and start training again tomorrow. Follow me."

"She would be stronger if she shifted," Henderson calls out to Silas's back, but he is already out of the room, ignoring him, and Henderson gives me a sympathetic smile.

I'm training with the devil, and he holds the only thing I want. Great.

Silas runs too fast out of the room, and I have to run faster than ever to keep up with him as we leave the mansion and follow a path through the forest of trees outside. This is going to hurt tomorrow…but I'm not giving up. A wolf never backs down after all, and it's about time I treat myself as a wolf instead of a sheep.

CHAPTER ELEVEN

*E*very part of me aches from the training yesterday, and not only was the two-mile run that Silas made me do enough to make me pass out, but the intense training afterwards was overkill. Everything from sit-ups to twists and weird movements Silas promised would strengthen my core so I could withstand a hit made me absolutely exhausted. I left training and went straight up to my room and slept ever since, ignoring the rest of the pack outside even though I am itching to go see the pack that I'm currently freely living in. The marks on my back seem to heat up for a second, reminding me of their existence and the forbidden god I'm now sworn to.

I roll over on the soft sheets that I'm just not used to, and my body still aches for the sheets I had back at the foster home, which had holes in them, and they weren't overly clean, but they were mine. The Fall Mountain Pack must have some sort of connection to the humans that my old pack definitely doesn't, because if this is their spare stuff, I don't even want to know what their expensive stuff is. Either way, this house and everything I've seen so far is more human than anywhere else. I'm curious if they talk to the humans we are not meant to have much contact with since the peace treaty between our kind was made so long ago, way before I was born.

I lie back and stare up out of the glass at the trees above, not liking how they don't move in the breeze. The view reminds me of the forest outside my foster home, and I might not be able to shift, but a deep part of me loves the forest. The trees, the smell of the forest and the safe feeling it gave me. Being homesick is normal, I decide as I stare out of the window. I'm homesick for a pack who would kill me on the spot if I went back there. I can't decide what that makes me, knowing deep down that I miss Mike, Daniel and Jesper more than anything the pack had. They were my pack, as dysfunctional as they were, and now I have to find a way to accept I won't see them again. I wonder what they know about the mating ceremony. Daniel saw what happened, but he couldn't stop the alpha, and I hope he is okay. I hope he can still keep his promise to look after Jesper, because I can't. Not anymore.

Deciding that I need to get up, I make a plan to explore the kitchen to get some food because I haven't eaten all day since I've come back from training. Climbing out of the bed hurts as I make my way to the new wardrobe in my room, which somehow appeared after I came back from training. One of the alphas did it, but I am in love with the beautiful wooden wardrobe that has red roses painted all up the sides and glass doors framed with oak wood. I run my hand down the door, knowing whoever made this put a lot of effort into its design. I'm surprised when I open it up to see several pairs of jeans and multiple tops, all in dark colours, and a load of lacy black underwear, which I was not expecting. I'm really hoping Seraphim helped with this, or the idea of the alphas going shopping for me and getting these clothes kind of freaks me out. For a second, I pick up the lacy black underwear, and a note falls out onto the floor. I lean down and pick it up, turning it over to read what it says.

"Guessed your size and chose something I would wear. Hope you like. Phim."

I chuckle as I pull them out and realise they're exactly the right size, right down to the fluffy socks made of a strange material that I've only seen on the upper class of the Ravensword Pack. I get myself dressed as fast as possible—which isn't as fast as usual because I'm sore—and quickly use the bathroom next door, taking note of the small room. It has nothing more than the toilet, a sink, and a bathtub with a shower, and all of them are plain, made out of porcelain, but the place is absolutely spotless, which I wouldn't expect from the fact that there are three grown men living here and one young boy. So someone is clearly cleaning around this place, but I'm yet to see them, so it might be the alphas. I plait my hair quickly to make sure it's out of the way before going back down and looking around the silent entrance hall.

The living room door is slightly open with light pouring through the gap, but I know not to go that way; the kitchen can't be back there. I know the back doors lead to the tiny rooms, so I search the three doors on the left, deciding on the middle door. The place is so quiet as I creep around, feeling foreign in this big place and like I'm not meant to be here. I make my way into the kitchen, not surprised to see it is again a massive room. It's filled with round countertops in the middle, shaped into a massive circle with dozens of leather stools all the way around them. The countertops are made of granite, and the cabinets themselves are made of dark wood, but light pours in from the gigantic windows on either side of the kitchen. So the place isn't dark at all, and I really like it.

There is a massive crystal oval-shaped lampshade hanging over the middle of the kitchen, which shines so brightly it's hard to look at. This is not something I was used to before. The lights were never this bright and playful, mainly because there wasn't enough electricity to go around for the foster home, let alone to make it bright. We lived off donations after all. But this place, it's spotless and bright, and there's a massive fridge that doesn't look old at all. It's made of stainless steel with several yellow post-it notes stuck on the door. I make my way to the fridge, reading some notes. Some are rude jokes that make me laugh, others are random food, and one is a riddle.

As the river travels, I go away. You're confused if you think I'm a bird, but we share our letters.

I SMILE and pick up the pen on the counter, staring at the riddle for a long time. I love riddles; Mike gave me a book of them, and I spent so many months figuring out answers.

This one is easy. I jot the answer below the riddle and put the pen back before opening the fridge. Inside, there are dozens of meals in tubs and loads of beers lining the bottom of the fridge, but little else and not a bit of vegetable or fruit in sight.

Who is the cook? I open up a few of the tubs, and I find one of the containers which just has turkey sandwiches in. I grab a few of those before starting to search the cupboards near the fridge, finding the plates and bottles of water in another one. After a few cupboards, I find some banana chips and some raisins and decide that's enough for me. I sit down on the stools to start eating in silence, wondering exactly where everybody else is and how this place is so quiet. But when I look out the window, I see the light is from lamps in the forest. Instead, it's coming from the bright streetlights that are outside the house. Just as I'm about to finish my sandwich, I hear Phim's voice shout through the house.

"Hey, where are you, wolf girl? I know they left you in this house all alone," she shouts out, her footsteps filling the house with some much needed noise. "They up and left to go to a party without you, and I know exactly why they did that, but I'm here to save you."

Phim walks into the kitchen and grins as she puts her hands on her curvy hips. Phim is dressed in a sparkling black dress that can't be covered in any more glitter if she tried.

Her long red hair is wavy, falling down to the middle of her back, possibly even longer than my hair, and she has strange markings around her eyes that make her look really pretty and her eyes really pop. Phim looks at me, taking in my casual jeans and black T-shirt, and rolls her eyes with a bit of a sigh.

"No, you can't go to the party dressed like that. No one is going to notice you, and everybody needs to notice you, especially when you're living here. We need to make a point tonight," she tells me as she crosses her arms. "You desperately need a friend, and I'm not usually the type to have friends, but I'm here."

"I didn't ask for a friend, and you don't have to feel sorry for me," I reply as I look at her in a bit of confusion.

"Tough shit, you're stuck with me now," she replies, waving her hand. "You don't seem to want to challenge me on sight like most of the girls in this pack. That makes us fast friends with you living here with my only friends, the alphas."

"They don't seem to be the type to have friends," I respond.

She laughs and changes the subject quickly. "We are going to make a point tonight. Make a point that you're living with the alphas, and you're not going anywhere. You don't need every skanky girl trying to challenge you."

I have no idea what to say to that as she comes right up to me and hooks her arm in mine, dragging me off the chair.

"Phim—"

"See, we are friends, you call me by my nickname. A clear sign of affection," she interrupts. "Irin, or do you like Mai? Either way, I'm sticking with Irin."

Giving up on resisting her pulling, I walk with her up the stairs as she keeps talking. "Look, there's a massive party going on tonight. It's a good party, it's the bi-quarterly moon party."

"Is it like a moon goddess party? We have those back—"

"No, don't mention that pack. No one talks about them around here. Everyone knows what they're like, and it's just depressing we can't kill their leaders and teach them how to be free," she tells me at the top of the stairs. That would be one way to sort out the Ravensword Pack. "No, the main party is, um, a freedom kind of party."

I look at her once again. "A freedom party? Do you want to describe that one a little bit better to me? What exactly are we celebrating?"

"Not celebrating anything other than the fact that we're free. But yeah, you need to be there," she tells me as Trey walks down the corridor, coming to a stop when he sees us.

"Hello, Mai," he calls out before he gets to the top of the stairs, and I sort of frown at the nickname that he's clearly picked up from the alphas.

"Hey, Trey. I haven't seen you around all day, but then again, I have been in my room. What are you up to tonight?"

"Watching reruns of this thing on Netflix that humans have, and it's the best invention since forever."

With that, he disappears down the stairs, and I turn to look at Phim. "What's Netflix?"

She laughs and shakes her head. "Wow, the Ravensword Pack are definitely living in the past. Crap. Even I said their name."

For some reason, I laugh with her as she bursts into my

room straight away without asking which one it is. Clearly, she knows exactly where she's going.

"I don't have anything to wear that's anything like what you're wearing," I tell her. She shakes her head.

"Now you do. I bought everything in here, so I know exactly what you have to wear," she answers me, and with that, she starts going through the drawers at the bottom of the wardrobe that I didn't open before and assumed were empty. Inside them, she finds this white dress, well, a slip of a dress, and holds it up in the air. I glance at her and then back to the dress.

"No, I can't wear that," I tell her outright. It's basically nothing. Phim throws it at me, and I catch it in the air.

"Get dressed in it and do your hair and then let me do your makeup. That's a beta command, Irin," she says with a wink and not an inch of wolf power in her voice.

I just stare at her in complete shock, wondering if I could just escape this, but one look in her eyes, she blatantly says, *No, no, you're not escaping this* without saying a word out loud.

"Look, it's part of my job to keep you alive. And trust me, you need to be at this party tonight. Not only are all the alphas there, but all the bitchy women of the pack will be, and they will be watching. You don't need the alphas walking all over you in this house and telling you what to do, so you need to make a point in front of the entire pack by coming tonight even though the alphas didn't bring you."

"Will they be mad at me?" I ask.

"Who cares?" she counters. "You aren't their mate, or theirs at all, so why do they get a choice? This pack is about freedom, girl."

"Freedom is new to me," I counter.

"I get it. Everyone's whispering about you, and it's about time you just show your face."

I frown at her but have a sneaky suspicion that she's right. Somehow she's become a beta wolf, a female beta after all. And for that alone, I'm extremely impressed, impressed enough to take her advice and walk into the bathroom and go and get changed into the dress. It takes me several times to get the really tight fabric on, which sticks to me, outlining all of my underwear. So I decide to shimmy out of the panties, at least so that they're not completely seen through the white dress. The white fabric is thick enough to hide anything anyway, and it falls just above my knees, with a slight slit that goes up to my thigh. There are gaps in the dress around my ribs, and the cut is so low, pushing my breasts up and making them look big. While they've always been quite big, this dress certainly makes things look bigger. I undo my hair like I was told, and run my fingers through it before looking at myself in the mirror.

The white dress brings out my blonde hair, making it look even shinier in some sense, and every part of me just seems brighter. My eyes look more alert. I suppose that's what freedom does to someone. It's what not living in constant fear does too. I don't know whether my old alpha will ever find me here, but part of me does feel safe even when I don't know these four alphas at all. I just get the feeling they are not going to hurt me. They could have done by now, and they haven't. And they don't seem like the type to play sick, twisted games like my old alpha did.

I suppose I'm questioning absolutely everything in my

life now; I have been since I got these marks on the back of my neck—no, scratch that—I have been since the mating ceremony went so wrong. I can still see the alpha's face as he held his hands around my throat before he threw me off that cliff. I shake the thoughts away, knowing that I need to fit in with this pack, and I can't do that if I'm constantly living in the past. Holding my head higher, I walk back to my bedroom where Phim is sitting on the bed, relaxed with her long legs crossed.

She looks up at me. "Wow. Yeah. You're definitely going to attract the right attention."

"I really, really don't think I will," I reply. She just laughs.

"Yeah. You have no idea what's coming. The alphas are not going to be happy. Well, they might be. I'm not sure, but it'll be funny," she says with a big smile. "Come on, let's do your makeup."

"No, I draw a line at makeup. The dress is enough. Let's go," I suggest.

"All right, Miss Bossy. Well, I didn't know that you had that in you," she says as I slip my boots on, and she looks at them but doesn't comment. I never got along with any of the females in my pack, and I'm struggling to trust Phim, even when she makes it easy to attempt to. The pack always saw me as an outcast, something that they weren't interested in. In some ways, I was safer at the foster home than I am walking around this pack when anyone could challenge me and the alphas wouldn't be able to stop it. Phim could if she wanted to. I know I'm being slightly paranoid, as she has only made me feel comfortable, but my past has taught me to trust no one. I'd be a fool to relax. We walk out of the house and start heading straight down the path towards the gates, and my boots seem really out of place with the white dress as they clunk across the stone ground.

I notice how I don't really care, and it's amazing. I never would have been this brave before, I'd usually hide from parties like this, and it feels good to be brave. The last time I went to a party, I snuck in the back and ended up running away. But this will be my home, and I can't hide forever.

WE HEAD out the enormous gates, which are left open, and down the steps as I breathe in how the pack smells like a mixture of forest and fire.

"How far is it to this place where the party is?" I question.

She smiles. "Oh, it's on top of the mountain where most of the adult parties are held. It's not far."

As I wonder if it's going to be freezing on top of the mountain, she all but drags me to the side of the steps and off them to a pathway to a staircase where several of the people are already heading up. Two men with dark brown hair walk behind a group of three women, all about the same age as I am, and they are equally as beautiful as each other. They look back at us for a brief second before turning their heads away and whispering to each other as Phim just rolls her eyes when I glance at her.

"Expect that for the rest of the night. This pack is so nosy, I swear," she laughs. "It's like one giant family when someone new is here, everyone's just got to know about them, especially if they start to live with the alphas like you did."

I go red from the attention because I've never really been the centre of attention in a good way, and I have no idea how to accept it or deal with it. Phim just kindly smiles at me as we head all the way up the stairs and come out into the cold night at the top of the mountain. It's a big circular area with nothing but jagged rocks at the sides.

"I thought you hated me when we first met, but you actually seem pretty cool, Phim," I tell her.

She flashes me a tooth-filled smile that is partly scary, and I have no idea if she's aware of it. "I thought you were a new hussy I would end up challenging because they got too attached to the alphas and tried to kill them. When I realised you weren't an airhead and you weren't in their pants, I lowered my guard."

"There is no chance of that. They might be…well, look at them, but I would never stand a chance," I reply.

She nudges my shoulder. "Just because you're rejected, it doesn't make you worthless. One alpha's reject is another's only desire."

I take in her advice and straighten my back a little, finally looking out at the top of the mountain. The stars are so bright up here, like I could just reach up and run my fingers through them. It might be cold, but the high shards around the mountain block a lot of the breeze. The place is lit up with lanterns all around the edges, the fire casting shadows around the several benches and cushions laid out all over the place. There are tables of bottles, food and glasses in the curves, and music I've never heard is being played from large speakers dotted around the edges. There is a massive bonfire in the middle, and fireflies float around in the air not far above my head, mixing with the stars, making a breathtaking view. They move around almost like they've been called here to dance to the music, to make the stars pop. It's really, really beautiful.

Most of the people are dancing around to the music. The melancholic hum is fast but still sensual enough to let them dance close together. It's really unusual to me and not like the music I've heard much before. After a few seconds, I realise a lot of the pack aren't just dancing, they're deeply kissing, their bodies pressed closely together. They move to the music like it speaks to their soul as they almost blend with whoever they are with. A part of me wishes I could be that close to someone, that open. To bare my entire soul to them, all my dark parts and secrets and be accepted.

A stray tear sneaks out of my eye, a deep-down feeling of unfairness making me feel like there isn't enough air. I suck in a deep breath and look for something to distract me, so I focus on the clothing. The women's lack of clothes is way too much to see, but they don't seem to care, and the men seem to like it, their eyes eating up the women. I feel my cheeks burning red as Phim pulls me through the crowd, unaware of my internal struggle. More and more people turn to look at me the further we go, and she pulls me all the way to the front.

That's when I notice the alphas are here. All four of them are sitting together, a genuine show of power if I have ever seen it. It's too much to take them all in, so I focus on one at a time, choosing Valentine because he has already looked away. I notice right away he is sitting with a woman in a red dress on his lap, and he's drinking straight from a bottle. The woman is kissing his neck, and a deep part of me hurts for a second even when it makes no sense that this would hurt me. After a second, the woman pulls back and wraps her red lips around her own bottle and takes a long drink. Valentine unsurprisingly slumps in the chair, completely out of it, and the bottle falls from his hand, rolling across the ground.

Look at them, don't be a chicken, Mairin. Silas's is the scariest gaze to meet, but sometimes it is best to get the hard things out of the way, so I look at him for a brief second. He is dressed in all black, his blond hair seeming even lighter than usual, and his grey eyes are nothing short of stormy. How I ever thought his eyes remind me of snow…he is a snowstorm, pure and simple. A storm that will take you under and bury you in its beauty if you let it. Ragnar and Henderson move at the same time, straightening in their throne-like seats. The sheer possessive look they give me sends shivers down my spine.

"What is she doing here?" Silas demands, treating me like I'm his to command.

"What do you think she's doing here? The whole pack was invited, and it's a great time for her to meet people," Phim answers, not remotely intimidated by Silas. I've got to ask her how to do that. I go silent, having absolutely no idea what to say as Ragnar gets up and walks over to me.

"Well, if you're here, would you like to dance?"

"I haven't really danced before," I answer. I've danced in

my room and to old wolf songs with Jesper in the snow, but this is a different dance altogether.

He smiles and picks up my hand, and I feel instant heat sizzle between our touch. I wonder how these alphas keep doing this to me. How one touch has heat coursing throughout my body. How one single touch just makes my mind fuzzy and all rational thoughts completely drift away. I shouldn't be here, and I shouldn't be here in this dress attracting so much attention, especially not from them, not when they make me feel this way. I don't seem to even notice as he wraps his hand around the back of my waist, and he guides me through the crowd. I can hear Phim arguing with the other alphas as we get near a crowd of several people, who move out of the way even in the sexual trance that they're in. I notice at the back of the crowd, there's more people, and moans, grunts and other noise come from them. They're sitting on chairs, wearing less clothing than the dancers are wearing, looking so close they seem to be completely stuck to each other. Ragnar pulls me to him, pulling our bodies together, holding me close as the happy music beats on, and I gasp from the contact. The way my body moulds into his, like we were made to dance like this and feel so good.

"You look beautiful, Mai," he tells me, his lips brushing against the tip of my ear, and it makes me shiver.

I lean back, needing some space as my heart pounds in my chest. "I'm sure you tell any woman you dance with that pickup line. It's generic and really doesn't compliment any of the things about me that I like."

He barks out a surprised laugh. "You're right, but the

problem is, I don't know who you are now. I only know the short story of your past."

"Do you want to know more?" I question.

"Yes. So where are your parents?"

"Right out with the hard question, huh?" I ask as he spins me around and back to him.

"You don't have to answer that."

"It's okay because the answer is, I don't know. I was found at twelve in the forest with nothing more than my name on my clothes, written on old paper. No one in the pack claimed me, and I was shoved into the foster home," I explain.

"That life must have been difficult. I see how they treat anything different back there," he replies.

"A new friend taught me that I might be worthless to them but maybe not to everyone. Maybe not to myself," I answer, meeting his eyes.

"Worthless is never a word I want anyone to use about you ever again. You are not worthless; in fact, no one in this world is. We are born with a purpose, and only the gods are allowed to judge us," he answers, slowly moving his hand up my back until his fingers graze my bare skin above the line of my dress. The little caressing touch makes my heartbeat all that faster.

"Is it my turn to ask a question?"

"Go on then," he replies.

"Who cooks and cleans in the house?" I ask.

He grins. "Henderson is the cook, and we all clean up and take turns with the clothes washing."

"How about I do the clothes?" I suggest. "I mean, I need

to help out, and I don't know much about cooking or cleaning."

"All right, the washing room is in the attic. Have at it," he replies with a big grin. "My turn for a question."

"It seems the song has ended," I answer as we both stop dancing.

"Then I'll hold you to it," he replies, and I smile, a real smile that feels full of hope before he nods his head at me and disappears into the dancers. Phim comes to find me seconds later, pulling me to the food and introducing me to random people for the rest of the night.

The only thing I notice is the alphas have gone.

CHAPTER TWELVE

Silas Fall

I stare at her, the woman I can't believe is here and alive, like my soul is commanding me.

When it comes to Mairin…it always has, but for her, she doesn't remember who I am. Gone are the memories we made, the connection we built, and instead she sees us as strangers.

But she grew up. If I thought I had a crush on her at twelve when I was thirteen, it's nothing to how fucking incredible she looks now. Her blonde hair is long, silky and wavy, begging me to wrap it around my hand and claim her pouty pink lips. Her curvy body is built for seduction, in a way only she could be.

No women here hold a candle to Mairin Fall. She outdoes them by just existing. The sexy fucking short dress she has on only makes her enchanting.

And makes me fucking hard in tight trousers.

"Are you coming?" Ragnar asks, patting me on my shoulder. He follows my gaze, watching Phim introduce Mairin to a group of women. "You could have asked her to dance."

"I don't ask women for anything. They give," I snap.

He chuckles low. "Not Mai. She doesn't remember you before, so you might want to tone down your normal dickhead self to get to know who she is now."

"She isn't her," I simply state. "Not anymore. We hoped for nothing."

He leans against the wall as a man, Lewis, walks over to her, holding out his hand. She shakes his hand with her tiny pale one, and he holds onto her hand for a second too long.

A low growl leaves my lips. When he steps closer and Mai laughs at something he says, Ragnar stops me with a hard whack against my chest. I turn and narrow my eyes on him. "What?"

"You're still as possessive and protective as you've always been with her. Trust me, she isn't interested in him," he tells me. "And you storming over will frighten her. Remember, she doesn't know us."

"How could I forget?" I growl out.

"She will remember, or we will tell her when the time is right," Ragnar states, like either of those two things can ever happen. Her memories come with a can of worms none of us are ready to open.

She is better off a million miles away from us, but now that she is here, I couldn't let her go a million miles away again.

Fuck the world.

Fuck the gods.

Mairin belongs here, with us, in our pack. In our home.

Ragnar laughs as he leaves me hiding behind a rock in the shadows, where I stay for the rest of the night to watch Mairin. She speaks to dozens of people, most all of them seem enchanted by her as I am, and I hate it. I don't want to share her with anyone. Her smiles should be for me, her body should be for my eyes only, and my wolf fills my head with thoughts of biting her pretty neck, marking her as my own.

I've never felt a possessive thing towards any woman, and she makes me feel all of them. She makes me a possessive asshole, and I don't give a monkey.

I watch as Mairin and Phim leave the party, more than just *my* eyes following her. The second she is out of sight, I jump down from behind the rock and look for Lewis. I find him in the corner with three other men I don't remember the names of.

I catch some of his conversation as I head over. "She has a fucking nice ass, doesn't she? I can't wait until she is out of the alphas' house, and I…"

He drifts off when he sees me, cowering even before I pick him up and slam him against the brick wall. I hold him up by his neck as the party goes silent. "Mairin Fall is not to be talked about or touched. I challenge anyone who goes near her. Am I understood?"

My voice echoes around. Lewis doesn't meet my eyes. "Yes! Sorry, alpha. I'm so sorry!"

I drop him onto the ground and walk through the crowd,

feeling everyone's eyes on me, wondering what Mairin is to me, no doubt.

The truth, that I don't like to admit, is that she has always been far more to me than I am to myself.

Even if she doesn't remember.

CHAPTER THIRTEEN

"Enough," I say. Silas just looks down at me lying on the floor and rolls his eyes at my answer to why I look like I'm dying and not getting up off the floor. Every inch of me aches, and I'm not a damn superhero like he is. I've never been worked this hard before, and I hate it.

"It's not enough," he snaps, crossing his arms. "That was barely two miles."

It's been like this for the last week now. It's not gotten any easier with Silas, aka Mr Constantly Moody and Full of Angst. In fact, all we do is run around the house until I drop in a breathless, sweaty mess and he laughs.

Asshat.

"We only run, and you haven't even taught me how to fight! You haven't taught me how to do anything but run!" I snap, getting to the end of my rope. "Newsflash, alpha, I learnt enough of that in my own pack!"

"Then it shouldn't be so hard, should it?" he counters, and I huff as we stare each other down for a long time. Those stormy eyes that I can't read feel like he is burying himself into my soul to find out my secrets. I wish I knew what was going on in his head. Why he hates me so much. I climb to my feet and look at the door just as Henderson comes in.

"Hey...wow. Everyone looks in a really great mood in here," he sarcastically comments. Henderson looks amazing as usual as he brushes his black hair to the side.

"If your trainee is terrible, the mood cannot improve," Silas coldly replies. Ouch.

"Hey, I'm doing my very best," I all but growl out, making them both chuckle—even Silas, who quickly realises I made him laugh and goes silent with his eyes narrowed.

Henderson just laughs at our squabble, and Silas walks out of the room, not saying a word to either of us. I pick up the towel in the corner of the room and wipe the sweat off my forehead as Henderson gets to me.

"Is he always this moody? Does he have an asshole off button?" I ask.

"No, but if you find that button, let me know," he says, making me laugh. "I was wondering if you want to do some shifter training. Just something a bit more, well, better than this?"

"Anything's better than running two miles and doing sit-ups for an hour. Then more sit-ups and yeah, just more sit-ups," I reply.

Henderson laughs and cocks his head at the door. "Come on, I'll teach you how to call shifter energy to shift. You might not be able to actually do it. Not until Silas gives you permission, but you will at least know how to do it. I thought it could be fun, anyway."

"No, I'd like that. That sounds really good," I answer. Much better than having a shower and hiding in my room for the rest of the day, like usual. He smiles and we both walk out of the training room. In my week in the alphas' house, I've learned Silas is the moody one. Well, Valentine might also be classed as moody since he can be found in the bottom of a bottle all the time. Henderson is kind of funny, but also very protective. Ragnar is the one who spends all his time in the garage, and I'm pretty sure he loves his cars more than anything else. And then there's Trey...he pretty much lives in this world of his own, and he is too mature for his young age. He doesn't seem to do any kind of kid-like things. I did learn that he can outrun me when he literally outran me three days ago when I was doing two more sprints around the house. Now, after that embarrassing time, he no longer comes into training, but I see him around. I have sat down and watched several of these movies on Netflix with him in the evenings when no one else is around.

Henderson and I leave the house and go out of the back doors into the forest. The back area is covered in decking with nice, picturesque, fenced areas around it. There are some planters around the outskirts with soil in it, but nothing's been planted in them for a long time by the looks of it. We go straight into the forest, and I'm quite eager to explore more of this forest, as I felt too nervous to leave the house without one of the alphas so far. Except for the party, but that was with Phim, and I felt safe with a beta. But I haven't seen much of her since the party to ask her to take me into the pack. At some point, I need to be brave and leave, but I am giving myself a week. We walk through the forest for a while before Henderson randomly sits down, and I sit opposite him and cross my legs in the way that he has. He smiles at my little gesture and looks up at that beam of light that is shining through the side of the mountain that falls on my shoulder, making my hair look almost white.

"You know, you don't have to stay in all the time. If you want, you could just ask and one of us will take you out," he suggests, and it almost freaks me out that he read my thoughts so well, but I realise I haven't been hiding my fear for the outside of the house very well.

"Is it that obvious I'm going a bit stir crazy?" I ask.

"Only to us," he answers, and I sense a deeper meaning to his words I'm not getting, but I leave it. I look down at the ground and pick up some branches on the floor.

"It's not that. It's just like you said, I don't want to be challenged. I've always stood out everywhere. And no matter where I've gone in the pack, as much as it seems different here, I don't want to stand out that much."

"You did stand out at the party. As I've heard, you made a great impression on loads of people," he counters. "How would exploring the pack with me at your side be any different?"

"That was different because Phim was the confident one, and I only had to talk after her," I answer.

"No, it was different because it was you. It's okay, your confidence will build the longer you stay here," he answers. I suck in a deep breath.

"Okay, so how do we call the shifter energy?" I ask.

"Well, I'm guessing you were not taught any of this?"

"No one ever mentioned how to call shifter energy, how

to change into a wolf. We were just told that when we mated, our mate would tell us everything that we needed to know. That they would control the shift so we wouldn't have to worry about it."

"Yeah, that's what I thought. But okay, so we start from scratch," he replies, running his hand through his soft hair, and I track the movement. I wonder what it would be like to be closer to him, to run my hands through his hair, to feel his body pressed against mine...or lips touching. I shake my head and focus on what he is saying. "Our shifter energy is from the gods. That's where it comes from. That's where it's always come from."

"Why doesn't everyone know that? No one in Ravensword does!" I whisper in shock.

"Because some alphas lie," he answers easily, and I nod. "When the five packs were alive, all of which once ran this world, we all had different gods that we worshipped. It was never just the moon goddess, as you were told, or the forbidden god. There were five different gods, and the gods feed off the power of our worship."

"Our belief in them gives them magic?" I ask, and he nods.

"So if there ever comes a day where no one believes in any gods, there will be no magic for us to shift. It's important that we have our moon marks to connect us to our god, to make us that much stronger, more than usual. It's important that we believe in the gods. And that's exactly how you're going to shift. It's exactly how you call shifter energy. You need to believe in the forbidden god," he answers.

"Is the forbidden god strong?" I question. "Because he

only has this pack, and it's quite a bit smaller than the pack that worships the moon goddess."

"Yes, he is stronger because of the connection we have with him. But I agree with you, we do need more numbers, but don't worry about our problems with the pack politics. Just try to focus on the forbidden god," he suggests.

"That's the problem, I know nothing about him," I reply.

"Yeah, well, that might be an issue I have an answer for," he says as he pulls out a small book from his pocket. The small little book fits easily in his palm, and he hands it to me. I peel open the first page of the black leather book, which has nothing on the outside, and inside are detailed pages filled with writing and paintings of moons very much like the marks on my back. "Do you want to read it? It's the history of the forbidden god, what he stands for."

"Yeah. I mean, thank you. Did you write this?" I ask. He shakes his head, not saying another word. I look down at the book and start reading about this forbidden God.

"The forbidden god, like many of the gods, went by a million different names. Many knew him as Hades, many knew him as the brother of Zeus, but he has always stood for worshipping the moon and the changes it can bring. He stands for the darkness in the corners of the earth, the darkness which is always treated as evil when it is just misunderstood. The forbidden god was once exiled for his many, many crimes."

I PAUSE at this point and look up. "What crimes did he commit?"

"Many crimes that were very bad. Let's put it that way and say no more on it," he says, leaning back against the tree and stretching his legs out. "The forbidden god lost everything. He lost the only woman he ever loved and who loved him. All parts of his soul, and he knew he would never find her again."

Henderson looks up at the beam of light. "For further punishment, the forbidden god was separated in four parts, never to be whole again."

At this point, I realise I don't really need to read the book because, in some way, it's better that Henderson explains as he tells the story with so much passion, like he was there and he is simply telling me his past.

"What do you mean four parts?" I question, wanting to know more.

"His soul was separated into four parts. His soul was divided so that he could never have a pack following him. That was the idea, of course. Magic and shifters always seem to have a way around these awful little rules, just like the moon goddess found her own way."

"How did she find her own way?" I ask.

"Well, she had to because she was also in exile and had her own punishment to escape," he answers. I feel like my whole life has been a lie, every lesson I had in school, every book I read in the Ravensword Pack is nothing more than lies, and I was fed them for so many years. "The exiled gods made shifters."

"I never knew that. It was not what we were told in school," I reply.

"That's not too surprising to me, but, yeah, all of the gods that were once worshipped, that shared shifter energy of the world, every single one of them was an exiled god. That's why they are ruling down here and not in the afterlife with the other gods."

I've always wondered what happens when we die, just like everyone has, and the Ravensword Pack never had an answer for me. They always said the moon goddess would decide...but now I'm seeing it wouldn't just be her decision after all. Or if at all.

"So how exactly is it that the pack here is very clearly ruled by this forbidden god with four parts of his soul separated?"

"Well, that's the biggest secret of all. No one really knows the answer. All we know is that we do worship him," he replies...but I get the suspicion he is lying to me.

"But you are the first to worship him, right?"

"Maybe," he answers, looking like he wants to change the subject.

"Does that mean that you're keeping a secret from me right now?"

"Some secrets are kept for a reason," he warns.

"Yes, but I want to know this one," I reply.

"Maybe sometime soon. For now, I've told you most of what I can—" He pauses and looks to the left, hearing something I can't, by the looks of it. While relief clouds Henderson's face, a man walks into the forest. This man is small, shorter than I am, but he's extremely muscular, and his head is completely bald. Despite his strong appearance, he has very kind eyes, and he's dressed in strange navy clothes with a gigantic belt on with a big steel part in the middle.

He bows to Henderson before looking to me.

"Hey, you must be Mairin," he says, holding his hand out for me to shake. I climb up off the ground and shake his hand, and he nods once at me before looking to Henderson. "Alpha, we got a problem."

He hesitates and looks to me, a clear question of whether he should talk while I'm here. Henderson nods his head. "You can say it in front of her." Looking at me, he adds, "This is Beta George."

Beta George clears his throat. "By the main houses, there has been a big fire. We're not quite sure what's caused it, but at least three houses have gone up in flames quickly. We've gotten everybody out, and we are working on the fire, but they want to see the alpha. And you're the first one I could find."

"Okay, thank you, George. Mai, I have to go. Stay in the house," Henderson warns. I nod as they both step back, their eyes bleeding into red. They suddenly shift right in the middle of the air. They're black wolves, but Henderson's wolf is huge, twice the size of George's. They quickly run through the forest, moving like shadows through the trees. I watch them go until I decide to walk into the house, feeling restless because I can't help. I walk through the training room at the back and into the entrance area just as Trey comes running down the stairs. He slams straight into me, knocking us both to the floor, and I hurt my arm as I land.

"Trey, what the hell is wrong?" I ask, rubbing my arm.

He looks at me, and I see nothing but the frantic panic in his eyes that makes my blood go cold.

"I saw someone upstairs, and he's not from this pack," he tells me, grabbing my arm to drag me to my feet. "We have to escape!"

"What do you mean someone upstairs?" I ask, and I look up just as a massive white wolf appears at the top of the stairs.

I push Trey right behind me as I can't hear anything over my fast-beating heart. "Trey, run and don't stop running until you find someone."

Instead of listening, the brave boy grabs onto my hand tightly. "Not without you. We need to run together!"

But it's too late for either of us to do anything. The white wolf jumps off the stairs, and I jump to the side, missing its claw by an inch as Trey falls over his feet, and I stumble but manage to stay on my feet. I pull Trey back up and turn to the wolf, who is clearly here to kill me. The burning houses are the distraction, and this is Alpha Sylvester's way of getting rid of me. He will kill me, but he doesn't have to kill Trey. I stand my ground as this massive wolf looks at me, blood dripping from its mouth. I take a few steps back, and it growls, the noise making the ground vibrate. As my mouth goes dry, the wolf takes one more step forward, and at this point, sheer panic slams into me. I'm not ready to die. I realised that when I was thrown off the cliff, and I'm certainly realising it right now.

"Who sent you here?" I demand, almost screaming the words out at him. Of course, the wolf doesn't answer me. It just growls and steps forward once more. He's toying with me, taunting me at this point, like a game. He could kill me if he wanted to, but I think he's enjoying the hunt. He wants me to run like prey.

But if one of us is going down, it's going to be me and not Trey. I have to save him.

I look to Trey for a brief second. "Run to the door and do as I told you."

I kiss his cheek before I take off on my own, knowing the wolf is going to follow me, and I have to pray Trey listens to me. Looking back, I see the wolf chasing me as Trey runs straight to the door in the opposite direction. I head to the training room, hoping that I can get outside to the forest for some way to hide. I barely get halfway across the room when something hard slams into my back and I'm thrown across the room. The air is knocked out of my lungs when I hit the floor hard, and the wolf lands on top of me, his claws drawing lines of blood down my back, ripping my clothes open. I roll over, wanting to face my fate, and I look up just as he is about to bite my shoulder when a black wolf slams into his side, knocking him off me. All I hear next is the clawing of wolves being ripped apart, the snarling of their teeth, and the ground being torn by their claws. I feel hot blood spraying everywhere as I shakily stand up. The pain of the scratches on my back burns as I turn to watch every second of the wolf fight. The black wolf is so much stronger, so much more powerful. The white wolf, my hunter, didn't stand a chance.

It's over soon, and the black wolf stands up straight, red

blood marking its beautiful fur coat, and he shifts back. Silas is stood in front of me seconds later, completely naked, covered in blood, and I couldn't be more relieved to see stormy eyes. The storm saved me.

"Thank you," I whisper just before I pass out.

CHAPTER FOURTEEN

The flickering lights of the room slowly wake me up as I confirm that I'm safe while the memories of what happened before I passed out rush into my mind. I'm in my room, lying in bed under the warm covers, looking up at the glass ceiling above me. The unmoving trees outside that I've stared at for so many days, for so many hours, are a welcome relief to see. My back aches but is nothing compared to the pain I was in when I passed out. Silas saved me. Having him save me is still so surprising, and I feel like I've dreamt it. Dreamt that he wants me alive for whatever reason, and I doubt it's anything like the thoughts that I am feeling. The way I can't stop thinking of his muscular arms, the look in his stormy eyes I just want to stare at. I'm addicted to thinking about the alphas in inappropriate ways. He was the last person I expected to run in to kill that wolf for me. And the very fact that wolf was here at all makes me more nervous of what's to come for my future. At the end of the day, Alpha Sylvester is still hunting me. He knows I'm alive. The mating bond, even unfinished, means I can almost sense that he is alive as well, and I hate that there is any connection between us. I know deep down that this means he'll never stop coming after me. I'm not sure how to face that. How to face a future where it will be me fighting him for the rest of my life and putting everybody near me in danger.

"You look sad." Trey's voice makes me jump, and I turn towards the door to see him come in. He looks a bit sheepish for making me jump as he comes to the bed and sits on the end. Trey offers me a glass of water he carried in, and I accept it, taking a long drink and knowing I needed that. He takes the empty glass and places it on the floor by his foot. "The intruder is dead, you don't have to be scared or sad."

I sit up straight and cross my legs on the bed, keeping the blanket around me as it's slightly cold.

"I wasn't sad because of that," I start off and realise I can't explain this to him. He is a kid. I shake my head. "Never mind, how are you?"

Trey looks straight into my eyes. "You saved my life. There are not many people who have done that for me outside of the alphas who brought me up. Thank you."

"No problem, I'd do it a million times over. You know you talk like you're a lot older than you actually are," I tell him.

"Well, because I've grown up around these alphas, and I've always been treated as an adult rather than a kid," he answers. There is something sad about that, about his lack of a childhood. I wonder why the alphas took him in and not a normal family.

"You're really brave," I tell him, feeling proud. "You tried to stay with me even though it was dangerous. I really appreciate that, Trey." He looks really shy as he blushes and looks away.

"I was taught never to leave women in danger. I feel really bad for running the opposite way when you told me it was okay, but I thought maybe I could find someone to help you."

"It was the best thing that you could have done, and I'm really thankful that you did. I couldn't live with myself if you got hurt instead of me," I tell him, making sure he understands he did the right thing. "You remind me of a kid in the foster home I was in. His name was Jesper, and he was about your age. Also brave and stubborn."

"Hopefully you get to see him again," he says, seeming to understand too much for his young age. I guess the trauma of his life, of his parents sending him as a rejected baby, has made him grow up a lot more than many adults. "The alphas asked me to come and watch you and make sure that you're okay. There are guards around the house now. They're pretty mad. Want me to show you where they are?"

"Yes, that's like a really good idea. Let's be quiet, though," I suggest. He smiles as I climb out of the bed. Looking down at the nightdress that I notice I've been changed into, I don't even want to think about who changed me out of my ripped clothes. I feel my back with my hands, noticing that there are bandages over the cuts that were there, but they don't feel as deep as they once were. Some part of me is healing even without being able to shift. I'm changing. I can feel it, my body is stronger, and it's nothing to do with Silas's training. My connection to the forbidden god is growing, and I know it is magic healing me.

I grab a few of my clothes and tell Trey I'm just going to the bathroom to change. Once looking at myself in the bathroom mirror, I guess I must have lost more blood than I thought, because my skin is so pale. My green eyes look brighter, but I look really exhausted. I think I slept long enough though, and I need to get moving around. Every movement on my back hurts just a little as I drag my T-shirt and jeans on. I pull my hair up into a ponytail so the strands are not hitting against my back.

Once more I look in the mirror and stare at my green eyes, having no idea what I should do for my future. My plan to hide here is just not going well, and I can't expect these alphas to protect me forever. They'd be crazy to do that, but they said they were only here to train me and then they were going to let me go out into their pack. But if I'm going to bring constant danger, how can I do that? I shake the thoughts away, knowing Trey is waiting for me, and head out into the corridor. The once silent mansion is filled with noises, and I soon recognise it's the alphas arguing not too far away from us.

We get to the end of the corridor where Trey leads me, one I've not been down because I assumed it was just more bedrooms. There's a room right at the very back of the corridor with large double wooden doors and a staircase off to the side, which I assume goes up to the attic where the washing is that I'm yet to actually explore because the door is locked and the alphas believe I need rest before doing housework. I tiptoe to the doors and press my ear against them, not wanting to disturb the alphas but also wanting to hear what is going on. Trey does the same thing as I do and smiles at me in a cheeky way as I overhear some of the alphas' conversations.

I'm pretty sure it's Ragnar who shouts. "They are clearly here for her, and Ravensword have made it clear they will kill anyone in our pack to get to her. Four wolves are dead, and we can't stand for it."

"That's one problem, but there is another. I couldn't sense them. I couldn't hear them. I was in the garage the whole time, and I didn't hear any intruder. It was like magic protected them, and I don't know what magic could do that. It was impossible. Very impossible," Silas growls out.

"The Ravensword Pack are hiding something we don't know, and we need to fucking find out what before they come back here," Henderson states. They suddenly go silent.

"Come in," one of them shouts, which I'm pretty sure is Silas. My cheeks go bright red as I push the door open, and Trey makes a run for it down the corridor.

All four of the alphas are staring at me as I walk into what I assume is their study. The room is littered with books on every wall, so many they are stuffed into the fitted bookcases. There are several bookends and ornaments littered around on the solo desk, and piles of paper look like some have fallen onto the floor. A big window lines the back of the room, flooding the space with light.

There are four red leather chairs, and Silas and Henderson are sitting on two of them. Valentine is leaning on the wall, a bottle in his hand as usual, and his dark eyes are watching me. Ragnar walks straight over to me and places his hand on my back which is mostly healed, guiding me into the room to a spare seat.

"You should sit down. You just recovered from an attack."

I nod once as I sit down according to Ragnar's advice, even though I'm feeling so much better than when I woke up. Ragnar looks straight at Silas. "Silas, if you give her your permission to shift, then all of this would be solved."

"You know exactly why I'm not yet. She's not ready," he counters, his voice strong and firm.

"I do want to earn it from Silas, so that's not necessary," I put into the conversation as it is about me. I meet Silas's stormy gaze. "Thank you for saving me, by the way."

He doesn't say a word in reply, not that I was expecting him to. He just watches me closely.

I glance around the room. "Thank you for still keeping me here when I'm clearly a big danger to you all and your pack."

"No, this wasn't your fault. We took you into our pack, and that means you are pack. End of discussion. If you're in danger, then we all are," Henderson firmly tells me, and how none of them disagrees tells me they have all decided the same thing. My chest warms as I relax back in my seat.

"Our discussion is currently debating on how we're going to move forward, because it's clearly not a hundred percent safe here like it should have been. I would have sensed the wolf usually, and I did, but he must have been hiding there all that time. Something is amiss," Ragnar states, placing his hand on the back of my chair, his finger brushing across the back of my neck. The little touch soothes me in a way I never thought a man's touch could.

"I agree. It doesn't make a lot of sense." Henderson rubs

his chin as he replies. "Valentine, when you were in the house, did you hear anything?"

"No, of course he didn't, because he was drunk…as usual," Silas bites out. I feel bad for Valentine as everyone's eyes fall on him.

He looks directly at me.

"I should have been awake," is all he simply says before walking to the door, opening it and walking straight out with it slamming shut behind him. All of them sigh in annoyance.

"Well, at least he said some words for a change that were different from 'Fuck, where's my drink,'" Silas says, crossing his arms.

"Is Valentine always quiet?" I ask, because in all the time that I've been here, I haven't really heard much from him, except for that first day where I thought I saw the brief kindness of a man. But now there doesn't seem to be much, that it's just him, how he is.

Henderson is the one who answers me. "Something happened, and he's been like this ever since. He prefers the bottle to any of us."

I know that many people in my old pack prefer the bottle; they lived in and out of the pubs and bars. And Mike himself wasn't a stranger to a nice bottle of whiskey and drinking it until he passed out in his chair occasionally. I never really understood the addiction to the stuff.

"So, what are we going to do next?" Ragnar asks a pointed question towards Henderson.

Silas is the one who answers. "We get the betas to come and move in here for protection. They can live in the basement rooms, and then they can take turns patrolling. With that many eyes around, it appears unlikely that the wolf would get in here once again. And I think someone should always be around Trey and Mai just for the time being."

"What do you think?" Henderson asks me.

"I think I'm putting all of your lives at risk by being here. I never should have thought I could escape him. I'm not like all the other rejected here in this pack. I'm the alpha's rejected, and he wanted me dead. He just couldn't do it because his wolf wouldn't allow him to, so he let the sea kill me, but it didn't work. But he warned me, if I somehow survived, that he would hunt me." I pause, not able to look at any of them. "I'm being hunted, and I don't want to take anyone else to the grave with me when he finally gets to me."

"He will find his grave years before you do, Mai," Ragnar warns.

"If that's true, I need to learn how to be better and quicker in my human form. I need to learn how to fight well and fast. If you won't let me shift into a wolf to fight, which I don't think would work against him anyway as he is an alpha, I need to learn how to fight with weapons."

"We will begin the first thing in the morning with an alternative plan of training," Silas responds. I nod at him, respecting him for changing his mind.

"That's sorted, then. Perhaps we should go downstairs and have a relaxed evening? Don't know about you, but I'm a bit stressed from yesterday's events," Ragnar suggests.

"Yeah, that's a good idea," Henderson agrees, stretching

his arms above his head, and I watch the movement for way too long.

"How about pool?" Silas asks, cracking his fingers.

"We should ask Val to play. He usually comes out for a game," Ragnar replies.

"How do you play this pool?" I ask as I get up with them and follow Henderson to the door with Silas and Ragnar following. Ragnar moves quickly to my side, placing his hand on the back of my waist, and Henderson gives him a strange look, but all I can focus on is that Ragnar is touching me. That he is this close to me.

I wonder if it's because he feels that need to touch me, to have that connection that I'm searching for with them as well, or he is just being kind. I am quite happy for his constant contact when we are close as we head down the corridor together.

Henderson answers my question I'd almost forgotten I asked. "Pool is a game where you have a table and a certain set of balls on top, and you have to hit them into the holes until you can hit the black and win."

"Yeah, that was the worst explanation of pool I've ever heard," Silas sarcastically quips as we head downstairs. Trey appears at the bottom of the stairs with a big smile and a bowl of food.

"I brought snacks for pool night," he says.

"Someone's been using their wolf hearing," Henderson jokes, messing up Trey's hair before he escapes, and I can hear his laugh as he runs into the living room. This almost feels like a completely normal thing, even as Valentine stomps into the living room from the kitchen, holding a piece of paper in the air.

"Who solved the riddle that has been on the fridge for over a year?" he demands.

All of us go still, and all of them turn towards me. Once again, I have all the alphas' eyes on me. And what should be extremely intimidating just doesn't feel like it. It feels normal, relaxing, and that on its own is just terrifying to me. I shouldn't be this relaxed around alphas I've only known for a week. The alphas rule our packs; they are the most powerful wolves that can rip enemies to pieces in seconds. But here I am completely relaxed, wanting to be closer to them, staring at them constantly. I just need to get my desires under control. I need to get my heart to stop beating so fast around them, so fast they must be able to hear it. But right now I'm just nervous about the riddle and interested to find out it's Valentine's riddle, though.

I look down at the floor for a second. "I'm sorry, I didn't know you didn't want it answered. I just saw it and had to answer it."

"I wondered who'd done it," Ragnar says with a long laugh. "I saw it a few days ago."

"No. That's brilliant. No one else seems to love my interest in riddles," Valentine says with a smile. "I might put a new one up."

"That'll be nice. I like riddles. I used to read loads of books on them I had, so I find them interesting to answer," I reply.

"Wanna play pool?" Ragnar asks Valentine, patting his

shoulder. He looks down at me, and I feel the pressure of his beautiful eyes on me.

"Yeah, go on then. Only if new girl's playing," he answers.

"Sure, I'd like to learn," I say, making him smile. He really has a sexy smile. We all head into the living room and straight to the pool table. Silas and Trey sit on the sofa, right before Trey throws a little popcorn at Silas's face. It's just hilarious, and Silas laughs, surprising me. Trey is in a fit of giggles at this point, and Silas picks some more popcorn up and throws it at him. I am truly interested to see a playful side of Silas that I've never experienced or expected. A light side to him that clearly comes out around children.

Henderson grabs two sticks from the wall where they are clipped in, and he brings one to me. His is a lot longer and taller, but mine is about the right height for me. I watch them as they set the balls up in a triangle shape in the centre of the table. The black ball is at the front, and all the others are one of two different patterns.

"Okay, this is really a game for two, but I'll be sort of your trainer for today," Valentine playfully suggests. "We can team up on Hens as he always wins."

"Can't blame me for being brilliant," Henderson replies, making me grin.

Valentine instructs me on what to do as Henderson removes the triangle shaped frame, leaving the balls in the perfect triangle shape, and he places a white ball a distance away on the table.

"Ok, you need to lean over the table like this." Valentine shows me how to hold the stick, and he steps back.

I copy his position, and then I freeze when he comes up behind me, moving my hips a little with his large hands. Every single touch of his makes me shiver in a good way. I've never had a man close to me like this, standing behind me, having a hard body pushed against mine in a good way. He covers my hands with his and moves me into place. Even over the smell of whiskey that flows off of him, I can smell how he has a warm undertone, a masculine side, a scent that you just can't hide, and it's nice. He steps back once he's got me in the right position, and I still feel everywhere his body touched me.

"Okay, now just hit the white ball," Valentine instructs. The room goes still as I hit the white ball and it rolls, barely touches the triangle balls, shaking them a little bit out of shape, but they don't really go anywhere.

"I'll be honest, that was a bit weak handed, but don't worry, you can only get better," Valentine says with a playful chuckle.

Henderson smiles. "You're just making it easy for me, aren't you, Mai?"

I laugh. "So you're not going to give me an easy win on the first time?"

He shakes his head. "No, no, no. You're beautiful, but I can't lose."

I laugh again at his competitive nature, kind of liking it in some sense as he lines up and hits the balls a lot harder than I did. Two of the solid-coloured ones go straight into the holes in expert speed that could only come from playing this game repeatedly.

I'm so going to lose. I go next and get myself in the right

position and try to hit one of the balls into the corner, but it just bounces off and hits the side.

"Maybe this is going to be a long night," I say.

"Luckily, we kind of have a lot of time. We're not going anywhere," Henderson replies with a smile. We keep playing, with Silas, Ragnar and Trey watching and talking between them, almost watching TV at the same time. Henderson and Valentine soon realise I'm terrible at pool, and I don't think I will get better at this game any time soon. Henderson looks happy until Valentine takes over and somehow expertly beats him in three moves. For more than a second, it's completely normal between all of us. A normal, slightly weird pack relationship going on, and I can pretend that the outside world really isn't there. It was exactly what I needed to forget the attack, because starting tomorrow, I'm going to train until I can go back to Ravensword and kill the alpha hunting me.

There is no other way.

CHAPTER FIFTEEN

Ragnar Fall

Rubbing oil off my hands onto my jeans, I stand up and stretch my neck before staring down at the car I can't get to work. Every wire is in place, everything broken cleaned up and replaced, but it's still not working. It's fucking frustrating. Truth be told, nothing has been right since Mai turned up, and none of it is her fault or something we can fix. The alpha bastard of Ravensword let pure gold fall through his fingers, and in a way, I'm thankful he did. We have searched for so long for her, but the fear of losing her is real now. The wolf intruder nearly killed her. He nearly got away with taking her from this world, and then we would never be able to find her again.

"Ragnar!" Trey calls, sounding near the entrance of the garage, and I pop my head around the car to see him walking into the room. His top is covered in mud but still very clearly purple, and his jeans look a shade close to pink, and I can't help but laugh.

"Can you tell Mai to stop washing our clothes? All my tops are pink," he complains, just making me laugh more. I ruffle his hair and rest my hand on his shoulder.

"We all have strange shades of clothing since Mai started washing the clothes," I remind him. "But she will learn, and it would be rude to say anything."

He groans. "Can't you give her some tips? Please? The boys at school were—" He pauses mid-sentence, and I turn him to face me. Trey is like a son to me, and both my wolf and I see him as such. He has never called me anything other than my name, but I accept that he has a hard time with his past. We all do, but ours is more hidden in secrets.

"What happened at school?"

He looks away, a very un-Trey-like move. "I don't want to talk about it."

Trey walks off, and I let him go, rubbing the back of my neck. I don't have a clue what to do other than going and scaring the shit out of his classmates at school with simply a look. Maybe I should ask Mai. She seems to have a connection to Trey, and it would come with the added bonus I get to spend more time with her. With my brilliant plan, I head out of the garage and round the back of the house to the training room where she spends most of the day with Silas. Lucky bastard.

Not that he acts like it, but I know Silas has an issue revealing his inner feelings and opening up to anyone. Mai, even though she is our past, is a stranger in some sense, and I understand his hesitation to trust her. Something changed after the wolf attack. I don't know if it was him nearly seeing her die or that she risked her life to save Trey or the fact she is in danger now. He has lowered the guard surrounding him an inch, and I see Mai is relieved about it.

Maybe not about the intense training that wipes her out, which she has been doing for the last two weeks. Beta George passes me on the way to the training room, and he bows once as I go past and nod at him. Having the betas around has been a new struggle, something I'm not used to as I've always liked my own space, but I'd have the whole fucking pack in here if it meant keeping Mai safe.

The back door is slightly ajar when I get to it, and I carefully open it fully, hearing grunting and shoes sliding across the floor.

Then I see her, and it's like nothing else in the world even exists. A layer of sweat covers her beautifully pale skin, making the freckles on her nose and defined cheeks stand out more. Her silky blonde hair is in a braid that hangs over her one shoulder, and she is in much tighter clothes than I've seen her in before as she fights Silas. The material looks soft and clings to her thin waist, her curvy hips and strong, long legs. The top is small, just holding her breasts and showing off a thin line of skin around her ribs. Her ass looks spectacular as well.

The sight of her makes me as hard as a fucking tree, and I struggle to hide my reaction to her, especially when she is dressed like this.

Mai is faster than I expected to see her as she dodges Silas's sword and spins around to block his other one. She moves in perfectly planned out steps, one after the other, the training we all had a long time ago that makes you a damn good fighter. Silas isn't moving half as fast as he could, and he is definitely making it easy for her as he attacks, but she can only defend and avoid.

It's still better than nothing, and I'm proud of her.

Silas kicks her arm, smacking one of the swords out of her hand, and then his sword is under her neck. She breathlessly glares at him, and I chuckle. They both turn to me as Silas lowers his sword.

"Hello," Mai says, waving at me as I walk over. Silas nods in my direction but looks generally pissed off with my interruption.

"I was—" I get cut off as the clicking of heels makes me look to the door to the house as Eleline walks in, followed by Phim.

"I can't stop her from being stupid. Why did you have to sleep with her stupid ass?" Phim asks, and I see Mai flinch a little. Fuck.

Every woman before she came back feels like a massive mistake. We used them. Pure and simple. They were a way to relieve tension and forget about the world for a night, but it never meant anything. Eleline was just one of the women who were clingy and stayed around for much longer than they were welcome.

I see what she is going to do way before the words leave her mouth. "I challenge you, Mairin Fall, to a weapon challenge. I will be waiting on top of the mountain for you at midnight. May the forbidden god judge us and choose a winner."

Mai stands still, but her hands shake at her sides as she nods once. Eleline gives me and Silas what I think is meant to be a sexy smile before walking out. I have a personal rule not to kill females unless they are trying to kill me, but I want to rip Eleline to pieces.

I let out a low growl.

"Fuck!" Silas shouts, throwing his sword across the room where it slams into the brick wall.

"Follow her and make sure she leaves. Then lock the gates," I snap at Phim before running my hands through my hair. It isn't her fault, and I know that, but fuck we are in trouble.

"I'm going to die, aren't I?" Mai asks, her lost and frightened voice cutting through me harder than that sword in the wall.

Silas and I look at each other before I meet Mai's eyes. Her hauntingly green eyes seem to find my soul and pull it out of my chest for her to decide what to do with. "Eleline is a skilled fighter, but I watched her train. I know what her weaknesses are, and I will help you. Don't give up yet, Mai. Not yet. Not ever."

Mai gives me a shaky nod. Not an inch of her is full of any confidence as she looks to Silas. He wordlessly picks the sword up off the floor and holds it out to her. "We have training to do. Don't we?"

"O-okay," she replies, wrapping her hand around the sword. I pull my shirt off and throw it across the room, grabbing one of the swords on the floor and twisting it in my hand. I look up to see Mai's eyes on my chest, her cheeks flushed and her breathing a lot faster than it was a moment ago. Red hot desire burns throughout my body, and my wolf all but demands for me to kiss her, claim her, make her mine.

In time, wolf. In time.

CHAPTER SIXTEEN

I couldn't be more nervous if I tried, but if I thought I was nervous to go to the mating ceremony, this is nothing compared to the nerves I am currently experiencing right now. Simply knowing I'm going into my first challenge has me shaken down to my core. One way or another, someone is going to die tonight, and I am directly the cause. I shake out my hands, hoping to calm myself down a little as I walk to the mirror. I'm dressed in tight black clothes that are made of soft material. The top is all lace on my back but holds my body tight and my back straight. Dark black paint streaks are marked against my cheeks and hands. As Phim explained it, the marks are meant to be warrior markings to protect you, but I don't feel like any kind of warrior or protected in any sense. I've had two weeks of training, two weeks compared to no doubt Eleline's had her entire life to get this right. I just don't see how I'm going to be able to get out of this without getting myself killed. Phim comes up behind me and looks at my eyes, clearly seeing the fear there.

"Look, you know exactly how to do this. You've been

trained by the alphas of Fall Mountain, who are fantastic fighters, the best that I've ever seen. Don't count yourself out just yet. I know you're going to be able to do this," she tells me, and while having a friend believe in me is nice, it's another thing to actually be able to win this.

"Yes, but I've got no idea what she's going to use against me. I'm only trained in swords. I can't do anything else. If she picks an axe, how do I win that without losing my literal head?" I ask her, the nerves swimming back to the surface, and I can't hear anything other than my heartbeat as I walk away and start pacing.

"Calm," Phim suggests but makes no move to step in my way as I pace up and down. "You have survived this long, I believe you're not going to die now for some hussy who's jealous that you're living here instead of her. That's no end to your story."

"Do I have to kill her, Phim?" I gently ask, coming to a stop. "Can't I just let her live and win somehow?"

"Yes, she must die. It is the wolf way. We are not sheep, and we do not forgive death threats," she sternly warns me. "If you don't kill her, then women will just keep challenging you. One after the other, knowing that you'll give them mercy. Eleline herself will come straight back and challenge you once again, and it will just be an ongoing thing; you have no choice."

"I've never killed anyone."

"I know, it's always hard the first time you kill someone. Sex or death, the first time is always shit and haunting," she tells me, and I blush. She doesn't comment on it but laughs slightly before she focuses on her point. "The first person you kill always stays in your mind. But remember, she brought the challenge on, and she will try to kill you. You don't have a choice."

"Did you have a choice with the first person you killed?" I ask her. Phim looks away, a flash of anger in her eyes, and she crosses her arms.

"Yes, and I still chose to kill him, and that's a story for another day when I'm drunk and so are you so you're unlikely to remember," she states.

"I've never been drunk," I tell her.

"Try it. It's easy to forget who you are and the past that won't disappear. That's why Valentine is like he is," she tells me.

"We should go," I say, knowing I want to ask more about Valentine, but now isn't the time. I wipe my sweaty palms on my tight trousers that are stuck to my skin and walk out the door. My boots are clean, and I refuse to wear anything else. These boots were from Mike. He made them himself, and I need a bit of his strength for what is to come. I wonder what he would think of me right now.

The alphas are waiting in the entrance hall for me, each of them dressed in blue shirts and black trousers with the Fall Mountain Pack symbol on their chests over their hearts. I've seen the symbol around the house on random things, it's a mountain with wolves running in a circle around it, and the middle is filled with stars. The guys look imposing, terrifying, and to me, my solace. Trey is also there, looking equally as nervous as everyone else.

"Can't you tell her that you'll just move out or something? Then she'll stop, right?" he asks, stepping in front of the alphas to greet me first. His voice is nothing short of upset, and it hurts my chest.

"That is a good idea," I gently tell him. I immediately notice that he's more frightened than I am, and I need to be brave, even if it's just for this tiny second. He needs me to be brave because that's the right thing to do. I take a deep breath, walk up to him, place my hands on his small shoulders, and he looks straight up at me. I realise I'm probably the only real female figure he's had in the house. Someone who he's been close to, I mean. Phim might have been around, but I highly doubt she's much of the mothering type.

"I'm going to be okay, you know I'm going to come back here, and we can have dinner and play chess. I still need to learn what the knights do," I tell him, making him smile.

"You might die," he whispers.

"I'm not going down that easily. Don't count me out yet, Trey. You have hardly known me that long, and you don't know what I've got up my sleeve. I can do this."

He does not seem to believe me, and I really don't believe that much in myself either. I plaster on a brave smile and give him a quick hug before walking out the door, the alphas following behind me like it's a normal thing for us to walk like this.

If I ever tried to walk in front of or even beside a beta, I would have been beaten for it, as I've seen many people hurt for accidentally doing exactly the same. Instead, these alphas don't seem to care where I walk, and it's freeing. It makes me want to fight to live, for this pack, for the freedom they can give me. We end up walking in a line towards the gates and the steps in content silence, even with where we are going hanging over our heads.

Henderson's hand brushes against mine, a slight bit of comfort without actually touching me for too long. Even a simple, slight touch of a hand does things to me that I can't explain. My connection to them grows each and every single day. I'm fearful of what's going to happen when they do ask me to move out, when I have to leave them and pretend that they're just my alphas. I can't stay, because in the end, they will find their mates, and an alpha female would not want me around. I'm no alpha female. I'm not strong enough. I've got a sneaking suspicion they would've never taken me, anyway. They seem like the type that are quite happy living in their homes and taking women for any pleasure and nothing more. I think I am just here because they don't want me to die straight away and then have that on their conscience.

"Why are we fighting on top of the mountain?" I ask them.

"Our people in the pack believe the top of the mountain is where the gods can see all. People go up there to pray for a miracle, to party in celebration of the gods, to make love for the blessing of a child," Ragnar tells me, his voice poetic. "Everything is done up there, including fights to the death for anybody that we kill for any reason and challenges."

"We believe that their soul can travel straight to the gods with nothing in between them," Valentine says, and we all turn to him, the usually silent one. He looks away and takes a long drink from a bottle of god knows what he has brought with him.

I nod, wanting to understand. "The gods are always in the stars, right? That's what I was taught."

"Maybe they came from the stars, but I don't believe they live up there anymore." Silas's indifferent response surprises me.

"What does that mean? They can hardly be down here with us." I all but laugh.

"Why not? Why do you think the gods are not walking this earth right now with us?" Silas counters. Ragnar, Henderson and Valentine give him a sharp look, which I know means they want him to shut up. But why?

"They would lead all of us, and they wouldn't let alphas rule if they could themselves," I reply. "The gods are all-powerful."

No one replies to my comment, making me feel almost stupid for my answer, even though I get the feeling some of them want to say something. We walk in silence out of the gates and down the steps towards the path to the stairs that lead to the top of the mountain. I hear the drums first, slow beating drums that go on and on, filling the air with tension with every single beat. The drums even seem to match my own heartbeat, which is beating hard in my chest, making it so hard to focus on anything. I carry on up the stairs until we come out in the clearing, with Henderson at my side, Silas and Ragnar coming out afterwards, followed by Valentine, then we all stop, standing in line and looking at everything. There's a large crowd of at least thirty to forty people gathered around the edges, here to see what exactly happens. The drum players are at the back, five massive fire torches circling them. The lit torches

Her Wolves

line the sides of the mountain top, their embers flickering around in the air.

Most of the crowd are female—I get the feeling that most of them are love interests or want the alphas or they've had the alphas—and therefore want to know whether challenging me straight afterwards is going to work if I let Eleline live. I know I've got to prove myself today because these women will tell the pack every little detail or fight me to the death. My eyes flicker towards Phim, and she nods once, confirming my suspicions about these women, reminding me that I've got to do this. I've got to stand up on my own and fight for my life. I just hope no one ever challenges me to a shifter fight, considering I can't shift yet. And I highly doubt Silas is friendly enough to just offer me his permission to shift. I haven't gotten close to cutting him in our practice fighting, but I'm hopeful for the day that I do.

I take a deep breath and walk straight to the middle of the clearing. The ground is rough, meaning that it's going to be hard when I fall. I walk straight to where there is a stone table that looks old, and it has six different weapons resting on top of a pile of flower petals.

Two swords, two daggers, an axe and a bow with arrows. Each of them looks dangerous and old. But thankfully, Silas has made me hold each one of these weapons this week. First of all, we know that I'm crap with the bow as I can't aim. We know that the axe is too heavy for me. I've got no chance of picking up the daggers because they are too lightweight and mean I have to be really close to her. I also don't have the aim enough to throw them. But swords. Swords is where I am good at. Even if these swords look heavy. But

I've been training with heavier swords today, and I know that I will be able to fight, using them with at least some ability.

Eleline is dressed in pretty much nothing but tight black shorts and a very small black top showing off all her flat and toned stomach with zero curves to her hips. Her hair is braided, and she has warrior marks all over her body, from her cheeks to her arms to her stomach, all in the shade of red, which I think is meant to portray blood. My marks are black, which are here just to represent the pack. To represent the forbidden god and hope for his personal blessing today.

Ragnar leans close to me. "You've survived worse than this, you can survive this, I know you can."

Silas gently touches the back of my shoulder. "We're going to be here for you. You don't let me down, okay? I have not trained you to lose, and between us, you have shifter strength now. You've had it for days, so you are not fighting alone. Your wolf is with you."

I glance back at him, meeting his gaze. "I know I'm not alone."

But I wonder if he realises I mean him and the other alphas.

Silas is going to take it personally when I get beaten up and lose. If I get beaten, he's got a point. I've got to stop putting myself down. Part of winning something is believing in me. So here I am, believing that I can actually do this.

I meet Valentine's eyes, and he looks away, taking a long drink. He is going to be drunk by the end of this. Henderson just looks at me once, his whole body shaking with the need to take this fight for me. To step in, to make me safe again. But we both know that can't happen this time or ever. I need to stand my own ground. This is a fight between girls. It's a fight that's coming directly at me, and I've got to do it. Silas moves to stand in the middle of us. He looks straight at Eleline, who is already staring at him. "If you cancel now and walk away, there will be no payback for this."

"You can still survive this," I whisper, and her eyes snap to me, whatever calm was there bleeding from her eyes into pure anger as her eyes take on a red tint. Her eyes look up at him once more. I can tell she really thinks she loves him. But it's not love, not the love I've read about in books and heard in Mike's voice when he speaks of his dead mate. If you love someone, it's painful, it's consuming and the most dangerous thing in the world. It's dangerous because you have to put them first, even when it rips your heart out. You have to let them go. You have to let them be with someone else if that's what makes them happy. You don't force them to be with you. And you certainly don't try to kill the person they're with. That's just not going to get you exactly what you want, and it's no way to show someone that you love them. At the end of the day, you have to let them go sometimes, and Mike told me it's hard to be in love. I'm yet to fall in love with anyone, and a part of me fears it as much as I want it.

It's exactly why being around these alphas is so dangerous. They make my soul move and my heart beat like no other.

I take a step forward, and Eleline looks to me again with such hate, hate that has likely been brewing since we met. But I don't think she will stop until I'm dead—and every woman is dead who goes anywhere near the alphas she thinks are hers. I wouldn't be surprised if I'm not the first person she's challenged for being anywhere near them. I sense she is powerful from how long she can hold eye contact with Silas, how the women here look at her. She could have been a beta with that kind of power, like Phim, but now she can't.

"The challenge will continue," she says. My heart feels like it drops in my chest, and my blood goes cold, knowing for certain that there's just no way out of this other than me killing her or her killing me, and I really don't want to die yet. I was given a second chance at life, and I just can't die right now. I'm well aware what that means for this day.

Eleline picks up one of the swords, brushing her body against Silas, and something like a growl leaves my lips, shocking me and her. Silas raises an eyebrow, making his point very clear. My wolf is fighting with me. I feel a bit of relief that Eleline took a sword as I walk and grab the second sword. She's definitely got the better one of the two. It looks lighter than mine, but mine is okay to fight with. It's gold plated, and the tip is extremely sharp. The handle is made of some kind of soft leather, and even though it looks heavy, it's quite lightweight and balanced. It fits nicely in my hand when I hold it up. Silas walks into the middle of the clearing, while Eleline and I go on the other side, and we stand a respectful distance apart with him in the middle of us. Silas looks up at the stars above us, the stars that light up the sky so bright, it really is beautiful for a tragic night. Midnight under the stars, with the gods watching as a life is taken.

It's at least a lovely place to die.

"May the gods judge this challenge and rightfully find a

winner. May you play fair. The alphas have accepted this challenge."

When the last word leaves his lips, he walks past me and back to the other alphas, his eyes staring at my face until he can't anymore. I don't look at him, because I keep my eye on the person I know is going to attack me any second.

She lets out a very low growl, a warning threat, before she swings around her sword in her hand and comes a little closer to me.

"You could run away, you know? You sure you didn't run away from your first pack and tell that little rumour you made about being the alpha's rejected mate?" She laughs a little. "No one believes it, by the way, did you know that?"

We circle each other, and I make sure to stay a good distance away from her. Hold my sword ready for her attack. I try not to let her words get to me, but it's hard. She's obviously picking things she knows can irritate me. "Did you have anybody you care about back in your old pack? Were you just happy leaving them behind?"

She tries to catch me with her sword, but I jump out of the way, making her smile. "You know, if you actually were the alpha's rejected mate, I bet he killed anyone who knew you and was close to you. I bet he killed and tortured them."

"No," I bite out over the heavy sound of the drums.

"That's all your fault. Do you know that? Do you care about anybody other than yourself?" Her words get to me this time, and I end up shaking in anger without really thinking about it. I run at her, attacking her first with my sword as she blocks it effortlessly and elbows me hard in the stomach. I gasp, all the wind leaving my lungs as I fall backwards. She swings her sword hard at me, hitting my arm but not doing too much of a deep cut as I slide out of the way. I breathlessly straighten myself up as the wind harshly blows around us, whisking escaped strands of hair into my face.

Eleline just smirks and twirls her sword in her hand.

I know what her plan is, how she's going to win. She is expecting me to attack every time, hit her again and again until I'm too weak to defend when she finally attacks me. This is not what I planned for with Ragnar and Silas. This is not what her weaknesses are. She's meant to be weak because she hits from the right all the time, and she's not as athletic as she looks because she's too strong, muscled, so she can't be flexible. But that's not her plan today. She knew Ragnar would tell me that, so she came up with a new plan. To bait me. To make me mad. And of course, I'm taking the bait.

I grit my teeth in annoyance as she keeps on talking. "What's it like being the alphas' whore? We all know you are. No way have they just kept your pretty blonde ass in the alpha house without expecting you to be on your knees for them or bent over their beds."

Hot blood drips down my arm from the cut as I try to block her out, to try and calm the storm of anger building in my chest. I want to kill her, I sharply realise. I want to end her when I take a calming breath and a way to spin this, to win, comes to me.

I cock my head to the side. "I've never been on my knees for them, but I know you have, and apparently they didn't like it, because they certainly didn't come back for more, did they? You were forgettable."

Her eyes light up with anger, burning bright red, her wolf not liking the disrespectful comment. Two can play at this game.

She runs at me this time with more speed than I expect her to, and I barely manage to defend myself with my sword as she tries to hit me. She hits me again and again, harder and harder. Each time the sword clangs in my hand, the vibration shaking the bones in my arms. My feet scrape against the floor with each movement as I step back again and again. She hits and hits and hits until sweat is pouring down both our faces; I jump to her left and swing my leg out, kicking hard in the middle of her back. She stumbles a little, and I swing my sword round, hitting her on her side and cutting her just below her ribs. She cries out and moves out of the way, lifting her sword up again. Her eyes are burning with anger, glaring from her wolf.

But I know she can't shift, and I know her wolf wants to. Her wolf wants to rip me to pieces.

"How does it feel being rejected? Because I was rejected by my intended, and I know exactly how it feels. But it's worse for you, isn't it? Because you weren't asking him to mate with you. You're just asking him to sleep with you, and they still didn't want you. This is the only way to get their attention, and they still aren't looking at you," I tell her, knowing that I've acted like a total bitch, but I just can't see any way out of this. I need her angry. I need her to attack me. Her eyes burn so hard with fury that I can almost feel it.

And for a second, a part of me just wants to say I'm sorry, to tell her that she can find her own fate and mate, she just needs to look for them somewhere else that is not with the alphas. But we both know that we're far past that point. She will not stop, and I need to survive. And when it becomes a game of surviving, it's no longer something that's fair or nice. I have to do what I have to do. She attacks me once more, this time just as hard. But her movements are slower. She's wearing herself out, her plan has backfired on her. And after all, it's a very good plan. She attacks me again and again, and this time she nicks me a few times. Eleline cuts a few strands of my hair as she makes a sharp turn to her right, and then she has me almost backed into a corner. People move out of the way for us, and I see my move.

I see it before I even think about her. I get close to the wall, and as she swings, I duck so she hits the wall, her sword smacking hard enough to loosen her grip. And I move to the left, using up her weakness for her left side, and slam my sword straight through her stomach in the pause, the force of my move harder than I thought it would be.

Not just on my arm, but on my soul.

The world seems to go still in this second. I realise I've won, and I realise I'm killing someone. I'm actually taking a life. And it feels wrong, just wrong on so many levels.

I let go of the sword, with it still buried in her stomach as her eyes look up at me, and I catch her as she falls. I hold her head up on my lap and brush some of her hair out of her eyes.

"I'm sorry," I tell her, because I really am. "And for what it's worth, I don't think it was ever you with the alphas. I think it's them. I don't think they know anything about commitment or how to love someone. They are lost, and neither of us is a bright enough light to guide them back. I don't think anyone is, not even the gods."

My words are gentle and true, because they certainly do not love me. I tell her this, knowing that that will make her feel better in her last moments, that's all that matters right now. I want her to think she has won, to feel something good. Her eyes flicker shut, and that body goes still in my arms, and nothing moves for a long time. I know her soul has left her body, and I know that it was me who caused it. And there's nothing I can do to take back that innocence, to take back what I've been forced to do. My life has changed. This pack has changed me, but I'm alive. Whatever it means to be now.

CHAPTER SEVENTEEN

"You need to get up," Silas coldly tells me, not an inch of comfort or understanding in his voice. He no doubt heard what I said to Eleline when she was dying, and he sounds pissed. I don't stand up, even when it's been too long that I've been on my knees, I don't want to let go of her dead body in my arms, knowing that if I get up, it's more real. The surrounding crowd are cheering my name, drowning out any of my senses. Silas's hand rests on my shoulder, and I pull away from him.

I look up to them. "This is your fault. All of yours, and I was forced to do this. To be a killer."

Henderson looks down at me. "She would have died one way or the other. Her obsession never would have stopped. Her wolf was obsessed, and our wolves are not easily swayed from what they think is theirs. Our primal side is hard to resist, even for us alphas."

"Some people are meant for others, and some people are not. That is just the way it is," Silas states. I'm surprised he knows anything about feelings and love, let alone mates.

Henderson leans down, and he picks Eleline's body up out of my arms and carries her.

"Let's go and bury her together," he suggests. "She had no family as she was rejected from your pack as a teenager for sleeping with someone who wasn't her mate. I don't think she had many friends or anybody really she lived with to say goodbye in the pack, and no one has come forward. We could go together if you wanted and bury her at the place where we bury most of our pack."

"I don't think I should be the one who buries her," I whisper.

"I believe it should be. Come with me, Mai," Henderson replies, staring into my eyes, and eventually I nod.

Silas, Ragnar and Valentine don't say anything, because I stand up and follow Henderson out. Phim reaches out and gently touches my arm. "I'm very proud of you, even if you're not proud of yourself right now," she says. "One day you will see that surviving is worth everything."

Maybe for her.

"Maybe surviving isn't something we should all just aim for. Maybe living with ourselves should be more important," I reply, feeling the alphas' eyes on me, taking in every one of my words. She doesn't have an answer for me, and I don't really expect one as I turn away. I head down the path with Henderson, and we go down the stairway, onto the steps and straight back to the house. Henderson never looks back or pauses, and he certainly never lets her body drop to the floor. I appreciate the level of respect he gives her as we go to the garage where he finds the keys on the side of the wall and unlocks the car. I help him open the boot of the car, a small, silky red car with quite gigantic wheels. It looks weird, but I guess it's one of Ragnar's inventions.

Henderson lies her body in the boot of the car gently, and then he goes and finds a white blanket, and I help cover her. When he covers her face, I can't help but look, feeling the guilt hitting my chest hard. It's impossible to know that I took her life. It's just nothing I could forget. Her blood soaks the white blanket in seconds, and Henderson shuts the boot, jolting me out of my thoughts. We get into the car, and I sit in the passenger seat, wrapping my arms around my knees as he reverses and takes off down the path.

We head around the back of the house, through the forest, and we come out to an archway of gates hidden by the trees and built into the mountain, flooding in light from outside the small cavern in the mountain wall. Henderson gets out and opens the gates, and I see that there are two betas waiting by the gates on the other side. They bow and hold the gates open for Henderson as he comes back. We drive out and down a flat path, which goes all the way down the mountain, and my eyes take in the view over the sea and how beautiful it is here at night.

It's really too beautiful for a night like this. Henderson leans over and puts his hand on my knee. And that's all he does to comfort me, but it's all that I need before I cry. Tears fall down my cheeks as I break into sobs, and I just can't stop. At some point, I put my hand over his and just hold on. Just needing that connection to someone else, someone real, as I take in everything I've just done. I don't stop crying until we get to the bottom of the mountain. We drive down the plain dirt road, which is lit up with tiny lanterns, but with the headlights of the car, it is bright enough to see where we're going.

Eventually, we come to a clearing, and I can see that it's a graveyard filled with blue gravestones. Each one of them has a shining rock on top, making it eerie and pretty here. And silent. There isn't a noise in the world after Henderson turns off the engine of the car.

We both look out, and Henderson hands me a tissue from a box in the back. "Thanks," I mutter before wiping my eyes and blowing my nose.

"I killed a man when I was twelve, right after he murdered my uncle in front of me," Henderson tells me. I go still and look up at him. "We were on the run and knew they were close. My uncle fought hard to save me, but he was outnumbered. He took down two of the others while I hid behind a tree, shaking from head to toe in my wolf form. When I saw my uncle die, I lost it, and my wolf ripped the man to pieces. I still, to this day, have never forgotten it, and I understand where you are right now."

"Thank you for sharing that with me."

"And for the record, you were right. We are too broken, and it was never Eleline's fault," he quietly tells me. "We've been broken since we were born, and there was only ever one person who could save us."

"Where is he?" I ask.

"She," he corrects, meeting my eyes. "And in every sense, she is gone from us. Untouchable."

"Did you love her?" I ask, feeling more than jealousy burning in my chest. I feel a need to know this answer.

"Why do you want to know that?" he asks. "I have a feeling the answer will do us both no good."

"You're right, it wouldn't," I quickly say, looking away. "I shouldn't have asked."

"You should have," he counters. "But now isn't the time for the answer. I will start digging a hole for Eleline, and could you walk to the beach for a nightstone? It's just down that lit up pathway."

He points to a path on the left through the forest, which has fire torches lighting up the way.

"Nightstone?" I furrow my brow.

"Oh shit." He pauses. "We believe nightstones are made of pure magic and they guide souls in the afterlife. Every wolf should have a nightstone on their grave, chosen by someone close to them."

"Shouldn't you pick it then?" I ask. "I wasn't close to her."

"Neither was I," he counters, his words ringing truthfully. "Get the stone. Call if you need me."

"Okay," I say, opening the door. I head into the forest, welcomed by the many noises of the forest and the cool breeze that leaves goose bumps on my skin. My breath is taken away when I step out onto the beach and see the nightstones littered everywhere. The nightstones stand out, bright glowing green against the blue waves and sand. I lean down and pick up the nearest one to me and brush the wet sand off it. A stone to mark the end of a life is so simple and special…and I have to bury my guilt. I did what I had to, to survive, and surviving is all I have now.

CHAPTER EIGHTEEN

After climbing out of the shower, I braid my hair in a complicated way that Phim taught me before tying it in a hairband. She says it's a fishtail braid that she learnt from humans, and it was easy to learn after a few tries. I find myself always wanting my hair put up in that way. After pulling on my clothes, I look at myself in the mirror. My hair seems to have gotten longer over the last few weeks, ever since the challenge that haunts me. Thankfully, no one else has come to challenge me, and it's been quiet around the house, even with the looming threat of the Ravensword Pack sending someone after me. The alphas and betas never leave me alone, not for long. They are around a corner at all times. I have a feeling if the Ravensword alpha sent anyone after me again, he would be dead before he stepped close to the house. My green eyes stare back at me in the mirror, the colour looking duller than usual, a mixture of how I feel inside.

I still can't get the image of Eleline dying in my arms out of my nightmares. Sleep has definitely not been my friend over the last couple of weeks. I rest my forehead against the cold mirror for just a second before I straighten up and head down the stairs to find some lunch to occupy my swirling thoughts. I spent the morning training with Silas, who says I'm getting better, which is a big compliment from him because he spends most of the lesson now being grouchy for reasons I'm yet to understand. A very strange but usual routine has fallen over the house, and it's so normal I don't know what to think of it. The alphas seem happy, the betas are kind, and I can see why the alphas chose each one of them. The betas are always around circling the house, always listening, and they join us for dinner in the evenings while two of them stay outside. It's been a good way to get to know them and understand why they became betas. For most of them, it wasn't a choice based on simply being a strong wolf. It was their acts as a strong wolf that got them chosen. They are each good people and loyal to the alphas down to the bone.

It's how a pack should be run, in my opinion, from seeing two completely different packs. Trey walks past, waving at me with a big grin before heading into the living room. He reminds me so much of Jesper in his own special way. He's different from Jesper though, who was always so serious, and Trey is funny. I get along with him more than I thought I would. I walk into the kitchen, smiling when I see a new riddle on the fridge.

I am beautiful, up where the gods can only reach.
I am seen by all, wished for by few, yet I cannot appear on a wish alone.

Her Wolves

> To wolves, I bring light, to some gold.
> I am eternal, and there is no end to my existence...
> What am I?

I GET myself a bowl of rice with chicken with some sauce before I sit on the stool and stare at the riddle as I eat my food. I struggle to figure it out for a second until I focus on the line about wolves and light, then it clicks. Wolves see everything in the dark, but in the day, there is one thing that looks like pure light, and it fits with the rest.

When I'm finished, I wash my plate and grab a bottle of orange juice from the fridge before I stop to write the answer on the note with the pen I found on the side. I leave the kitchen and listen for any sounds in the silent house, wondering what I should do. I could go and watch something on Netflix with Trey, but when I peep into the room, he isn't there. Eventually I decide to wander around on the top floors of the house and see if I can find something to do. I go up to the attic and look to see if there's any more washing that needs to go into the machines that wash clothes. For some strange reason, the guys have been doing their washing in the night and beating me to it. I think they have done more washing than ever before in the last few weeks, judging by how there used to be piles of washing and now there is nothing. Everything seems washed before I get to it, seems like they are only interested in me drying and folding the clothes at this point. It could be something to do with how some of the clothes had been coming out in strange colours, but I'm not quite sure how to stop that.

I wander back down the stairs to the first floor and look towards the open study doors at the end, knowing that I really shouldn't sneak around in there. But still, I walk towards them and peek inside the room, looking over my shoulder to make sure no one is around. The study is empty, which is rare because the alphas each spend a lot of time in here with the doors closed.

I sneak in, leaving the door open behind me, and see there is a single book on the large desk. All the messy papers that were once here are gone. I walk around the desk, running my fingers over the hardwood of the desk before sitting in the chair. The massive chair makes me feel much tinier than I am as I rest back on the leather, smelling the alphas' scents in here on everything. They smell too good, too addictive. I shake my head and try not to focus on them for a second. The book in front of me is made of some maroon leather that feels old as I place my hand on it. Suddenly something like a shock zaps my hand, and I jolt away, feeling the tips of my finger pads are a little burnt.

"What the hell?" Whispering to myself, I look at the old book and around the table, finding a pencil on the edge. I pick it up and move back to the book once more. I damn well know I'm too curious for my own good as I use the pencil to open the book to the first page.

The book seems to be a record of some kind, all of it done by hand. There's a painting that looks like a dark-haired human, but strange bat-like wings come out of its back and stretch out at its sides. The wings look white, almost glimmering with a silver undertone. The human is bare from the waist up, and markings line the middle of the man's chest. The markings look like the outline of pomegranate fruit in red, and four red stars go down in a line underneath it. Whoever painted and wrote this book has incredible skill, and I feel spelled to read what is written below:

Once, a long time ago, before wolves hid on earth, before humans ruled the earth, there were creatures that did not have a name. These creatures had human bodies with wings made from pure nightlight. Wondrous creatures with a heavy temper and powerful instincts, they watched the fall and rise of every being on earth. They have extraordinary powers, powers unlike anything that the world will ever see born again. Eventually, these creatures became known as angels. They twisted human stories to the point where humans worshipped these angels without knowing what they worshipped. They were made to believe angels came to save them all.

But they never were.

The only way the angels survived was from drinking animal blood. The angels soon realised human blood was the most desired and fulfilling of all the animals on this earth.

Nature itself came up with a natural enemy to ensure the survival of humans. It came up with the shifter wolves. These new creatures, connected deeply to the moon and given powers, were created with a mixture of angel blood and human.

The shifter is the only creature in this world that is poisonous to angels' existence. One bite and—

I JUMP, nearly letting out a scream as the book is slammed shut in front of me, and stare at Henderson's burning red eyes as he leans over the desk, his face directly in front of mine. His wolf is here, not really Henderson, and his power feels very dark as it surrounds itself around me. Dark and powerful...and alluring. I almost forget everything as I settle into the darkness pressing against my soul, letting Henderson's wolf see how much I am affected by him.

I don't know why I'm not frightened.

I can feel his power, the shadows of his magic, of his essence, breathing in the air around me like it has a life of its own. Henderson's eyes slowly bleed back to pale blue that reminds me of the sea at night. "We don't make many rules in this house, but it's an unspoken one that this room is off limits to anyone but alphas unless invited."

I stand up off the chair and hold his gaze. Even if my hands shake a little bit from doing so.

"Maybe I should be told about this rule in advance. I wasn't aware that reading books was against the rules."

He tilts his head to the side as I speak, and I don't breathe as he leans forward. His nose gently touches the side of my face, and I hear him breathe in my scent. Everything about how close he is to me makes my legs feel weak until he backs off, and I suck in a breath.

"You're right. There are no rules for reading...just not

this book," he tells me a little more gently. Henderson walks to the bookcase and slots the book back in a place where there is a gap for it. "Some books hold more secrets, and trust me, this is not a secret you want. You need to forget everything you read in there."

"What are angels?" I ask instead.

"Nothing more than fairy tales," he replies.

"Are they real, Henderson?" I ask, wanting a real answer and not the spin on it he just tried to pull.

He looks me dead in the eye as he answers. "As much as the gods walking this earth are."

I have no idea what to think about that answer as we stare at each other. That was more of an avoidance of an answer, but I decide to leave it. I shake my head; I never seem to get a clear answer from any of them.

"Okay, I'm going back to my room," I tell him as I walk around the desk and try to go past him, but his hand reaches out and clamps around my wrist, stopping me.

"No, you're not. I'm taking you out for the night. I was coming to find you to ask if you wish to come on a hunt in the forest," he asks.

"Hunting with someone who can't shift? Why would you want me there?"

"We think you should come. It'll be good for you. I know you've not shifted yet, but your wolf will be able to sense and understand the hunt," he explains, stepping a little closer. "Please come on a hunt with us."

I've always wanted to go on a hunt, truth be told. Many of my classmates went on them with their parents and loved to brag about it back in my old school. The thrill of hunting something is natural to a shifter, shifted or not. It's electrifying. It's all about the hunt. Wolves look to chase and kill, it's natural to us.

I nod with a small smile. "Yes, I'd love to do that."

"Good," he replies, but he doesn't let go. His thumb rubs a circle against my arm, and I close my eyes at the strange pleasure his touch sends through me.

"I-is it safe for me to leave the house? With the Ravensword alpha on my heels?" I whisper, the words feeling too loud for the small room.

His finger touches my chin, and I open my eyes as he tilts my head up, our eyes clashing. "Let him come when we are at your side. I will rip through an army of wolves to protect you."

My heart pounds faster than ever before as he lets me go and walks out of the room, leaving me to ponder if he meant what he just said.

A voice inside my head tells me he did. It tells me I'd do anything to keep him alive too, and that is more dangerous than I can admit.

FOR THE NEXT FEW HOURS, I help Ragnar pack the car with tents, boxes of snacks and water, and everything we need to camp for the night. I pack myself a change of clothes and some things out of the bathroom that I need, like my toothbrush, into a small bag before meeting them at the car.

Ragnar and Henderson are near the car, talking quietly,

when I come into the messy garage. When I come in, they suddenly go quiet and look at me, like that's not entirely obvious they were talking about me.

"Ready, Mai?" Ragnar asks, walking over and taking my bag from me. He places it in the trunk of the car as Henderson crosses his arms, avoiding my eyes.

"Ready," I answer with a small smile, despite how awkward I feel.

"Good," he replies with a grin and opens the car door for me for the front passenger seat.

"Since when am I not sitting shotgun?" Henderson quips.

"Since women always come first," Ragnar replies, sharing a smirk between him and Henderson.

"Touché," Henderson replies with a chuckle. It takes a few seconds for me to understand the insinuated joke that I missed, and my cheeks turn red. I slide into the passenger seat, and a few minutes later, Trey, Phim and Henderson climb into the back. Ragnar shuts the boot of the car and gets in a few moments later.

"It's been too long since I've hunted," Phim says and leans forward, patting my shoulder. "Are you excited, Mai?"

"Yes," I tell her, and she leans back, looking at Henderson over Trey, who has headphones in his ears and his eyes closed as he lets out a long yawn.

"You seem tense today, Alpha Henderson," Phim points out.

"It's been a strange day," he bluntly answers. I feel a little bad for snooping in their things, but I want to find out more about them. I can't shake this feeling about them. Like something isn't right. It's no doubt something to do with the secrets that I haven't figured out about them yet, like where they came from, what secrets they are desperately trying to hide from me. We drive in silence through the pack, and I find myself almost drifting off to sleep after an hour of driving out of the city into thick forest land.

Eventually, we go off the path altogether and straight in the forest on what looks like a dugout dirt path before randomly stopping near a clearing. We all climb out, and Phim hands me a torch light so I can see what we are doing. This one is bright and powerful and works far better than any torches I've seen in my whole pack, making me curious how they got this. So many things in the pack look so new it's like humans recently sent them here, but that's impossible. Humans haven't come over the border in years, and we don't have much contact with them anymore. I don't say anything at the risk of annoying them, though. While Ragnar and Henderson make the tents up, Trey, Phim and I go in search for sticks to make a small fire. When we come back, we light the fire—well, Phim does with expert skill—and sit down around it, watching the alphas. It doesn't take them too long to put up the two grey tents and click on lanterns inside of them.

"I'm sorry, but I do snore, and you're sleeping in a tent with me tonight. I bet the alphas didn't mention that," Phim chuckles. I shake my head, making her laugh.

"So the alphas and Trey are going in the other one?" I ask.

"Yeah, it's got three zip-up spaces," she explains. "Ours has only got two."

"Okay," I reply. I've never exactly camped out in the middle of the woods on my own, unless you count when I was twelve and was found in the forest, but I don't. But it should be interesting.

"I'm happy you're not one of those girly types who never want to go camping," she says. "It's nice to have a girl out here instead of just guys."

"I'm glad to be here," I tell her.

"We're going to team up," Ragnar announces, clapping his hands together. "I will take Mai, and you three can go together."

"That's not fair. We all know you're the best hunter," Phim says with a pout. "There's no way we're going to find the prey before you."

Henderson just smirks. "He won't be the best this time."

Ragnar just grins back. "Bring it on, brother." I love their banter and smile to myself as Ragnar nods his head to the side. I pick up my torch light, and he takes it out of my hand.

"No, not this time. I'm going to shift, and we need to stay in the dark. The moonlight will guide us," he gently tells me, putting the torch down.

"I can't see in the dark like you can," I remind him.

He moves closer, and my breath hitches when he reaches out and tucks a stray strand of hair behind my ear. "You're a wolf, Mai. Let your wolf guide you."

"Okay," I whisper as he steps back and starts undoing the buttons of his shirt.

I look away, hearing more rustling of clothes and then inhaling the telltale sign that they've shifted when everything smells like magic for a brief second. I look back, shocked and in awe at the black-furred wolves, which are just beautiful. All of them are pitch black, but Henderson's and Ragnar's wolves really do stand out compared to Trey's and Phim's since they're quite magnificent wolves. They are literally twice the size.

Henderson's wolf looks over at me, bright red eyes glowing in the dark and looking like embers dancing to the beat of a flame. His wolf's eyes bore into mine before he growls once, then runs off into the forest, kicking up the ground with his giant paws. Trey lets out a long howl before running off in the direction Henderson went, followed by Phim, leaving nothing but a pile of clothes on the floor. I quickly fold everybody's clothes for when they get back, and put them in the tent before grabbing a coat from my bag and putting it on. The coat is black with silver buttons and made of thick sheep's wool, keeping me warm. I will have to thank Phim for buying me it. My wolf keeps me warm, but it is bitterly cold in the forest. Ragnar's wolf is waiting for me when I come back out of the tent.

I see so much of Ragnar in his wolf, even the way his wolf stands tall and proud screams Ragnar.

I stand very still as Ragnar's wolf comes closer to me. Each footstep on the ground crunches across the snow, broken leaves, and the occasional twig in between us.

His wolf nose gently brushes against mine, his hot breath blowing against my skin. I stand staring into the eyes of an alpha wolf. Who never really should let me get this close to him. The wolf should be forcing me to be on my knees right about now in submission, like he would do to any wolf who stared him down.

These alpha wolves make no sense. They break every rule known to shifters. They break rules like they aren't anything at all.

And I should be very frightened...but I'm not. Eventually, he moves back and circles around me before walking off into the forest slow enough that I can jog to catch up with him. It takes me more than a few seconds to get used to the forest once the light at the campfire has drifted away, and I breathe in all the scents that I can smell. I can smell everything from the damp leaves littering the floor to the frosty snow that's stuck to all the trees around us, and of a scent that comes with the forest, like the musky scents, the trees themselves. My ears twitch, hearing the distant sounds of other animals that roam around, like rabbits and squirrels. Nothing big to hunt that I can sense.

My eyes take time to adjust, but I see better than I ever have in my entire life. Ragnar stays close to my side, occasionally sniffing the ground before changing in rapidly different directions for what seems like hours on end. My legs tire after a while, but I don't pause or slow my pace as I enjoy the hunt. It is peaceful in the forest, even as we hunt, and I spend a lot of the time thinking about the alphas more than I should. I stay close to Ragnar's side, trusting him completely, and then he comes to a sudden pause. He crouches down low, and I do the same at his side, looking across the clearing in front of us. Right there in the middle of the clearing, there's a huge stag. The grey stag is giant with massive antlers that stretch up into the sky.

He is far bigger than the alpha wolf next to me, and each one of those massive antlers could easily kill us. I don't think that's going to stop the wolf at my side; he isn't just a wolf after all. He's an alpha, a magical being with such power that I can't even understand. A power that comes from a forbidden god that is clearly more powerful than anything I've ever seen. Suddenly, he moves quicker than a bullet through the trees, leaving me far behind with no chance of catching up. He's across the clearing and landing on the heels of the stag, who tries to bolt off. A growl echoes through the forest from Ragnar as he chases the stag, cornering him in some trees within seconds and jumping on his back. I run into the clearing just as Ragnar's wolf digs his massive teeth into the stag's neck, and it lets out a long whine that sends shivers through me, a thrill through me that I've never felt before. The stag collapses underneath the wolf, and Ragnar lets go, taking a few steps back before shifting into his human form. I walk over to see Ragnar crouching down, nothing more than a naked man in the middle of the forest, blood coating his lips and dripping down his chin.

He wipes it off and looks over at me before going to the stag. He leans down and places his hand on the stag's forehead.

"The gods thank you for your sacrifice and welcome you to the afterlife. May you roam in peace."

His deeply spoken words make me shiver, feeling like the gods are watching for a second. I try not to stare too much at his naked body as he stands and looks at me. He looks anything but human right now, and he feels like raw power. Raw, possessive and commanding power. I find it hard to look away from his gaze.

"Are we ever going to speak about the unspoken between

us?" he asks. I assumed my attraction to him was a one-sided thing. He could have anyone...why would he want a rejected mate?

"I don't know what you mean," I reply, wondering if he meant something else. He can't mean what I think, what I feel.

"Any wolf can pick up a scent of attraction," he tells me what I already know. I can ignore my reaction to them, but my body is clearly betraying me.

"Being attracted to someone doesn't mean it would be a good idea," I gently tell him, rubbing my arm. "You're an alpha...you know the rules."

Everything about him is toned as he stands up, and I stare. He suddenly shifts back into his wolf, leaving our conversation at a very strange end. It's only then that I hear the crackling nearby and turn around just as Henderson's wolf comes out of the forest, followed by Trey and Phim. Henderson's wolf lets out a long growl, which Ragnar returns. I look over to see Ragnar with his paw on the dead stag, claiming his prize.

Phim makes me jump when she speaks, and I turn to see her naked at my side for a second before I look away. I will never get used to how most wolves care little about anyone seeing them naked.

"The alphas will carry the stag back. How about we three walk back to the campsite?" she suggests. Henderson walks over to Ragnar, and they growl at each other.

"Sure," I say to Phim as Trey comes to my side, his wolf brushing against my leg.

I gently run my fingers over Trey's fur just a second,

feeling how soft he is. When I look back, the alphas are still watching me, and instead of being hunted, I feel like it is a protective stare.

Eventually, I manage to pull my eyes away and continue down the forest back to the campsite, with Trey and Phim nearby, knowing the alpha wolves are on my heels.

"I'M surprised you know how to do this," I say to Henderson, sitting down on the log next to him around the fire. "Cook the stag, I mean."

Henderson and Ragnar made quick work of stripping the stag, cutting the meat and cooking it with a bunch of things they brought with us.

"We learnt from our parents," Henderson tightly says, but then a ghost of a smile appears on his lips. "My mother was the hunter, and Ragnar was the only one who inherited that skill from her teachings. My father preferred to cook, and I learnt from him."

"I never really asked, but are all four of you blood-related brothers?" I ask. "Only you look—"

"Different. We aren't blood-related, but we were brought up together from infants," he explains to me. "You can ask me anything, Mai, but I might not be able to answer everything."

"So where exactly were you brought up?" I question.

"I get the feeling you're going to keep asking that until one of us slips up and gives you an answer," he replies.

I smile. "You've got the right feeling."

He laughs and shakes his head. "We're not going to tell you. We haven't told anybody here where we came from, and it's best that way."

"I'm going to find out. I'm too curious," I reply.

He looks me dead in the eye. "I bet. But how about you tell me something about you. Like perhaps what you liked to do before you came here, in your spare time."

"Drawing," I start off, rubbing my icy hands together. "I never had much, but there was always paper and a pencil around. I used to take it around with me and draw parts of the forest. There was a waterfall nearby the foster home that I loved to draw in different lights of the day and night. My favourite was at sunset one day when it was almost purple in the sky and cast pink lights on the water."

"Funny, you're not the only one who likes to draw," he counters.

"Do you like to paint?" I ask, and his eyes narrow.

"Just a little bit, and yes, I wrote the book. You might as well just ask exactly what you are thinking."

"It was a very good painting of the angel creatures," I answer, but I won't ask anything more because I see I have pissed him off in my quest to find all the answers. "I can see it's a tense subject for you."

"I am going to sleep," he answers before walking off, leaving me alone by the fire as Trey and Phim went to sleep over an hour ago and Ragnar was getting more wood for the fire.

Ragnar comes back to the camp a little later as I stare at the fire.

"All alone?" he asks, and I nod. He sighs, dropping the

wood by the fire and adding a few logs he has found before going to his tent. I'm surprised when he comes back out with two tumbler glasses and hands me one as he sits next to me. I take a sip, tasting a fruity and rich drink that I've not tasted before, and it burns my throat on the way down, but somehow makes me feel warmer.

"What did you do to annoy him this time?" Ragnar asks, suggesting I always annoy him.

"Do I annoy him a lot?"

"You're annoying him simply because he can't be everything he wants to be around you," he answers.

"And what does he want to be around me?" I ask.

"I think we both know the answer to that. You're not as innocent as you seem," he counters, raising an eyebrow.

"Henderson should forget about me. I'm not an alpha female, and I don't want to stand in the way of whoever comes along to be one for you each," I respond, even if it hurts to say that out loud. I've been thinking about it for so long, and it needs to be said.

"What makes you think you're not an alpha female?"

"It's very clear that I'm not," I answer.

He shakes his head and looks down. "Being alpha female is about being chosen by an alpha and nothing more. Nothing less."

"Alphas are chosen by the gods, be it female or male," I reply. "The gods have not exactly blessed me."

"You're alive, aren't you?" he replies, then takes a long drink. "I call being alive as being favoured by the gods."

"I enjoy being just friends with you all. It will make it easier when I have to leave."

"Nothing about you leaving will be easy," he replies, turning his gaze on me. "They say you have to let the things that belong to you go. If they are yours, they will come back."

"Who ever said I am yours?"

He leans closer and presses a single kiss to my cheek, making my heart pound, and everything in the world disappears so it is like it's only us. "Goodnight, Mai."

CHAPTER NINETEEN

I wake up in the water. Deep, cold water surrounds me as I stare at the expanse of the sea in front of me. The sea pushes me around with every movement, hurting my sore body as I struggle against its power. I search all around me for some light, somewhere to swim towards as I panic, sucking in more water and choking on it. But there's nowhere. There's nothing but ocean for as far as I can see. The waves keep pushing me harshly in the sea like they want to rip me apart, and they might do just that. Nothing but the cold water surrounds me. I can't focus on anything but my beating heart in my chest. Part of me wonders if I'm in a dream. Part of me wonders if this is some sort of memory. My blonde hair strangles me in the water as I'm pushed further and further away, and my hands grab hold of nothing but seawater in my struggle. Suddenly the sea goes still and I'm floating, staring at a shadow. There's someone else there, someone just on the tip of my vision. I try to swim towards the shadow, but every stroke I swim, the shadow gets further and further away.

Like I'm chasing a memory and just getting nowhere. Just as

I'm about to get closer to the shadow, seeing the outline of a man, everything disappears, and the world goes completely black.

I wake up with a chill in bed, covered in sweat, my damp hair stuck to my cheeks as my body shakes from head to toe. The dream felt so damn real...real enough it could be a memory of before I was twelve for all I know. Sucking in a deep breath, I have to calm myself down as I look up at the trees above, reminding myself where I am, safe in my room.

Dreams like this have become recurrent in the last few weeks, and I don't know why. I don't know what's caused them, and I never know why I'm in the sea or how I got there.

I always feel so lost and scared. If it's not dreaming about the sea or chasing shadows through a forest I've never seen before, it's nightmares about Eleline. In my nightmares, she wins the challenge and I die. It's like she's haunting me now. I took her life, and I honestly don't blame her at this point for haunting my dreams and invading my conscience. I climb out of bed on my shaky legs and grab some new clothes before going into the bathroom to have a quick shower. I leave my hair down and wet, listening to the sound of water drops on the hardwood floor as I get changed into my clothes. Finally, I pull on a long red cardigan, which I like to wear around the house.

In the last few weeks, winter has moved into spring, and

everything's a bit nicer now that it's not so cold outside. There haven't been any new attacks from my old pack, and part of me wants to think that he's forgotten about me and moved on. But I'm not that stupid. I know he hasn't. And it makes me worry about what he's planning. I'll always worry. Panic and anxiety might be the main reason I'm not sleeping. The house is noisy, and I follow the noise to the kitchen.

I pause when I see Valentine opening all the cupboards one at a time, slamming each one when he doesn't find what he wants. He has no shirt on, and I search his muscular back for his moon markings, not finding them and wondering where they are. I stand there watching him quietly, seeing the anger and frustration pouring out of his every movement. Valentine is the quiet one, I've figured out. I see him every day, and I have absolutely no idea about him. I know nothing about him, nothing real and nothing from him. I know his past makes him reach for the bottle and that's about it.

Oh, other than his love for riddles and throwing stars, which he practises with drunk. I clear my throat and he pauses. He slams shut the cupboard he had open and turns back to me. The alpha looks wild in this moment, his hair messy and all over the place. His giant beard hides so much of his face, and I wonder for a second what he really looks like. He has an amazing body and soulful eyes, but a part of me itches to sneak into his room and shave all that beard off.

I see some kind of man, something familiar in his eyes, and it always puts me at ease when anyone else would go running from a man like this.

"You should be asleep, little wolf," he says, his voice a

warning laced in a kind tone. I'm sure this is how the sheep get lured into a wolf's den. Shrugging my shoulder, I walk into the room, feeling his eyes tracking me. I know exactly where the other alphas hid the booze they like and don't want Valentine to have. I walk across the room, and I open the cabinet under the sink and pull out the large box with several bottles of whiskey. There's one good thing about being trapped in this house pretty much all of the time, I got to know and see every single bit of it. I pull out two bottles and hand one to him.

"I've never gotten drunk, but I'm inclined to tonight because sleeping is not happening," I tell him, knocking my bottle against his.

He looks dumbfounded for a long time. He stares at me and then suddenly a big smile lights up his face. "All right, then. That is something I can definitely teach you to do."

"Good," I say with a smile.

"I'm certainly not the fighter like Silas, and fucking hell, I'm not the kind one like Ragnar or smart like Henderson," he tells me, pausing to run his tongue over his bottom lip, and I track the movement with my greedy eyes. "But getting drunk and being a bad influence, that is definitely my arena."

I follow him out of the kitchen, through the entrance hallway to the living room where he collapses on the sofa, spreading his large legs out at one end of the sofa. I curl my legs underneath me before unscrewing the top of the bottle. The strong smell is absolutely revolting as I get the lid off, but it has a sweet, musky undertone that I can deal with. Valentine is already downing his drink, and I take a sip of mine, coughing a few times as the burning liquid goes down my throat.

Valentine chuckles. "Take it slow, little wolf."

"Technically, I'm not a wolf shifter yet. I'm still locked up."

"Silas is an asshole. Sorry about that," he replies with a grin. I keep taking sips until the warm buzz of the alcohol takes over. Feeling very bold with the alcohol in my system, I glance at Valentine Fall. The mysterious mess of a man I feel drawn to for no explainable reason.

"Do you ever sleep?" I ask.

He doesn't answer for a while, taking a much longer sip like he needs it. "No," he replies. "I don't do much other than drink enough to get past my wolf's blood, which burns away the buzz, then I pass out. Then I'm back to finding more drink to block out memories... Sleep doesn't come easily."

"What happened to you?" I blurt out.

His forest green eyes find me. "How long have you wanted to ask me that?"

"Since we met."

He shakes his head and rests it back, and I have no idea if he is going to tell me or not.

"You can tell me as I drink this, and most likely I'll forget everything you say tomorrow, so it'd be like just talking to a wall," I tell him before taking another long sip to make my point.

He shakes his head. "It's painful how much you remind me of someone. Makes it more difficult to have you here."

"Who do I remind you of?" I ask.

"Just someone I lost," he replies through gritted teeth.

"Is that the reason you drink? Is that the terrible thing that happened?"

"No," he whispers. "Well, it's one of the reasons, but not the worst. One of the reasons is that looking at you is like looking at a ghost that I can never truly possess."

"I don't think you're meant to possess ghosts. I think they're meant to possess you," I reply, trying to make light in the tension-filled room. He tilts his head to the side, his eyes boring into mine. The tension seems to build up, making me nervous to even blink.

"This woman I would have fought the world to possess as mine. My brothers would say the same," he answers me. For a second, I feel almost jealous of this woman. She has their hearts, that much is clear, and I haven't even met her. That's why they all look at me strangely sometimes. It's most likely why they are training me and treating me so well. I remind them of someone they lost. I don't even know this person who obviously isn't here anymore.

He takes a long drink again, and I wrap an arm around myself. "Tell me about her."

"I suppose it could do no harm." He lets out a long sigh. "She was smart, curious and so beautiful it was almost like the gods made her in the image of themselves. For some insane reason, she liked hanging out with me and my brothers. When we were struggling with everything, she was there. She was always there for us."

Valentine looks at me, so I nod and take another drink before he continues.

"It was more like a family relationship at the start when we were younger, but then we grew and I noticed her as more than the girl we treated as pack. It became more. We wanted more. And I think she did too. None of us ever really said that to each other, but the attraction and deep feeling were just building."

He explains this to me with a soft chuckle. I don't dare interrupt him, break him out of the memories he has. "And just when one of us could have been brave and actually said that she was just like that to us…"

His drifting off says it all. "I'm sorry. What happened to her?"

"Something we had all been running from here," he answers, not really telling me anything at all. He stares at me for a second too long.

"Do I really look like her?" I ask.

He nods, but he doesn't answer with any words. The way he looks at me makes me think I'm missing some part of a story I don't understand.

"Tell me, little wolf, what are your plans for the future? What are you going to do when you move out of this house?"

"You're the only one who actually talks like I'm moving out," I reply.

"Are you not?" he asks with a teasing smile.

"Yes, I am. I want a life. I want a life where I'm not a foster kid or a rejected mate and just want to be me," I tell him the truth of how I feel. "For once, I want to not stand out. I want normal."

"Normal, huh?"

I nod before taking a long drink. "Can I ask what

happened that made you like this? If it wasn't losing this girl, what was it?"

"My brothers will kill me for talking to you about our past," he sadly laughs while I wonder why they are so adamant about keeping their secrets. "Part of me wants to do it just so Silas can beat the crap out of me and I could pass out for a few hours. Much quicker than this shit." He holds up his bottle, and I grimace at him. Part of me is worried for him, part of me knowing that he's crazy enough to actually do that. "All right. It's been hard to become alpha of this pack, hard because we had a pack before and we couldn't save any of them."

"Your whole pack died?" I whisper. In that moment, it takes me a second to understand them all so much better than weeks of being with them. I understand them on such a deeper level than I ever have before. Alphas losing all their pack. I can't even imagine. I can't imagine how they stay here and are so happy or how they even built up another pack who became who they are. Eventually, we end up staring at each other for a long time as he lets me process and doesn't answer my rhetorical question.

"Surely a few survived whatever happened?"

"They're all gone, all of them, Mai. There was nothing we could have done to stop it."

"How old were you?" I ask.

"Thirteen," he replies.

"Then you couldn't have been expected to stop it and save your pack. You were a kid," I tell him, reaching over and placing my hand on his arm. He freezes under my touch, even though he feels boiling hot. His eyes crash down on mine with a passion I can feel with one look.

"Thirteen or not, it was my job. I should have protected all of our pack."

"No one could blame you for not being able to do that at thirteen. You know thirteen-year-olds can't run a pack, let alone save everybody from whatever happened," I gently say.

"You don't understand. We were born to save them," he answers, and I furrow my brow, trying to work that out.

"What the hell does that mean?" I ask as he shakes my hand off his arm and stands up, but I get tired of being left in the middle of a conversation with half answers. I put my bottle down and block his path as he tries to walk out.

"No," I firmly state. "I don't know why you seem to think it's okay for you to just walk away from everything, drink to forget like you don't have a pack who need you right now to protect them, but I'm here to say it's not cool. I just asked you a question, and you should have answered. If you are absolutely certain you want to host a one-person pity party where you have no friends and no life, then fine. But you will actually answer my question, not be rude. I'm tired of being ignored by everybody like I'm a goddamn child."

Valentine steps closer to me, crowding my space as he looms over me. "You know, it's very dangerous to challenge an alpha like you are right now."

"I'm not like the others. You won't hurt me."

His hand reaches out and wraps around the back of my nape, pulling me towards him until our bodies are lined up and I feel all of him. He holds me there for a second, breathing heavily and smelling of that god awful whiskey.

"Tell me, why do you think I should let you get away with challenging me?"

"Because I'm like you," I reply. "I'm broken."

My eyes drift down to his lips and back up to his eyes, forcing myself to focus on anything other than the desire to lean closer and press our lips together. To find out what he tastes like.

"Being rejected doesn't make you broken," he counters with a slight growl, but I don't feel threatened at all.

"Whoever said it was because I was rejected that made me broken?"

He stares down at me like he can force the truth of my past out into the open. "What did they do to you, little wolf?"

"Wouldn't you like to know?" I reply.

"Actually, yes, I would," he answers. "I want to know everything about my little wolf so I can destroy any threat."

He stares down at me for a long time while I don't answer but feel like I can't breathe. Swearing to protect me is one thing, swearing to destroy the monsters of my past is a whole other. I reach over and take the bottle from his hand and gently pull it back from him.

"As long as you keep drinking this, you have no future or trust from me," I firmly tell him. "Your excuses for destroying yourself are just that, excuses. Trust me, if I can get up every day despite my past, then you can do it. We can do it together."

His hand slowly pulls away from the nape of my neck, stroking his long fingers through my hair, and he pauses. Valentine leans in and takes a long sniff of my hair, breathing in my scent and making my legs shaky with an unspoken need that I know he can scent. He may be lost. He may be so different from anybody I've ever met before, but my body reacts to him all the same.

The attraction between us is undeniable. Then his lips find mine. Just a brush of his lips, almost like it didn't happen, but I feel it. A strong buzz shakes through my body, and I lean forward.

He stumbles back after a few seconds, not a drunk stumble, almost like he can't believe he just did that. I stare for much longer than I should as he backs out of the room.

"I see how broken you are," he says, not looking at me. "And people like us, we don't just get to move on."

"Yeah, we do. We do because we were tested, and we survived," I say to his back, and he pauses in his attempt to leave. "I'm not going to give up on you, even if you give up on yourself. I'm going to show you how to move forward. I'm going to help you."

"No one, not even you, can help me," he replies and leaves me alone in the empty room, a bottle of whiskey in my hand. I lift the bottle and stare at it for a long moment before throwing it across the room, watching it smash into pieces against the wall. I'm getting rid of all the alcohol in this house because I am determined to fix Valentine before my past catches up to me.

CHAPTER TWENTY

"You're slow today." Silas clicks his tongue, narrowing his eyes on me. "Too slow. You'd be dead ten times over if your old alpha was here."

I swing around in anger, and Silas jumps out of the way. His blond hair is softly swept back and distracting as he casually runs a hand through it. "Stop bringing him up to piss me off."

He tilts his head to the side. "Making you angry is pleasing to me."

"Just when I thought we were becoming friends," I quip.

"Enemies first," he replies with a smirk. "Friendship is a big upgrade, and you aren't there...yet."

"Yet?" I ask as I block his sword with my own and push it away from me before spinning out of the way and swinging my sword around my back to block another hit.

His laugh echoes off the walls. "Correction: never."

For some crazy reason, I smile and go back to swinging my sword at Silas. He naturally moves out of the way, using his quick footwork to dodge to the side and swing his leg out, whacking me hard in the stomach. I go flying across the room, unable to stop myself but landing on my back thanks to Silas's training on how to land without breaking any bones. I gasp for air as I roll over. I don't hurt as much as I could have done if I let myself land in bad form.

The second I stand up, Silas is behind me, and his hand wraps around my throat, his whole body pushed to my back and his lips inches away from the tip of my left ear. I shiver.

"What has you so tired and distracted today, Mai?" he asks me, his words deep and seductive, his hot breath blowing down the side of my cheek. A rumble leaves his chest, vibrating across my back, and I feel nothing but Silas, like he is attacking my very soul.

I take a deep breath before replying, hoping my voice doesn't betray how I'm feeling. Letting Silas know I am attracted to him would just give him another thing to use against me. Part of me wonders if he is using that attraction right now.

Or if he just wants to be as close to me as I want to be to him. "I was up last night with Valentine," I reply.

"All night?" he asks, biting out the words. He takes a deep breath, pushing his nose against my neck.

"Does it matter?" I question. He laughs, wrapping his arm around my waist, his hand splaying against my flat bare stomach. The short crop top I have on means Silas has full access to my stomach, and his fingers drift up, brushing over my ribs one by one. My heart pounds in my chest, making me overfocus on nothing but him. There could be a whole war going on outside this room and neither one of us would notice, I don't think. I wouldn't. That's for sure. Not right now. Not in his arms. I don't know why he's holding me like this. Sometimes we get close, but never like this.

"Valentine doesn't get close to anybody. He doesn't make friends," Silas eventually replies, not moving his hand on my skin, his thumb slowly rubbing circles.

"No," I breathlessly respond. "You're friends with him, he's your brother, so clearly he does."

"Family is different."

"Valentine told me that I look like someone that you used to know. Someone you had crushes on as kids."

I nearly gasp as he spins me around so fast, his hands wrapped around my back, forcing our hips close together. He walks us back until I hit the wall, and he shoves a knee between my legs, making me suck in a breath.

He reaches his thumb out and slowly brushes it against my bottom lip as we stare at each other. Who knew being pushed against a wall by a possessive alpha is sexy outside the romance books I've read?

"What else has he been whispering to you?" Silas gruffly demands.

"Do I look like her?" I ask him instead, answering his question with a question—something they have taught me to do, because it's all they ever do. He growls, recognising that I'm using his own tricks against him.

And I don't stop.

"Do we have the same hair, the same eyes, the same body? What is it?"

"Everything," he bites out the word. "Absolutely everything except that you're not her."

"Clearly not."

"You're different. Broken," he growls out. "And I want to break every wolf that ever hurt you."

I blame my beating heart, my swirling, messy and complicated emotions as I do something stupid, reckless and dangerous. Something that I think I've been planning for a long time but not like this, not with feelings...not real.

I knew it would be the only way to get what I want.

I kiss him.

I kiss Silas Fall, alpha of the Fall Mountain Pack.

He pauses, my lips pressed against his, and I expect him to push me away. But when he doesn't, when he deepens the kiss, pulling me harshly against his body, I open my mouth and melt into his arms like we are two long-lost lovers. This is not what I had planned. His lips taste like perfection with a hint of something minty. He tastes like everything I've ever wanted, and our bodies fit together like we are made for each other as he pulls me closer with his strong arms.

I feel like I'm in the ocean and he is the strong storm to wreck everything about my life. His lips devour my own, hard and demanding.

If he asked me for anything, without a single doubt, I would give it to him in this moment. It takes me more than a few seconds to get out of the moment to remember what I need to do, the reason I kissed him.

The reason I opened a can of worms. His lips drift down my jaw, and pleasure shoots down my body when his lips press against my neck. I force my shaky hand to lift my sword and run it across Silas's thigh. He pauses against my neck, realising exactly what I've done and why I kissed him.

"I never expected that from you," he murmurs against my neck, and I don't move.

"You would never have given me a chance to win. I want to be able to shift," I say breathlessly.

He lifts his head, and his eyes full of fury land on mine. "I don't like being tricked."

"Tricking you is the only way I'm going to win," I reply, holding my head high, not backing down even if he looks so furious I should be scared. "I drew blood. That means I won, and you have to give me permission to shift."

He pushes away from me, a long growl escaping his lips that echoes around the room. "You don't know what you're asking for!"

"I'm asking you to keep your word, which you promised that you would!"

"I never said I wouldn't," he counters, not looking at me. "You're playing with the devil, Mai, and you should fear the outcome of getting what you wish."

"I've been learning from you all in the last three months. The alphas who are meant to be cruel and dangerous...but not to me. Why is that? What makes you different around me?" I question. "Because you can claim to be the devil, but all I've seen and felt are angels."

Whatever I said makes him sharply turn back and storm towards me. This time, I take a few steps back, actually fearing the anger burning in his eyes.

"Outside, now!" Ragnar shouts from the other side of the house, interrupting us with his tone alone, making sure to let us know something is wrong.

"We will continue this conversation another time," Silas darkly tells me. "Now stay the fuck in here."

He runs out of the door, and I keep my sword gripped tightly in my hand as I run after him, not listening to his rules. I'm nowhere near as fast a runner as he is, so he is out of the house way before me. If they're in danger, I can fight now and help them. I'm not completely useless, and I refuse to sit back as they run into possible danger, danger caused by my past. I've brought them a million problems, and they haven't turned their back on me.

For that alone, despite how I feel for them, I won't run and hide. I made my decision a long time ago that I'm not being a coward and hiding in the shadows. I run out of the training room, through the house and into the entrance hall, guessing they might be outside. Heading straight through the front doors, I see Valentine, Ragnar and Silas are standing around something by the gates. Henderson comes to my side as I run over, and I glance at him to see his eyes narrowed, slowly drifting to red.

"You should go back," Silas demands, stepping in front of me.

"Is anyone in danger?" I ask as Henderson comes to a stop at Ragnar's side.

"Let her past," Ragnar demands. Silas grits his teeth but steps to the side. My heart pounds as I take in what they are looking down at.

Right in front of the gates are five dead black wolves. Each one of them has got long cut lines in their neck, blood pouring down their fur, and they're very clearly dead. The wolves are laid out in a line with a letter of some kind pinned on each one of their chests, looking identical. Silas moves first as sickness crawls up my throat, and I have to look away.

I feel dizzy as I hear him pull one of the notes off and walk back to us. The alphas pass the note around, each one of them looking more annoyed and furious as the next before Valentine just holds it.

I leave my hand out flat in front of him. I need to read it.

"Mai—"

"Just let me read it, Val," I demand. He sighs and drops the letter in my hand.

Bring my rejected mate back to me, or my wolf will kill all the women in your pack. One by one.

THE NOTE FALLS from my hands as my blood feels like it goes stone cold. My hands are shaking as I realise that these must be all female wolves. Five dead women in a world where hardly any are born in comparison to men, no matter what pack we are from. Now there are five less in the world, and their blood is on my hands. They died because I'm alive.

"You don't have to fear him, Mai. He won't get you here, and what this says? This changes nothing," Ragnar gently tells me, but I hear it in his voice. The pure anger. But me being here? My very existence is going to start a war...and so many are going to die because I didn't die in that damn sea.

I turn sharply, turn my eyes to him. "This changes everything."

The sword falls out of my hands as I run from them, from their words and how I think they will try to tell me this isn't my fault. I don't know where I'm running. I don't even look back as I keep running. I don't get very far before large hands go underneath me and pick me up. I'm thrown over a large shoulder with a manly grunt.

"Let me go!" I scream, smacking my hands against Valentine's back.

"Nope," he casually replies as he starts carrying me towards the house. I shout, scream and smack my hands and legs to try and escape as hot tears fall down my cheeks. I fight as he slowly walks, but he doesn't let me go. He just carries me through the house, up the stairs and to one of the bedrooms I've never been in, ducking to go under the smaller door frame.

Valentine drops me onto something soft, and I sit up, seeing I'm on a green fabric sofa at the end of a large luxurious hardwood bed. Valentine sits next to me, blocking the way to the door as I wipe some tears away.

"Welcome to my room. Fair warning, you're the first girl I've brought in here in a long fucking time," Valentine says, leaning back and stretching his arms out. "Sorry for the mess."

Honestly, his room is cleaner than I expected it to be as I flicker my eyes around. There are piles of neatly folded clothes on a large oak chest of drawers, and there's a corner full of what looks like weapon woodwork. The silky dark blue bed sheets are even made, and even though there are about twenty empty bottles on the floor by the bedside unit, it's still not what I expected for his bedroom.

"I like it," I say, shrugging my shoulder. "But I need to pack my things and leave. No one else can die because of me."

Valentine looks at me, his eyes full of a wisdom I don't understand, and I don't move. "It's not your fault."

"I need to go back to him and let him kill me like he should have at the very start. Then no one else will die. I can't have them die for me. It's not their fault that I'm here," I whisper out, feeling more tears fall down my cheeks. "This is your pack I'm ruining. None of their lives mean less than mine."

"Your life means more to us," he softly tells me. "You are our pack, and we would protect you. Let us make that choice."

"The pack will hate me if I don't leave."

"No, they won't. No one has any love for the Ravensword Pack here, and no one wants the alpha to get his own way. We will get revenge for the women. Be sure of that," he vows. "Leaving will just let him win. Don't give your life up to let him win, Mai."

I gulp and eventually nod.

He leans over, tilting up my chin with his finger. "You said last night you weren't going to give up on me. I decided I'm not giving up on you. Trust me. Trust your alphas."

"When did you get so wise, or have you always been that way?" I counter.

He smiles, moving his hand away. "No...I just know how to accept what needs to be done for the greater good. I killed a lot of wolves under the previous alpha's rule to take over this pack with my brothers. We know death is something close to our souls in the position life has given us."

"I'm sorry I freaked out," I admit, letting out a sigh.

"As long as you understand it's not your fault and you don't try to run, you're forgiven for kicking me in the chest," he counters, and my lips twitch.

"I haven't drunk anything since last night," Valentine states. "And I'm not going to. I'm done...and that's down to you. You made me realise last night that I'm an arsehole and I need to man up. The bottle isn't going to fix my past and make me forget. It just makes me miss every moment I could have."

"I'm proud of you," I whisper, feeling tears prick my eyes.

"Having you here changes things," he admits. "And for the first time, this morning, I actually didn't feel like touching that bottle."

"Maybe we can find different ways to heal," I gently suggest.

"I'd like that," he softly replies.

He lets me lean over, and I rest my head on his shoulder, just needing that little bit of comfort that I've never really seemed to get from anyone before. We don't move for a long time, even after he slips his arm around my shoulders.

"By the way, you're not an arsehole."

He laughs. "I am, Mai, but never to you. Never again."

CHAPTER TWENTY-ONE

"I can never quite get the lines right on the trees," I say, looking down at my drawing. Henderson peeks over my shoulder, his arm brushing against mine and making me shiver. Not in a bad way. The funeral for the five wolves is happening right now, and Henderson suggested taking me out of the pack for the day, into the forest, just in case the funeral is another chance for someone to attack me. Five betas roam around the forest nearby us, and Daisy is parked up close by, just in case we need to escape. Five days ago, hours after the five wolves were found dead, we moved all women and children into the mountain for protection, making it like a fortress. Only male pack members can come in and out of the mountain for the time being until the alphas find out who has betrayed them in the pack. Someone must have. There is no way those wolves had been killed and moved so close to the house without a beta seeing it.

The thought makes me shiver. Since that day, one of the alphas sleeps outside of my room every night and follows me around the house. Despite Silas being close to me, he won't discuss letting me shift or say a word to me in practice training. Whereas I can't get that kiss out of my mind. Not for a second. I taste him every time I close my eyes.

Henderson's shoulder brushes against mine as he looks over at my drawing pad. He holds his hand out for it, and I pass him the pad. I watch him as he goes over the drawing of my tree on the one side, making it much wider than I usually would draw. When he stops and hands me it back, I realise he's made it absolutely perfect.

Realistic. I never had a chance.

"Where did you learn to draw like this?" I demand around a laugh. "You know, I've not seen you draw anything bad in the entire time we've been doing this."

I lean further, my back against one of the two trees. Henderson told me about this place in the forest where there are two trees joined, known as a place where love starts. I don't know why he likes to bring me here...or I try not to think too much about us coming here to draw. I glance up at the twirling bark, how it winds around all the way up to the top. Like two lovers wrapped so much in each other that they can't see the world around them.

The view of the forest from here is beautiful. Nothing but thick forest, and we are on a slightly raised hill, so it really is perfect for drawing.

"I'm just good at drawing. You learn over time," he says. "I'm surprised that you don't like any kind of music. I always hear you singing in the shower to songs I've not heard before."

"I've played nothing before," I explain. "The foster home didn't have expensive things like that. We had some at school, but of course, I wasn't allowed to use them."

He shakes his head. "Every young wolf should have an instrument. Wolves have a deep connection to sound. We hear it on so many deeper levels than any other creature."

"I am still thinking about how you've heard my terrible singing," I say around another laugh.

"It's not that bad," he coughs out, and I burst into laughter.

"You're a total liar. It's awful," I say, laughing so hard tears drop from my eyes.

"We've got some instruments in storage," Henderson finally says once we both stop laughing. "I could look for them. Which one did you want to try?"

"Maybe a violin," I say, thinking of the one at the academy. "I don't know, it just seems like a graceful instrument."

His eyes flash red for a second, confusing me, and then he jumps to his feet, moving in front of me.

"What is it?" I whisper, standing up and dropping the pad onto the ground.

Henderson doesn't reply for a long second, then he relaxes, straightening up, looking over his shoulder at me. "Just Ragnar. He must have felt left out."

I chuckle, looking across as I see Ragnar's wolf running fast towards us. He comes to a halt and immediately shifts back.

I divert my eyes from all that golden skin.

"We have a problem, and we need to get to the lighthouse," Ragnar states as I hear him walk closer.

"Another rejected?" Henderson asks.

"No, but an injured wolf from Ravensword. He woke up and asked for Mai," Ragnar tells us.

"Then I'm going," I say, placing my hands on my hips but not directly looking at a very naked Ragnar. Even if a part of me wants to sneak a peek.

"It could be dangerous. The alpha of Ravensword might have sent him here to kill you," Henderson cuts me off. "So no, you are not going."

"I am, with or without you. You must know by now I'm stubborn enough to find my own way to the lighthouse," I counter, staring him down.

"Fine," Henderson sighs.

Ragnar shifts back as Henderson and I go to Daisy, get in, and take off quickly through the forest. Beta wolves join Ragnar, running not far behind Daisy with him, and I look at them. How could one of them betray the alphas and want me dead?

We drive quickly through the forest as I wonder who is here from Ravensword, who possibly said my name. I just can't think of anybody. The alphas might be right. The Ravensword alpha could have sent this person to kill me. Or he could be a rejected wolf. Possibly. We drive down the beach after a long time, straight towards the lighthouse where I first went and met the alphas. The place where they saved me and swore me to the forbidden god. Healer Saffron is waiting outside the door, her arms crossed against her white coat as we pull up. She looks straight towards me with a warm smile.

"Hello, dear. How are you?" she asks. As I get closer, she wraps her arms around me before I can answer her. "It's good to see you looking so much better."

"I'm sorry I'm back under unfortunate circumstances," I say, breaking away from the hug.

"Me too," she replies before bowing her head at Henderson. I hear Ragnar shifting back nearby and likely getting dressed.

"Who is it?" Henderson asks.

"I don't know. He hasn't woken up again," Saffron says. "But when he did, he cried out Mairin. He sounded desperate."

I frown and take a step towards the door. Henderson wraps an arm around my waist and tugs me back from the door.

"It might not be safe. I'm going in first," he warns me, stepping around me, sliding his hand slowly from my waist.

Ragnar comes up the steps, in jeans and nothing else. I gulp at the sight of all that muscle. "You asked us to come here. We let you, but you let us go first."

Saffron interrupts. "I'm sorry. I don't mean to interrupt you, alphas. But the truth is, this man is too weak and too injured to do much. In fact, I think he's past the point of being saved."

"But you saved me from near death?" I say to Henderson. "How is this man different? Why wouldn't the forbidden god help?"

"I think he's poisoned by Nightshade," she softly answers me.

I glance at the alphas, finding both their eyes turned downwards, and I frown, questioning what the hell Nightshade is.

Dammit, who is this person anyway? I push past Henderson before he can stop me, and hear a low growl at my back as I walk into the room. I pause, my heart dropping in my chest when I see Daniel lying on the sofa where I was once. His skin is so pale, his one eye is closed shut from swelling, and he looks dreadful.

It's still good to see him...but not like this. God, not like this. I rush across the room and pick up his hand in mine, feeling how clammy and cold he is to touch.

"Daniel, I'm here," I whisper, my voice catching. I clear my throat and turn to Saffron and the alphas as they crowd the room. "What is Nightshade?"

"Who is this man to you?" Henderson demands instead of giving me an answer, his eyes focused on why I'm holding Daniel's hand.

"An old friend. Not a lover," I say to get him past the stupid possessive stuff I can feel rolling off him and his wolf in spades.

Ragnar steps forward. "Nightshade is the only thing in the world there is no cure for. They make it from an herb grown from dead wolves. It's unnatural, and the gods can't help. I'm sorry."

"No," I whisper, a sob escaping my lips.

"It kills you very quickly, within a few days. I've seen this once before, and I believe he's been out at sea for a while before he washed up here. He has several injuries, and his heart rate is so low," Saffron gently tells me, coming over to my side and placing her hand on my shoulder as I silently sob. "We can only take away his pain. Nothing else."

Tears fall down my cheeks, dropping onto the shiny floor at my feet.

"Then take his pain away so he can come home," I tell her and stand up on shaky feet, turning to my alphas. "Will you help me take him to your home?"

"Our home is yours and welcome to your friend," Henderson replies, nodding his head. "I'm sorry, Mai."

"So am I...he is a good man," I say back. "One of only three people in my old pack who defended me and treated me like a genuine person...and I can't save him."

Ragnar and Henderson come to my side, wordlessly giving me the support I need for what will happen next. Alpha Sylvester is going to pay for everything he has done.

I'm going to become his biggest regret.

CHAPTER TWENTY-TWO

"Mai!" someone shouts, someone I know well. I giggle and hide behind the wall, pressing my back into the cold stone. I brush my blonde hair out of my eyes and close them, reaching out with my senses. He is getting closer.

Just before he gets to me, I jump out, and he catches me, twirling us around until we are dizzy and laughing as we fall onto the grass.

"You're always going to be my best friends. All four of you. No matter where we run, we will find each other."

Waking up with a jolt, I find I'm still seated in a chair, with my back bent over the side of my bed where Daniel is sleeping in the middle. I lift my head from my arms, struggling to remember what I was dreaming about. I vaguely remember a boy with blond hair before the dream slips out of my mind like most of them do. Except for a single sentence which repeats itself in my mind again and again like a broken record:

"No matter where we run, we will find each other."

Shaking my head, I clear my throat and lean over to

place my hand on Daniel's forehead, hoping something has changed.

But of course, nothing has. He is still stone cold to the touch and unconscious.

Rubbing my tired eyes, I stand up off the padded chair. I walk around the room, no proper direction in mind but to stretch my legs, and I hear the door creak behind me. I look over to see Trey peeking in.

"Has your friend woken up yet?" he asks.

I shake my head and rest my arms together against my chest, glancing at Daniel. "Not yet."

"Can I come in?" he questions.

"Of course," I gently say. "When Daniel wakes up, I want to introduce you to him. Tell him about the cool kid who can run faster than anyone I've seen and eats way too much fruit."

He grins widely as he comes into the room and hands me a glass of orange juice. "I brought your favourite orange juice. I thought you might like it after waking up."

I accept the drink with a soft look and wrap my arm around his shoulders. He rests against me. "Thanks, bud."

"I'm sorry you're sad," he replies in a quiet voice. "I don't want you upset."

"It's very kind of you to worry so much about me," I reply, moving him to the door. "But being sad is part of life just as much as being happy is. You can't have one without the other."

"I wish you could," he replies as I take a long drink of the orange juice. He waves at me before leaving the room, even though I suspect he won't be far away. Once I finish the drink, realising I was thirstier than I thought I was, I place the empty glass on the chest of drawers.

Slowly I peek around the door, finding Henderson is sitting with Ragnar outside on the sofa, the one they dragged up the stairs to sit on or sleep on. Both of them are talking quietly, and they turn their heads my way.

"Any change?" Henderson asks.

I shake my head. "No."

"Anything we can help with?" Ragnar asks, leaning over and picking my hand up in his. I squeeze his hand.

"Do you think there's any way we could wake him up? I just need to speak to him."

They look between each other. "We both know what Saffron said. We know that he might never wake up."

"I can't accept that he might die before I ever have time to speak to him. Never know why he's here and what's happened back in the Ravensword Pack," I say, pulling my hand from Ragnar's. I know it's not his fault, but everything seems against me right now. "I will never get to say goodbye if he doesn't wake up. That's twice."

My heart hurts at the thought, and I rub my hand against my chest like I can stop the pain from taking over my heart.

"Loss is never easy, but you are not alone," Henderson replies. "Be with him in his last hours, Mai."

My feet feel heavily weighed down with every step I take back to Daniel, wishing he was better, wishing for a miracle that can never happen.

I stare at my best friend, another foster kid just like me. A million emotions run around in my mind. I grew up with this man. All of me remembers the last time I saw him, as he found his mate in the mating ceremony, and how shocked he looked, like it was yesterday.

I still remember his shouts and growls as he tried to get to me when he found out who I was mated to in the ceremony. I just have no idea what happened next. All I know is that he stuck up for me, defended me, and I can't save him like he tried to save me. I pick his hand up once more. "Daniel, can you hear me?" I ask, shaking his shoulder with my other hand. I hate how weak he looks. I hate that there's really not much I can do about it.

His eyes flicker for a moment, and I jolt up, leaning over him as he slowly opens his eyes, his big eyes staring up at me. Shock and joy make me smile at him, and I move some of his dark hair away from his forehead and eyes.

"Is it really you, Irin?" he groggily asks.

"Yes," I say, a swirl of emotions coming out in my voice. Happiness that he's awake, sadness that it doesn't change the outcome. "It's me. You're okay, Daniel. You're safe. I promise I'm safe."

He gives me a weak smile as I help him sit up a little with the pillows. "Do you need anything? A drink?"

He shakes his head softly. "No, it's just good to see you," he says. "It feels like it's been a much longer time than it has been."

I pause, not knowing what to say. I need to tell him he is dying. But how do you tell someone that?

"I bet you're wondering what happened," he fills in for me when I can't reply, and I feel completely speechless. I've waited so long for him to wake up, and I have no idea what to say.

He looks so pale, so weak as he squeezes my hand tightly. "After what happened with you at the ceremony, the alpha locked me in his house with my intended mate, who screamed the entire time. The alpha soon killed her when she tried to escape, and that was my fault. Instead of being happy about my mating, I saw only red and tried to save you. It wasn't right that they killed her," he admits.

"I'm so sorry," I whisper.

"How are you alive?" he questions. "Everyone thinks the alpha killed you."

"You could say the sea saved me when he threw me into it. His wolf wouldn't let him kill me," I explain.

He nods. "You've always been special."

"No, I'm not. I was just lucky," I reply. "How did you get here?" I ask him.

"Mike helped me escape the alpha's house and the pack," he tells me. "Brave old wolf that he is."

That's an understatement.

"I don't know what happened to him after I left," he warns me, and I gulp. I doubt he is alive. "But Mike came to the house to see the alpha, to demand that he give Jesper back to him at the foster home."

My heart pounds in my chest. "Why would the alpha have Jesper?"

"Things have changed, and he took in Jesper as a ward...no doubt to make sure they could hold him against you if you came back."

"What else has changed?" I ask.

"The pack's on lockdown, and no one leaves their homes. He's building an army, Irin." He grabs my hand tighter. "And you need one too. Don't let that bastard ever touch you again."

"I won't," I firmly tell him. "He will pay for everything, Daniel. I promise."

"When I was escaping his house, he shot me with an arrow which I pulled out of my leg, and they coated it with some blue stuff. I don't know what it was, but I could feel the poison seeping into my bones, into my wolf," he starts off, looking me right in my eyes. "I can feel what it is doing."

"I—"

"I could always read you like a book, Irin," he interrupts. "I see my death coming in your eyes. You are too easy to read."

"I can't lose you."

"You can, Irin, because you've survived this far. Tell me everything," he asks. So I give him a quick rundown of every important thing that has happened since I arrived to right now.

"He won't stop," he softly tells me. "And you have to save Jesper. He's too young, too innocent to see what the alpha is truly like. Jesper doesn't understand what the consequences of being the alpha's ward are. It's going to be nothing good for him."

"I won't leave Jesper with him. I will find a way," I reply.

He moves a little, his face contorting in pain. "Dying is not as easy as I thought it would be."

"I don't want you to die," I whisper around a sob that ends with me bursting into tears.

"Irin, look at me," Daniel demands, and I lift my eyes. "You're my best friend. My best friend I've been in love with since we were kids. I was never brave enough to tell you it."

"Daniel," I whisper in shock.

He gives me a smile. "I knew with no doubt that your feelings for me were not the same, and that is okay. It's all okay, Irin. I'm happy for the moments I got with you."

I push his admittance of feelings to the back of mind, knowing I have never felt the same way, and anything I say about it now, he doesn't need to hear. "Thank you for always defending me, even when it ended up with you getting beaten to a pulp. I almost understand why now."

"I saved you because it was the right thing to do," he tells me. "Even if it hurt...it was right. My feelings only meant I was around you more to do the right thing."

"I wish I could save you," I almost cry out.

"Don't be sad," he gently says. "Just stay with me. Let it just be simply us until the end and don't let go."

And I do. I stay with him, clasping his hand in mine.

I stay with him as he drifts back off to sleep; I stay with him as his breaths slow down, and I hear his heart rate beating slower and slower. I stay with him as he goes deathly still, and I feel all of his soul drain from his body.

And he is gone. Gone.

I release his hand on the bed and lean over him, using my fingers to close his eyes.

"Goodbye, Daniel."

Anger like I've never known it washes over me as I walk back in a haze, and I scream. I scream, grabbing the lamp off the bedside unit and throwing it across the room. I grab everything I can touch, throwing it and screaming in frustration and pain. Growls, almost sounding like howls, leave my lips as I burst into tears and smack my fists against the wall. I hit the wall, again and again, pouring everything out.

"Stop, you're bleeding!" I hear someone shouting, but I'm too lost in the anger, too lost in the emotions swirling all around me. My mind can't focus on anything, and I feel like I can't breathe without thinking much. I need air. My soul needs to be out of this house. Bolting out of the room, I head straight out of the house and into the forest behind. My legs keep me running and running, not knowing where I'm going until I smack into a tree and fall to my knees. I cry in gigantic sobs that shake my entire body, my cries echoing around the trees.

I hear them as they surround me. Four giant black wolf alphas here to comfort me. To protect me. To remind me I'm never alone.

"No matter where we run, we will find each other," I whisper, and each one of them howls into the sky. I might have lost my best friend...but I'm not alone. We will avenge him.

FUNERALS WERE NEVER something I attended in my old pack, mainly because I didn't know anybody well enough to lose them. I wasn't close to anyone to attend a funeral made up of family and friends, but I saw some funerals from a distance. I drew a few too. And they were nothing like the funerals the Fall Mountain Pack has.

This funeral is done under the moon in the middle of the night, solid beams of moonlight shining through the spaces in the trees above us. Daniel lies on a platform of wood with dozens of glowing nightstones in piles around him, all the ones I found on the beach today.

Daniel doesn't deserve just one nightstone. He always deserved dozens. Tears fall down my face as I stand in front of the platform with my alphas at my side. Trey and Phim are close by; even though none of them except for me knew Daniel, I feel their remorse for his death.

They trust me enough to believe me when I say he was a good man. A good wolf.

Sucking in a deep breath, I smell the damp forest and the alphas behind me. I feel the chilly wind blowing my hair around my shoulders, but I focus on Daniel. I need to say something about him.

I clear my throat.

"Daniel Ravensword was a good man, and he came from good wolves who all died, leaving him in the foster home where we met. The first day we met, he punched a wolf who was kicking me for fun, and then he became my protector. A protector I needed. He was a powerful wolf, and he died in a way that no powerful wolf ever should," I say, my voice echoing around the trees.

"I would have been dead ten times over if it weren't for Daniel, and I wish everyone I have become close to here could have known him, but I know I am lucky in my memories I will treasure of Daniel," I whisper. I don't say Jesper's name out loud, but I think it, I think of him and how upset he will be when he finds out Daniel is dead.

Ragnar steps forward. "Thanks to Daniel, it prepares us for the attack of Ravensword and a war that will cost a lot of lives. Daniel spared many, and I hope he is listening down on us as I thank him. Thank you for saving our Mai and for warning us."

"Thank you, Daniel," Henderson agrees. Silas and Valentine repeat the sentence. The power in their voices makes me shiver.

"I wish I could have saved him from this fight, but I couldn't. Daniel, you will be sorely missed and never forgotten," I say, ending on a sob.

Phim surprises me by walking to my other side. "May the forbidden god keep Daniel's soul soothed and welcome in the afterlife."

"Thank you," I tell her. She nods. Knowing it's time, I pick up the large fire torch off the ground and walk over to him. I stand silently for a long time before I drop the torch, feeling my heart go with it. The platform lights up quickly, and I step back, leaving us all silent for a long time as we watch. Ragnar gently puts his hand on my back after some time. "Gone, but not forgotten. Our wolves will run together in the afterlife one day."

I stare at the fire, feeling empty and broken inside.

"How many people I care about are going to die before I'm free?"

No one answers me because the answer is something none of them wants to tell me.

Death will always chase me. It has done ever since the moon goddess made a mistake.

CHAPTER TWENTY-THREE

"Has there been another attack?" I ask as Trey runs into the attic, with wide eyes and almost looking a bit frightened.

"I couldn't find you in your room. You've left!" he says, smiling. "And no, there hasn't been an attack."

"You had me worried for a second there," I reply with a soft smile, going back to folding the shirt in front of me, wanting to be alone. I haven't really left my room since Daniel died, and I still see him there on my bed. I felt like if I left, then he would really go. Even if I know in my heart and soul that he has.

This morning, two weeks after his death, I resigned myself to leaving my room for more than bathroom and food trips. I wasn't shocked to find the attic a mess of clothes like the first time I came up. It's easy to work and doesn't let me think too long.

"Sorry, but I think the world's ending, because Valentine wants you to cut his hair."

I cough out a surprised laugh. The first time I've laughed in a while.

"What?" I ask, wondering if I'm hearing things. The man with long overgrown, never styled hair wants a cut? I thought hell would freeze over before he'd let me near him with a pair of scissors. "Yep." Trey scratches his head. "Valentine asked me to come and get you so you can come and cut his hair."

"He wants me to cut his hair?" I question again to make sure I'm hearing him right.

He nods one more time with a big grin. "I have never seen him with a haircut. He's never cut it since I've known him. And that's like, you know, a lot of years."

"I wonder what he looks like under the hair," I chuckle. I glance around the attic, knowing the clothes aren't going anywhere. "Well, I guess I can come and cut his hair. I've done it once or twice in the past."

"I'll go get scissors!" Trey shouts, fist-pumping the air and running to the door. He shouts back as he goes through it. "Valentine's in his room!"

I know that this is probably a tactic to get me out of my room, to cheer me up, but I still smile. Out of pure curiosity, I head down the stairs and to Valentine's room. I knock twice before he calls me to come in.

I wrap my hand around the handle, heading into his room, and I freeze when I see him sitting naked on the floor in front of the bed. He has on nothing but a little white towel wrapped around his narrow waist, his thick thighs spread out.

I gulp.

He looks up at me, his hair dripping wet, and his beard is gone. Instead of a bushy beard that hides his face, there is nothing but smooth skin, showing how utterly gorgeous he is. Everything from his high cheekbones to his structured jaw and his long lips make him utterly stunning. So stunning that I'm completely speechless.

He turns his head to the side and breathes in a long breath, and his eyes flare at whatever he scents. I know he's scenting exactly how I'm feeling about him.

I clear my throat, hoping he doesn't bring it up. "I'm not great at haircuts, but I can give it a go. The no beard thing suits you."

He smiles, and it's a devilish smile.

"I'd like that. Come and sit behind me," he instructs. My legs wobble as I walk over and sit on the bed behind him as he leans forward. Valentine wraps his hands around my ankles, parting my legs and leaning back. The demanding and possessive move sends shivers through me. As he settles back, his large shoulders press against the inside of my thighs, so close to my centre.

And it's all I can think of as my mouth goes dry.

Valentine tilts his head back, his eyes finding mine. I can feel the tension building in the air as we look at each other, right until Trey comes running into the room, banishing all my thoughts, and he hands me a pair of scissors. Trey sits down on the sofa as I divide Val's soft, soaking wet hair with the comb I find on the bed. Valentine almost seems to sink back into my touch, and I try not to react to how much I enjoy touching him. Running my hands through his hair, brushing my thighs against his shoulders. I've never been this close to him.

I didn't know a haircut could be so sexual. But god, it is.

I get to work on his hair, but he stays very still the whole time. Trey watches me, likely wondering if I'm going to make a big mess out of Valentine's hair and also curious what he will look like with it gone.

I think I'm sculpting the hair of a god—in theory, he looks like a god—and revealing more of him is nothing short of dangerous.

"Can you do my hair next time?" Trey asks when I'm nearly done with Val's hair.

"Who says I'm sharing her, kid?" Valentine comments, a wave of possessiveness grumbling out of his voice.

I have to blink a few times to get myself to focus on finishing his hair as Trey laughs and rushes to the door.

"I'm going to tell them!" Trey announces when he is out of Valentine's reach.

"Get back here, kid!" Valentine shouts, making me laugh. "Snitch," he grumbles when it's clear he isn't coming back. I place my hand on his shoulder for a second, and he makes a low grumble in his chest, nearly making me cut his hair in a very wonky way.

"How are you?" Valentine asks. "I've heard talking about it makes it better."

"I can't be sad forever," I answer.

"For what it is worth, he seemed like a good man from your stories. He wouldn't want you sad," he replies.

"I know that, but sometimes it's easier just to hide in a bed and pretend the world outside isn't happening."

"I know what that's like, but trust me, it happens anyway, and it's just worse the longer you spend in that bed. Sometimes it's better to get up, take a shower and just get on with the day," he states. I glance around the room for the first time since coming in here, noticing how there isn't a single bottle in sight and it's even cleaner than it was before. In fact, Valentine doesn't smell of whiskey anymore...no, he smells like the forest, earthy and damp.

Addictive.

"Since when did you become so wise on self-help?" I question.

"Since I'm learning to be better for someone important," he responds, making my heart flutter.

"There you go," I say, brushing off strands of hair from his large shoulders. He stands up, holding a tight grip on the towel, but still making me come face to face with his narrow waist and stomach. I try not to count the lines on his flat and toned stomach. Not all eight of them. Not think about how much I want to kiss each one and see where that V line disappears to.

These alphas are too tempting. They tempt my heart, soul and body by just breathing.

"Holy fuck, he really did it!" Henderson claps, walking into the room, followed by Ragnar.

Ragnar just laughs. Silas comes into the room last, followed by Trey.

All of them look shell-shocked. "Good to see your face again, brother."

"Don't thank me, thank beautiful over here." He points a thumb at me.

"Can we thank you with dinner and a movie?" Ragnar asks.

I glance at Silas, who stares me down. "I will start cooking."

"I didn't say yes!" I shout at his back as he walks away.

"Your eyes did," he shouts back. Cocky alpha.

"What do you say?" Henderson gently asks.

I stand up, brushing hair off my legs. "Dinner sounds good."

It's time to leave my room. Daniel will never be forgotten, but Valentine is right...he wouldn't want me to cry over him forever. I need to enjoy the life I have...with my alphas for as long as I have them.

CHAPTER TWENTY-FOUR

"Don't move," a man darkly warns me, standing close to my back. My plate slips from my hand into the sink, and I want to kick myself for not hearing anyone come in. I stay very still when I feel something sharp press into my back and a hand brushes my hair over my shoulder. I glance around the empty kitchen, wishing I had woken Ragnar up before coming down for a drink of water in the middle of the night. I shouldn't be alone.

And whoever this is should never have gotten in the house without being sensed. His voice is familiar…but I can't place it.

"Who are you?" I breathlessly ask as he pushes his large hand into the middle of my back and shoves me forward. A deep part of me knows this wolf isn't from our pack, he doesn't scent right, and that means only one person could have sent him here.

"Keep walking, Mairin," he warns me when I try to stop. I glance behind me, frowning at a man in a golden cloak that hides his face.

I imagine Silas whispering in my ear, telling me to do

something, anything. To fight. I can't let whoever this is take me back to Ravensword. I won't go back there. Quickly, I swing myself around and punch my fist hard into the man's face, hearing a crack. I swing my leg around, hitting the middle of his stomach, and he jolts forward, pulling out a long sword. We circle each other as he pulls his cloak down, and I recognise him right away.

"Beta Valeriu?" I whisper in shock. The alpha must be getting desperate if he is sending a beta here. He grins, even with blood dripping down his cheek.

"Tell your alphas to let me fight you alone, or are you a coward?" he sneers. Ragnar jumps over the top of stairs, landing behind Valeriu and wrapping his hands around Valeriu's neck.

"Mai is the bravest wolf you will ever meet, fucker," Ragnar shouts, and with incredible strength, he picks Valeriu up by his neck as he struggles to get his hands off his neck. Ragnar's eyes are glowing red, a scary red. Silas, Henderson and Valentine come into the room. They instantly stand in front of me, blocking me from any harm.

Henderson looks back at me. "You okay? He didn't hurt you?"

"No," I reply. "Silas's training kicked in before he could."

Silas looks back with a proud grin. "For that, I might reconsider training again."

Valeriu goes crashing into the kitchen wall, making the wall shake and plaster drop off around us. I sneak around Valentine, who wraps his arm around my waist, holding me close to him.

Valeriu pulls himself up the wall, wiping blood off his

chin. "The alpha should have killed you himself when he took your innocence all those years ago. That was fun to watch. You screamed and screamed. Just like you will when—"

He never finishes his sentence as Ragnar snaps his neck, and his body slumps down the wall.

I feel like I can't breathe as all of them turn to me, and I pull away from Valentine.

"What the fuck did the Ravensword alpha do to you?"

I look down. "When we were sixteen, he pretended to be my friend and...well, it was a game. He forced himself on me. I never thought I'd ever recover from that day. The shame of it."

Ragnar walks right up to me and cups my face. I look directly into his eyes. "You have nothing to be ashamed of. He does. And I am going to rip him to pieces for this. I swear to you."

"You don't think I'm broken?" I ask, my voice cracking.

"None of us do," he vows, his words echoed by the others. He wipes away the tears falling down my cheeks as my heart pounds in my chest. I glance back to Valentine, Silas and Henderson circled around us.

"He told me I was nothing... They all did," I admit. "And I believed it. The pack believed him when he told them all I seduced him and didn't like what happened. That it was my fault."

"It wasn't," Silas firmly states.

"And we are going to tell you every single day how beautiful, amazing and strong you are until you believe that," Ragnar says, letting me go and stepping back so all four of them make a half-circle around me. I've never felt safer or more wanted.

Less broken.

"That's the thing… You have already been doing that," I say with a small smile. "And now you know my secrets; I hope you trust me with some of yours."

"We have wanted to tell you for a while," Henderson starts. Just as he is about to say something else, the world explodes. I scream as I go flying into the air, brick smacking into my body until one sizeable chunk hits me on the head and everything goes black for a second. I open my eyes, coughing at the dust around me and heaving from pain. My ribs scream in pain as I sit up, finding the world spinning in a dusty dark haze. I touch my head, seeing hot blood coating my fingers as my ears ring. Bricks keep falling around me, and I feel confused. What just happened?

"Mai!" I hear Phim shout. I turn in the direction of her voice, walking on shaky steps over bricks and rock even as it keeps falling. Bright light shines down suddenly through the dust, and I look up to see the top of the mountain is gone, letting bright light beam down on what is left of the house.

A hand wraps around my wrist, and I turn to see Phim, seeing her talking, but my ringing ears make it impossible to hear what she is saying as she pulls me with her. I stumble over rocks and onto grass outside, and I see we aren't alone as my hearing finally comes back.

"I found her. You could have killed her!" Phim shouts at a man. The man is tall with long white hair, glowing green eyes and a beautiful face. He pushes Phim out of the way and walks to me, stopping so close to me.

"Phim...what is going on? Who is this?" I demand, and I turn to look back at the house. "The alphas. You have to help them! Trey is in there!"

Two hands land on my shoulders, and I scream as the touch feels like ice. I shoot my eyes back to the man as I try to fight his hands off me, but I'm too weak or he is too strong. "Who are you?"

"The more important question is who are you, Mairin Fall?" he replies with an accent I've never heard. "Are you a lost wolf? A childhood friend of four of the most important alphas in the world? Or are you the soul of a goddess?"

"What are you going on about?" I demand, feeling myself getting weaker. He is doing something to me. I can barely lift my arms now to fight him, and my legs feel heavy. I still manage to scream. "Tell me!"

Phim walks to the man's side and looks me dead in the eye. "The alphas have been lying to you. You grew up with them because you're bonded. They are the four parts of Hades' soul, and you are Persephone's soul reborn to a half-wolf, half-angel hybrid. They aren't from this tiny bit of the world, and neither are you. They know it, and now, so do you. The reason you are so close to them is that your souls are bonded and have been for thousands of years."

I laugh, shaking my head. "You're insane. Insane! That can't be true. They would have told me! I would know if I were a goddess and was living with Hades!"

"She is not lying to you. I know this because I am your father," the man holding me states, and I look back at him as slowly golden bat-like wings stretch out at his back, appearing from nowhere. I jolt, realising the book I read on angels is real.

And Henderson wrote it. So many other little things seem to slot into place until the final one does. Valentine said I looked like the woman they lost…but he lied.

I am the woman they lost, and they lied to me. So is this man right? Are they really Hades? The forbidden god? Is that how they saved me?

"We are going home, Mairin. You belong to us and not them," the man claiming to be my father states as my legs give in and I collapse into his arms without a choice in the matter. "Seraphim, take my hand, daughter."

"Daughter?" I ask in a haze. Seraphim leans over me, and for the first time, I realise her eyes are the same shade as mine as they start to glow. "I don't want to go with you. Le-t m-e…"

"Hello, sister."

READ the next book by clicking here…

AUTHOR NOTE

Sorry to leave you there. My bad. Cliffhangers can be a real...B. Some books pour out of my soul, and Her Wolves was one of them. Her Wolves demanded to be written around lockdown, two kids, three dogs and moving house. I have to thank my hubby for his dedication to stopping the kids coming into my office every few minutes.

I've spent so many late nights writing away on Mairin's story, and I can't wait to share more of her with my readers. Wolf shifters have a special place in my heart, and this book is no different. Let me know if you liked this book with a quick review. I adore reading them.

Thank you to everyone who helped, edited, poured me coffee or inspired this book in my mind.

This is a trilogy and book two, Her Defenders, is on pre-order already. You can click here for the link.

Thank you so much for reading my story!! Lots of love,
G. xoxo

Her Guardians Series

Her Fate Series

Protected By Dragons Series

Lost Time Academy Series

The Demon Academy Series

Dark Angel Academy Series

Shadowborn Academy Series

Dark Fae Paranormal Prison Series

Saved By Pirates Series

The Marked Series

Holly Oak Academy Series

The Alpha Brothers Series

A Demon's Fall Series

The Familiar Empire Series

From The Stars Series

The Forest Pack Series

The Secret Gods Prison Series

G. Bailey is a USA Today and international bestselling author of books that are filled with everything from dragons to pirates. Plus, fantasy worlds and breath-taking adventures. G. Bailey is from the very rainy U.K. where she lives with her husband, two children, three cheeky dogs and one cat who rules them all.

A few random facts about her...

She loves tea. (She may be a little obsessed but what Brit isn't?)

Chocolate and Harry Potter marathons are her jam.

She owns way too many notebooks and random pens.

Please feel free say hello on here or head over to Facebook to join G. Bailey's group, Bailey's Pack!

(Where you can find exclusive teasers, random giveaways and sneak peeks of new books on the way!)

FIND MORE BOOKS BY G. BAILEY ON AMAZON...

LINK HERE.

Part I

Description

The alpha of hell is my fated mate and he rejected me.

I'm an outcast in my pack and have been since the day I was born. Shunned by most of the wolves around me, I've managed to stay out of trouble... until now.

Now The Alpha of Stormfire is hunting me, but he doesn't want to claim me as his mate.

He wants me dead.

Forced to leave my old life behind, I have no choice but to go on the run. Luckily, The Demon Hunting Trials is the perfect place to hide, even if it comes with a few obstacles.

Such as their leader is a total jerk, a wolf is blackmailing me to be his friend, and I swear my new, sexy as sin partner is trying to get us killed.

With demons running amok and the alpha of hell searching for me, I hope I can live long enough to get my revenge.

18+ Dark reverse harem romance full with a sassy and sarcastic heroine who finds her match.

Bonus Read of Alpha Hell....: Lilith Thornblood

There isn't enough booze in the shifter world to deal with alpha egos.

I take a deep drink of the red wine I stole from the teacher's lounge at Caeli Pack Academy before passing it to my best friend. The only person in the whole world (okay, just the academy) who I like. She's also the sole reason the alpha's sons are walking right over to us at this lame excuse for a party to celebrate the rare blood moon. Who throws a party for eighteen-year-olds without booze?

Aurelia Winters coughs as she takes a long drink and rolls her eyes at me when I chuckle. Although she tends to think otherwise, Aurelia is ridiculously stunning, and it's mostly down to her bloodline. She looks just like her mum, but her father's genes are strong and make her the perfect example of a Caeli wolf. Taking another sip from the bottle, Aurelia tucks her curly blonde hair behind her ears and looks past me at the alpha's sons with her big blue eyes. She is the perfect wolf at the Caeli Pack Academy, whereas me, on the other hand, I stand out as the outcast they put up with. I'm a red in a world of white with my dark-red hair and red-furred wolf. Other than the streak of white hair that falls down the side of my cheek, there isn't much about me that lets me mix in with the pack I have always lived in.

The Caeli Pack is hidden deep in the snowy Mountains of Alaska, where no one ever comes because it's too high up and the humans are afraid of us. Mostly because we're supernatural beings who don't mix well with them since they only see us as a means to protect them from the bad things in the world. Every pack in the world has its mission, its purpose, and Caeli's is learning and recording every event in the world of shifters. Basically, librarians with a bite.

"I stand out everywhere," I mutter to Aurelia.

"So? You're pretty and unusual here. That's not a bad thing," she replies. "Don't worry so much."

Says the girl who fits into our pack better than my ass fits into these skinny jeans. I don't hide or blend in very well. Aurelia is the opposite. At least, she is until we're at a party like this where she stands out far more than I do in some sense. It's all because of the mating season. In a year's time, most females will have chosen a mate, and the males all want the prettiest wolf in the pack which is Aurelia.

Finding a mate is definitely not on my to-do list. At least not with any of these wolves.

I take the bottle from Aurelia. "I think I should just leave at the end of the academy year in two weeks. Maybe join the demon-hunting trials in the Stormfire pack or something." Throwing back a deep mouthful, I wipe my lips with the back of my hand. "Hell, maybe I could look for my father and actually fit in there."

Aurelia gawks at me, then snatches the bottle. "Are you freaking crazy? You could also die in the trials. That's it. No more booze for you."

I glare at her jokingly. "Hey, I'm not even tipsy!"

"You're speaking like my aunt on New Year's Eve! Have you forgotten that you could get killed trying to capture those disgusting demons? They eat wolves for fun. Why would you even want that?" She shakes her head. "You're safe here. You shouldn't leave."

"My brother left."

With a sigh, she rests her head on my shoulder for a few seconds. "But he's a male and strong. There are like three female demon hunters in the whole of the Stormfire pack, and each of them are totally badass."

"So you're saying I'm not a badass?" I question with a raised eyebrow.

She laughs. "If you were brought up in Stormfire, taught to fight from a kid instead of how to read a book and study like our pack taught, we might be having a different conversation. But your circumstances are totally different. You were brought up a Caeli, and we both don't have a clue about fighting demons or capturing them. Come on, Lilith. You know this. Please tell me you weren't being serious?"

I don't answer her because I know she's right. But the thought of studying wolf history and doing nothing more than studying for the rest of my life makes me feel sick. It's like my pack is squeezing the life out of me with each passing day, and the only way to stop is to find an escape.

"We can talk about it later," I say, shrugging my shoulder. "They are nearly here."

Aurelia raises her head and straightens her tight, sparkling yellow dress that shows off her long legs. I cross my own covered legs, the movement straining my jeans and knocking mud off my heavy boots. Aurelia decided that we both needed to dress up and come to this party at one of her friend's houses, something that I would never attend before now because honestly, parties are not my thing. I'd much rather be drinking this bottle of red wine on my own back in my room, but I can't always be unsociable when my best friend is a big extrovert. I need to compromise sometimes, even if that means leaving my bedroom. C'est la vie, right?

The alpha sons stomp over from the dance floor that we can see at the end of the corridor we are sitting in. The blasting music vibrates through the room, shaking the floor almost from the noise of it, and pop song comes on that sings about humans shaking their asses. Another reason I tend to avoid these things. Why does the music always suck? I'd much rather they played some rock. Hell, if they put on some Guns N' Roses, I might even bust some real moves. None of this swaying, grinding nonsense.

Beside me, a dancing Aurelia knocks my shoulder as she sings the song word for word. I can't help but smile at her. I thought I could hide back here with her, but now the alpha's twin sons' shadows hang over us, I'm thinking my hiding skills need work.

This was a really bad idea.

They're both looking at her like she's the answer to their prayers, the very air to their lungs, while their mating scent invades my own lungs so much that I nearly gag. They never stop staring at Aurelia even as they finally come to a stop, and I know why. Everyone knows she's going to be an alpha female at some point because her wolf is strong, a born leader, and her human incomparably beautiful.

All the things you need to be on the alpha's sons' radar.

As for me? Everyone knows I'm only ever going to be the outcast. It's because I really, really don't belong in this pack. Caeli is all about reputation and utmost control, of unrivalled intellect and centuries-old knowledge that are the very bones of our existence. Each pack in our world has its own unique purpose. Caeli's is record-keeping and the continuous search for better, more proficient pack medicine; something that has been installed into me since I was a pup.

Learn for the Pack—the motto every wolf here lives by.

Every wolf except for me.

As my mum puts it, I've always been too wild, too uncontrollable, and in general too nosy for my own good. I'm sure that's the sole reason most of the teachers at this academy absolutely hate me and most likely the reason that my adopted brother sometimes pretends I'm not really his sister.

Being an embarrassment to the shifter world is weirdly something I can live with. But being an embarrassment to my own family is the only thing that's kept me from running away.

Damn, I need more wine if I'm going to think about my family.

The alpha's sons, Dumb and Dumber as I've nicknamed them, just gaze with wide eyes at Aurelia. Their expressions are almost panicked. Aurelia watches back and sighs. It always makes me laugh how the simple fact she stares down future alphas who will no doubt one day fight for the chance to be pack leader, and subsequently, choose her as the alpha female if she chooses them, too. But I don't know if she will. Aurelia is picky about her guys, a lot like me. Not that many have been interested in the girl who doesn't belong here. Beyond their curiosity, I'm usually too different for them to look at twice.

The alpha sons may be handsome and muscular, both of them built like dump trucks, but for as strong as they are, there's not a lot going on upstairs under their thick, white-blond hair. My point is proven when they both stumble for a second on what to say to Aurelia. They scratch their heads, no doubt in search of a cheesy, overthought chat-up line, and then one of them says something that surprises even me a little.

"Would you like to come and dance to the song that is playing? I heard you say it was your favourite once."

And for whatever reason in the world, Aurelia appears almost happy that one of them noticed she likes the song that's playing.

She looks at me, and I nod. "Go. I'm going back to my room with the wine."

"Okay, see you back there later," she replies with a big smile.

The two of them quickly wander off down the corridor, and I hear her laugh a while later as I take another long drink of the bottle. A warm buzz floats down my body, the wine finally kicking in, but then I notice I'm left alone with the other alpha's son who I can never remember the name of. Every girl at this academy, other than me and Aurelia, has got their names memorised and written down in their diaries with love hearts. I know she doesn't do silly stuff like that just because we share a room and have done since we both came here when we were eight, like every young pack member. Their names come back to me now I gaze at them; Mathi and… Dammit, I can't remember what the other one's name is.

I stand and fake a big yawn before trying to walk away. But Mathi reaches out and grabs my arm, stopping me. I knew it was never going to be that easy. These alpha-holes rarely ever take a hint.

I narrow my eyes on his brown ones, a big contrast to my light grey. "Let. Go."

A smirk slides over his lips. "No. Why should I?"

He moves closer to me, lining up our bodies, and the disgusting thoughts circling in his head are written on his face as clear as day. This asshole better back off. He can't touch me; his father himself accepted me into the pack, which means I have the alpha's protection until he isn't alpha anymore. Of course, I worry about what will happen to me if the next alpha, AKA Dumb or his brother, Dumber, become alpha. But that won't be for some time yet. Right now, my focus is to get this unwanted paw off my body.

At the sight of me trying to wiggle my arm free, his smirk deepens into a malicious smile. He tightens his grip and pulls me closer, bringing his lips to my ear.

"You and I both know no one would notice if you went missing. You are just the outcast, the red wolf in a pack of white purebreds." He jolts me harder against him, his hands leaving bruises on my arm, but I refuse to turn away, to even wince at the pain. "Actually, that begs the question as to why you are still here. I'm surprised my father let you into the academy at all, half-breed."

Searing rage slams into me at the insult. Half-breed is the delightful nickname purebreds use for wolves like me; a subtle reminder of our so-called inferiority. Well, that's what they like to think. Anyone who's called me a half-breed usually walks away with a black eye.

I ball my hands into fists. "Maybe your dear father likes my mum a little too much. He does always seem to be admiring her."

The wolf's smile fades, and I inwardly chuckle at his stupid expression. So easily provoked, these young alphas. However, my satisfaction is short-lived. With a growl, he slams me into the wall, and I gasp from the impact. He presses his thick forearm against my neck, holding me in place, and the air dies in my lungs.

"Is that… any way… to treat a lady?" I choke out, unsure why I'm using my last breaths to anger him further. Then again, the fury burning on his gaze does make my sacrifice worth it. Besides, it's not like I'm unused to assholes like this one asserting their authority over me. Alphas love putting unruly wolves like me in their place.

Too bad I've never quite learned how to stay in mine.

Despite the black spots seeping into my vision, I stare up at him, wondering what exactly he's going to do. One thing is for sure—this dickwad has solidified my desire to leave his pack as soon as possible. I'll never follow an alpha who treats their packmates this way.

"Do you want to die, half-breed?" he growls.

I resist the urge to give him a sarcastic reply. I may be brave, but as my brother puts it, I can be pretty stupidly brave.

And I know that challenging an alpha son is really not a good idea.

I might be able to fight well, thanks to all the training the Academy has taught me. But even I know that you can't beat a guy twice your size in a small corridor like this, with no weapons on me, and his forearm pressed on my windpipe.

He gazes down at me and raises an eyebrow, but something burns on my arm.

In the corner of my eye, my wolf mark in the middle of my arm burns vividly. The swirls that form a wolf shape glow a deep, vibrant red, at first burning painfully but they quickly fade into a dull ache that fills my entire body.

Mathi follows my gaze to the mark and smiles.

"Seems like your parents are calling you home," he snarls, loosening the pressure on my throat. "Did your mum's mate ever realise that you weren't his?"

This asshole knows damn well my dad knows I'm not his.

I was conceived and born before my mum ever mated. Everyone in the pack knows it. It was a big scandal, and to this day I still hear the boring wolves talking about it. Caeli wolves love to gossip because they have nothing better to do.

I grit my teeth at the jab. "Fuck. Off."

He raises his free hand as if to strike me. I don't flinch, and that seems to piss him off. He grabs me by the scruff of the neck and slams me against the wall again, drawing everyone's attention.

"Go back to your little family, half-breed. But just remember that when I'm alpha, your kind will never be welcome here." He releases me with a derisive scoff. "Off you go now, run back home."

I don't reply despite the tinge of fear that his threat elicits in me. My wolf, however, bares her teeth and snaps her jaw at him in retaliation. I need to get out of here before I shift and try to take on an alpha twice my size. The fading burn from my family's mark sears in my mind, screaming down to my soul for me to move.

Biting back my spiteful retort, I jog down the corridor and take a left out of the noisy house, dodging students who whistle and tease me. The cool night air lifts my hair over my shoulders when I step onto the porch. I take a deep breath and jog into the snowy outskirts that surround the house. Snow-capped trees line the distance, and I make a break for them. The cold doesn't bother me, even when I duck behind a tree and strip off. Once I'm fully naked, I bundle my clothes into a ball and shove them into the small bag I always carry with me.

I rest my head against the tree and gaze up at the moon

cutting through the frozen leaves. My breath comes out in puffs of smoke, and for a moment I stay there, thinking about how much I'd have liked to punch that alpha-hole in the throat.

But my family needs me.

I dig my feet into the earth and arch forward, spreading my fingers through the snow. Shifting is an effortless, painless task for me, almost like breathing. I transform into my wolf easily, letting my body change until my red paws sink into the ground. Picking the bag up with my fangs, I run through the forest back towards the towering academy hidden in a clearing shrouded in blankets of untouched snow. It's eerily silent at this time of night. Most people are sleeping, and those who find themselves awake under the light of the moon, venture into the woods to hunt.

The side door of the academy is always left open, and I slip through it. The wood corridors echo every hit of my wolf's claws on them as we dodge around corridors of lockers. We keep running until we get to the main stairs and head straight up to our room and pause. My wolf drops my bag on the floor, and we use our advanced hearing to make sure no one is around before shifting back. Most wolves don't care about nudity, but I'm not one of them.

I unlock my door and head inside with my bag, quickly getting back into my jeans, plain black tee-shirt and boots. I search the messy floor for my phone next. I push a few items of clothing around before I find it and try ringing my parents, but it goes straight to voicemail. I ring my adopted elder brother, but again, straight to voicemail. My family are bloody useless with phones. Instead of trying to keep ringing them, I decide I might as well just go and see them since it's not too far to walk. It's a weird thing for them to use a wolf call with my mark, but I'm sure everything is fine, even if something in the back of my mind doesn't think so. My mum never uses the mark to summon me, and my dad definitely hasn't done it. He likes to pretend I don't exist. That only leaves my brother, but Leo's too busy working as a new demon hunter to bother summoning me. I guess there's only one way to get to the bottom of this.

Time to go home and see what the hell is going on.
ALPHA HELL (THE REJECTED MATE SERIES #1)...

Lilith Thornblood

CHAPTER TWO

Lilith Thornblood

Burning leaves.

It's all I can smell when I emerge from the trees surrounding my childhood home. The scent clings to my snow-covered fur and permeates the night air like a sceptic perfume. I pause on the outskirts of the forest and lift my head towards the sky. A stiff breeze sweeps over me and carries the scent downwind, meaning it's coming from the direction of my house.

The scent can only belong to a Stormfire wolf, but why would one of them trespass into our territory? Unless my parents invited them. Could that be why I've been summoned?

I slip out of the trees and run across the field towards my home. The three-storey, red-brick building has been in my family for generations. The slanted roof is covered in a thick blanket of snow, and icicles dangle from the gutters to overshadow the wooden porch. My dad's car is parked in the driveway, and the shed, which we use for shifting, has been left open.

Slowing my gait, I scan the ground. Fresh paw prints. They're triple the size of my own when I step into them. I take a cautious sniff, and sure enough, burning leaves cling to the indentations.

I hurry into the shed and shift back. Rummaging through my bag, I dress quickly, lock the door behind me, and climb the porch steps. Only the kitchen light is on. Mum must be cooking dinner. My stomach clenches, and a feeling of dread washes over me when I touch the door.

Someone with magic has been there. The only creatures who can use magic nowadays are demons. Not even the headmaster at the academy is able to cast spells; he has to summon a demon to do it for him.

I take a deep breath and open the front door. One step, two steps over the threshold, and my heart clenches at what I see inside our little kitchen. My mother, held by the throat by the largest man I've ever seen, and my father standing beside her as pale as a ghost. The unfamiliar male towers several feet above the both of them, and his grasp on my mum's throat.

"Welcome home, Lilith Thornblood."

His deep, powerful voice sends a shiver running down the length of my spine. He's completely naked from the waist up. His torso is covered in symbolic tattoos the same black colour as his hair. Thick gold bands encircle his arms, and a black medallion with a ruby centre hands around his neck. The jewel glows just like his crimson eyes, all of them cutting into me like molten shards.

"I believe introductions are in order," he says, flashing the tip of his fangs in a smile that doesn't reach his eyes.

My mother's wide, terrified ones never leave my face. It kills me to see her so afraid. Even my dad has cowered a little in size; a gesture meant to convey submission in the presence of an alpha.

"I know who you are."

He lifts a scarred brow. "Oh?"

I peel my gaze from the hand on my mother's throat to glare at him. "You're the alpha of Stormfire. You guard the Gates of Hell. Apparently, you have quite the temper and once wiped out an entire pack just because their alpha stole from you."

The alpha inclines his head. "The very one."

He regards me through the barest slits of his eyes. A minute shake of his head threatens disappointment as he looks at me. Look isn't quite the right word. The Stormfire alpha is dissecting me into pieces, stripping me naked with his gaze until I'm only flesh and blood. From his stony expression, I appeal less to him than a mildly interesting object, and for some insane reason it raises my hackles.

Despite everything my parents and pack have taught me, I make a point of holding the alpha's gaze as boldly and firmly as he holds mine. "What do you want?" I practically spit out at him.

My dad crosses the length of the kitchen and slaps me so quickly I stumble back in surprise, my body thudding into the back of the door. I'm used to his temper, and his fists, but still, I didn't expect this hit.

"Show the alpha some goddamn respect!"

The impact forces me to break eye contact, but not before I catch sight of the alpha's eyes glowing a deep shade of black.

"Touch her again and you'll lose more than a hand." He adds just the slightest bit of pressure to my mum's throat, and the tips of his claws dent her skin.

She doesn't so much as draw a single breath. Dad takes a big step back from me in fear for my mum, his mate's, life.

The alpha cuts his gaze to me. "Come."

He drags my mum from the kitchen, and my dad slowly takes up the rear, his expression a little grimmer than before. My heart thrashes so violently I can scarcely make out their footsteps as they head into the dining room. For a moment I just stand there in the kitchen, and then I follow suit, each step laced with a growing, burning hatred for this alpha. And my dad. Why is he letting this alpha treat my mum this way? It's almost like he couldn't care less about her. While he's always been like that towards me, he's never disrespected my mum. I don't even care if he's only doing it because there's an alpha in our home. It's unacceptable.

If my mum didn't appear so terrified in the alpha's presence, I'd grab a knife from the kitchen and swing at the alpha, then I'd take my mum away where my dad can never find her again. She's always deserved better than him.

We both deserve better.

Once I reach our open-plan living room, everyone is seated at the dining table; the alpha where my dad would usually sit, my mum beside him. I sweep my gaze over the surface, unsurprised to find it set for only one. Of course the alpha would eat before any of us. It's customary in packs that alphas should eat first and, usually, alone. With a wave of his tattooed hand, a thin chain slithers around my mum's wrist. It wraps around the table leg, binding her to the alpha's side. She glances at me standing in the doorway, her eyes wide and stark with fear, and more searing-hot fury consumes me.

The alpha pulls out a chair and gestures to it dismissively. "By all means, have a seat."

Everything about this male pisses me off. From the arrogant way he struts around my home like he owns it, to the manner in which he curls the edge of his lips and looks at me like I'm a piece of meat… So typical of every other alpha out there, and yet so, so much worse.

He doesn't even wait to see if I'll obey his command. With not a care in the world, he claims the seat at the other end of the table and reaches for the bottle of red wine. My dad sits across from my mum, leaving only the pulled-out chair at the end for me. My every instinct screams to shift and challenge this alpha, but I'm not an idiot. Not only does he hold my mother prisoner, but I'm willing to bet his wolf is three times the size of mine. I'd be dead before I could so much as sink my teeth into his throat.

There's really nothing for it. If I'm to figure out what the hell is going on and get my parents out of this alive, I need to play nicely; something I've failed to do so far in my eighteen years.

I settle down on the opposite side. The silence is so tense I could cut it with the alpha's butterknife. Instead, I lift my eyes from the polished surface of the table and look at him.

"Why are you here?" I repeat, ensuring my voice is firm. "And what do you want?"

My dad slams his fist on the table and prepares to stand. "Dammit, child! How many times have I told you? Do not speak unless spoken—"

The alpha's voice stops him. Dad freezes in his half-crouched position, and his worried eyes flick to the other end of the table.

"You'd do well to follow your own advice, Valerio." The alpha narrows his eyes on me. "At any rate, I see no problem in answering her questions. She is my mate, is she not?"

Lilith Thornblood

CHAPTER THREE

Lilith Thornblood

It's clearly a rhetorical question, one that sends my heart shooting to the pit of my stomach. Did he just say what I think he did? My pulse skyrockets, and I clench my hands underneath the table. For the first time since entering the dining room, my mother isn't looking at me. It's as if she can't bring herself to. I've never seen my mum as anything but the beautiful and graceful wolf with long white hair I wish I had. I can't ever remember seeing my mum scared or weak. I know her expression scares me far more than the alpha behind her and calling me his mate could ever do.

"I'm here to collect what's mine." The alpha pours himself a glass of wine and sniffs the contents before taking a sip. His eyes cut over the glass to me. "That would be you."

A nervous laugh bubbles in my chest and quickly escapes my lips. "W-what? You can't be serious?" I glance at my mum, my chest rising unevenly. "Mum, what the hell is going on?"

But she doesn't say a word. The colour has completely drained from her face. She seems like she's about to be sick.

"One thing you should know about me, little mate," the alpha says in a dangerously low voice, dragging my attention back to him, "is that I am only ever serious. You belong to me and you are my fated mate. The Crescent Mother wills it."

The glimmer of anxiety that had gripped me a moment ago vanishes, replaced with more searing-hot anger.

"I don't belong to anyone," I spit back at him. "Especially not a wolf who came here uninvited and raised his own hands to my mother!"

He picks up my mum's favourite cutlery and begins cutting his meat. "Who says I came here uninvited?"

My dad shifts nervously, and my mum's face turns a violent shade of red. This doesn't make any sense. If they invited him, why would he threaten to hurt my mum? There's no way my mum would invite the alpha of another pack to our home. It's unheard of unless it's to the house of another alpha. And as much as my dad likes to pretend he's an alpha behind closed doors, he's nothing of the sort.

I straighten. "I don't know how things work in your pack, *Alpha*, but shackling your host to a table isn't something we do in Caeli."

He chuckles and shoves a slice of meat into his mouth. "You've got fire in you, little mate. Good. You'll need it when I take you home."

"*This* is my home," I snarl at him.

The alpha dismisses my retort and continues eating. "I see your mother failed to inform you of your situation. Allow me to explain." He wipes his mouth with a silk handkerchief and then tosses it on his near empty plate. "Eighteen years ago, your mother and I came to an agreement. In exchange for helping her flee a rather complicated situation, your mother promised me a mate worthy of the Stormfire alpha. I've come to see just how worthy of a mate you truly are."

The air clamps in my chest. It's like the alpha has thrust a paw into my chest and is squeezing my heart with his razor-sharp claws. Through the tears blurring my vision, I glare venomously at my dad. He used to say there would come a day when my past would catch up with me. Until this very moment, I never understood what he meant. But it was that I'd been promised to an alpha who would one day come to collect me. And he knew.

My *mum* knew.

I wonder if my brother and Aurelia were aware, too.

The thought twists my stomach into a pile of knots, and a rush of anxiety trickles down my spine. This can't really be happening. It's like I've fallen through a portal to an alternative universe where my own family would betray me. I glance at my mum, searching for something, anything, that will tell me the alpha is lying. But she only looks away as her lower lip trembles. She really did do it.

My mum promised me to an alpha when I was just a baby.

I snap my head to the alpha in question and glare at him. He just fucking smirks at me like this is an amusing game to him. But then something changes. His lips thin, and he sniffs the air. His prior amusement melts from his countenance like wet snow, and he rises from the table. Slowly, he comes towards me, and I struggle to hold his gaze this time. There's something darker about it, something primal and deadly. Power radiates off him like an all-encompassing shadow. His presence alone swallows up everything in the room, and despite my best efforts, I shrink a little in my chair.

He stops beside me and picks up a strand of my long, auburn hair. A muscle ticks in his jaw, and a crease forms between his brows when he lifts the strand to smell it. His eyes darken into a deeper onyx. Faster than I can blink, he leans forward and brushes his fangs along my neck. I grip my thighs and close my eyes. I know what he's doing. He's taking in my scent to see whether or not I'm 'worthy' of him. From the way my palms turn sweaty and my heart convulses, he can no doubt smell the whirlwind of emotions wreaking havoc within me.

"You smell of weakness," he breathes, the tip of his fangs sweeping over the pulse in the side of my throat. "Weak wolves do not belong in my pack."

"My daughter is a lot of things, Rizer. A half-breed and nuisance, sure, but no wolf of my line has ever been weak," my dad says.

In my shock, I open my eyes to gawk at him. I've never heard him defend me like this before. Even when our own pack ridiculed me, he said nothing.

Did nothing.

A foolish part of me actually hopes to find compassion when I face him, but there's only that same old, familiar coldness. I wish I knew what I did to make him despise me so much. The fact that he just said I'm part of 'his' line means he does see me as part of the Valerio family, so it can't be that I'm not his biological kid.

"Your line is also descended from cowards and liars," Rizer growls, moving behind me.

Again he sniffs my hair, and I dig my fingernails into my jeans. My mother holds my gaze, but ever so quickly, she glances at the front door.

"That I could ignore. But weakness? That is disgusting and cannot be tolerated. You should not be allowed to exist."

I swallow the nervous lump in my throat and watch my mother drape her free hand over the alpha's knife. Her glancing at the front door was a signal for me to run. But I can't just run while she's chained to the table. However, before I can so much as protest, she throws the wine glass onto the table. The glass smashing against the wooden floor rouses the alpha's attention, if just for a second. That's all I need to jump up from the table and out of the way, moments before the knife whistles through the air towards the alpha.

The blade pierces him in the chest, and for a second, he just stands next to me, his eyes wide.

"*What have you done?*" My dad's chair falls over and he shoots up from his chair. He rushes over to the alpha and stumbles to his knees beside him. Shaking hands hover over the dead body, but they can't quite bring themselves to touch the bloodstains on his chest. Unfortunately, the alpha won't remain dead for long; alphas always regenerate, usually once the source of their death has been removed from their body, but there's rumours that alphas don't require that.

I doubt a knife to the heart will keep Rizer dead for long.

"He'll kill us," my dad chokes out, his hands trembling so violently his whole upper body shakes. "He'll kill us all!"

My mum doesn't even glance at him. "Lilith, go. We don't have long."

Blood pounds in my head and I shake it in disbelief. "The chain—"

"Go without me!"

I flinch at the volume of her tone but keep shaking my head. "N-no, I can't. I'm not leaving you here, Mum!"

As I rush over to her side, my dad continues muttering about how the alpha will kill us—him—once he wakes up. He really is a coward. I'm glad he's not my real dad. Once I reach my mum and look down at the chain cutting into her skin, the tears I've been struggling to hold back finally fall from my lashes. She follows my gaze, and instead of being scared or upset, she just smiles at me. Slowly, she tucks my hair behind my ear and pats my head like she's done since I was a kid.

"Don't worry, sweetie, I'll be right behind you." And with that, she pushes me towards the front door, her chain scraping the table. "Take the backpack hanging by the door and go. Don't turn back. I love you, baby."

A sob bursts from my trembling lips. "I love you, too, Mum."

I quickly hug her, grab the bag, and then I'm taking off through the front door without so much as a glance at my dad.

My boots barely hit the ground when I shift into my wolf, take the bag into my mouth, and run. I never feel the cold, but right now I'm as cold as the snow crunching beneath my paws. My breath streams out in harsh, rapid puffs but I head into the trees as fast I've ever ran in my life, not even bothering to bring my clothes. I keep going until a deafening howl cuts through the air in the distance and my fur instantly stands on end.

Rizer.

His burning-leaves scent carries on the downwind, and my stomach roils with a mixture of fear and anger. I pause by a frozen creek and stare down at my reflection on the icy surface. My wolf looks as dejected as I feel. Did my mum even make it like she said she would? A small part of me hopes she did and that I'll see her soon, that she will catch up with me. But the rest of me, no matter how much I want to refute it, shatters as if I knew all along: my mum was never getting out of that house alive.

A sick, twisted piece of me hopes my dad never made it out. He'd been perfectly willing to hand me over to the alpha like a bit of discarded meat. My mum had been nothing but terrified from the moment I entered the kitchen. My eyes water at the thought of her, but I quickly push them aside and continue. There will be time to mourn for her later. I need to get out of here before the alpha catches up with me.

With this shadowing over me, I run faster through the forest. It's a little ironic that I've spent my childhood exploring these woods. I know every tree, every creek and clearing, and yet I don't know where to go. I could go back to the party and get Aurelia, then come up with a plan. But I don't want to drag her into this. My best option would be to seek refuge in the academy. That means going east.

Another howl echoes in the near distance, followed by

another. Their cadence is so different to what I'm used to hearing amongst Caeli wolves, which means these ones aren't part of my pack. They must be from Stormfire. Damn it! They've blocked out the academy. West will just take me to Aurelia, and I don't want to endanger her. All I can do is head north in hopes that I find a place good enough to hide.

After hours of running, my limbs ache from exertion, and I have no choice but to stop to rest. The Stormfire howls stopped about a mile back. I'm not stupid enough to think they've given up hunting me. Leaning against a tree, I glance up at the bloodstained moon, and a powerful urge to howl at her fullness consumes me. My mum used to say that the Crescent Mother was more likely to bless her wolves on the night of a full moon. It's a slim chance, but right now, I'll do anything to get out of here.

I need your help. Please tell me where I should go. Give me a sign. Please. Something. Crescent Mother, help me.

In answer to my prayer is the cloying smell of more burning leaves, and the low grumble of a howl rumbling in the back of a wolf's throat. I whip my head around in search of the wolf. Through the shadowy trees, I'm able to decipher an enormous red wolf surrounded in tendrils of smoke. The medallion around its powerful neck gleams in the moonlight.

Uhh, Crescent Mother... This isn't what I quite had in mind.

Rizer snaps his bloody jaw at me and takes a step. The blood on his lips carries my mum's scent. A low whimper escapes me, and I instinctively back away from him. I lower my head and press my tail tightly between my hind legs. More howls resonate close by. There's no way I'll be able to fight off Rizer let alone the others.

In the corner of my eye, a light flickers in the darkness around me. The bright glow pulls me towards it like gravity. I turn my head ever so slightly, and relief washes over me. A huge staircase stands proudly on the forest floor, and right at the top is a bright orange light.

A portal.

I don't even stop to question where it might lead me.

I charge up the stairs and dive head-first into the blinding, beautiful light.

Lilith Thornblood

CHAPTER FOUR

Lilith Thornblood

I *really* hate portals.

I stumble through the light, my stomach feeling like a thousand bees are bouncing around in it, and smack hard into the stairs on the other side. I stand, my wolf shaking our head, just as the edge of the old, cracked steps to the portal gives way under my feet.

My wolf whines as we fall down the steps, right off a damn cliff of all things. My body smacks across the rock side, sharp pebbles digging into my calves. My wolf tries to dig its claws into the cliffside to stop us. Roots and branches snag in my fur and against my legs as I keep falling, unable to find anything to stop us. I briefly see everything is red and burning right before I crash into something that instantly burns my back.

Standing quickly, I move off the tiny pool of lava under me, letting my wolf heal the brief burns. Breathlessly, I take a second to glance around me and I freeze. My blood runs cold when I realise exactly where I am.

The Stormfire pack.

Also known as—Hell itself.

What the hell? I'm not even on Earth anymore.

In my horror, I look up at the portal on top of the mountain, wondering why the alpha isn't right on my heels. He should be able to follow me.

This is his frigging pack, after all.

Shit. Shit. Shit.

My brother once told me Hell was a really beautiful place, but I never quite believed him. How could a place where demons and wolves live be beautiful? Until this second when I'm staring at all of Hell right in front of me, I never once imagined it was like this. A giant tree has grown from below the city and its entangled roots stretched everywhere they could. I remember the tree being called The Tree of Ignis. The tree has made winding paths that swirl around the main trunk, lit up with red fire on its edges. Pack homes are also woven into the branches and roots, almost like they are part of the tree. Sharp and steep rocky mountain walls make a circle around the outskirts of the city, one of them I've just fallen down, which must have one of many portals to Hell on it.

No wonder that hurt like a bitch. The fall must be about thirty feet.

I didn't even know there was a portal to Stormfire near my home. In fact, it should be impossible for that portal to even exist. *Problem for another time.* The Stormfire city surrounds the major part of the ancient and wondrous tree. The looping roots and gnarled vines hold much of the city together. There are tall towers of apartments wrapped in vines and red flowers, that are like flames, on the edges of the city. Closer to the middle are large stone buildings that seem untouched by the tree themselves, and perhaps newer.

The tree isn't the most beautiful and fascinating part of the city.

No, it's the leaves.

Burning leaves constantly fall off the branches at the top of the tree. They flutter down and then disappear into nothing but embers before they hit the ground. I stare around in awe at the place I've always wanted to come to see.

Terrified awe.

What the hell am I going to do? I bite my backpack in my mouth a little tighter, wondering what Mum packed inside it for me and if she is still alive. My wolf whines softly, our pain shared between us, threatening to take over the fear we need to focus on. It isn't safe here. I glance back up at the portal at the top of the massive hill that I've just fallen down.

Rizer is going to follow me here soon. He is too powerful for me to fight head-on, and there's no way I'm going to get away from him in his pack's territory if he spots me now. I glance back at the tree and Stormfire city resting around it.

There's only really one thing I can do to survive: hide in Rizer's pack of millions of Stormfire wolves and make sure he doesn't find me.

He won't think I'm brave enough to hide in his own pack. *Hopefully.*

At least I won't stand out in Stormfire, not with my red fur wolf, as they all appear the same as me, something I've always wanted. Just not like this. Except for the white streak of hair, but I can disguise that with a hat or something in human form. Not so much as a wolf. I lean back on my heels and tighten my grip on the backpack before I break out into a run. My wolf bolts across the rocky terrain that seems like it's on fire, but it does nothing but heat my paws. In fact, I feel warm but not on fire like I should do.

"Outside the gates of Hell's city burn all those who flee and do not belong."

My academy teachers' words come back to haunt me as I keep running and come to a large river made of clear, crimson water. Sharp rocks sit at the bottom, and a few strange fish swim around them. *Let's hope none of them bite.* The current of the river flows fast, and I don't see a bridge in sight or anywhere I can cross.

We'll have to swim.

Feeling my wolf's reluctance to go into it, and I'm completely in agreement with her, I figure we don't have a choice. We're not great at swimming. It was never one of our bonus points at the academy, but there's no way around it. I pull the backpack tightly into my mouth, knowing I need to hold on firmly to it in the river.

We can do this!

I dive into the water, and my wolf uses all our strength to swim to the other side. We try not to get pushed too far down by the current, but the river is deeper and bigger than we thought. The water is warm, almost painfully warm, but I try not to focus on it as we swim as fast as we can to the other side. Soon we realise the current is much wilder than we predicted, and suddenly we are being pushed harshly around. My wolf dives underwater, and we bare our teeth, holding the backpack to push through the current. It directs our path. I know I need to let the current take me and not fight it, even as I can't see or hear anything but red water.

It's official. Hell sucks, and they even ruined water.

My wolf pulls free of the current eventually, and we break out of the top of the river, gasping for air around the backpack. We end up just being pulled and pulled farther down the river, not able to get out of the current to either side. My legs ache, and tiredness takes over with every brush of a wave of water against us. The only good thing is that Rizor is unlikely to find me now. The dreadful thing is that rivers like this can only end in two ways. One could be a pretty lake and the other a deadly waterfall.

With my luck, it is definitely going to be a waterfall.

No sooner do I think that than the rushing of a waterfall in the distance carries to my ears, and pure panic makes me struggle around in the water. I want to shift back, but I know it's not a good idea. My wolf is stronger than I am. She goes back underwater with the current, and we try swimming tougher when we come back up, but it doesn't get us anywhere. I glance around as quickly as possible, looking for anything to help us get out of this damn river. That's when I see it, a big rock ledge on the left side, next to the edge of the waterfall cliff. If I could just land on to that, I can climb out and be on the right side for the city.

I swim as hard as I can towards it, pushing my wolf to her limits, begging our body not to give our tiredness.

We really need to work on our cardio and swimming skills if we survive this.

We just about slam our body into it, my lungs gasping from the impact, and I nearly drop the backpack out of my mouth. Pulling myself up onto the ledge, I reel my weak legs across to the side of the rocky pathway and finding a hidden space between a few roots of a stray tree that will hide me for a bit.

Fucking hell, I think to myself, letting out a small, frustrated whine.

I shift back, needing to be human for a moment, and take a deep breath before breaking down in sobs as the pain of everything that has happened catches up with me. Wrapping my arms around my knees, I don't know how long I cry for. Knowing that my mum's gone, knowing my dad is most likely gone, too, and I'm the alpha's intended mate.

And he rejected me.

Being rejected by someone who you're meant to mate with is unheard of in the pack world. At least I've never heard of it. But then it's also unheard of for the Stormfire alpha to take a mate. I know he has one son whose mother he murdered, but she was never his mate. Just his breeder.

How he ever thought I could be his mate is insane to think about. I'm no alpha female and I never want to take a mate. I don't want to love someone because magic forces me to. Too many times I saw my mum resist her mating bond because her mate was an asshole.

Sorry, Dad, but you were one. RIP. Hopefully.

I grit my teeth, and my wolf lets out a growl that echoes in my chest when I think of Rizor calling me weak. *I am not weak.* Taking a deep breath, I try to control my emotions, try to push down my urge to shift back. To run and run until we get out of this world, to somewhere safe from him. But I know we need to be smarter than that right now. I don't have anywhere to go back to. The alpha of Caeli won't fight the Stormfire pack for me, which he would have to do if he protected me. Rizor will never stop until he kills me…even I don't understand what he wants with my death. I can't go straight to my brother because that's exactly where he'd think I'd go. Watching my brother is going to be his first move, no doubt. I search my brain for an answer for a long time before I come up with the perfect (ish) idea.

I look up at the falling embers that drift down around me, matching the same colour as my hair. I think of my brother's best friend who lives here in Stormfire. The boy who always smelt of burning leaves and bad decisions.

Caspian Hardling.

I met him a few times as a young teenager and I fixated on him because he was Stormfire, new, interesting, and most importantly, gorgeous. His parents let him spend two years training in Caeli Academy as part of a student exchange programme to help with peace between the four packs. Caspian is a good guy, and I can trust him. My brother said he trusted Caspian with his life, and I really have no one else to turn to here. I doubt Caspian is even going to remember me; I haven't seen him since I was thirteen and blurted out I had a big crush on his handsome eighteen-year-old ass.

I was a dork who had just discovered wine. *A bad combo.*

I have to ask him to hide me until I can come up with a plan. He's a bounty hunter, or at least I heard that he was in the bounty hunter trials last year. My brother never said if Caspian passed them, like he did, but I doubt Caspian failed. When he sets his mind on something, he always gets it in the end. He told me that himself when I was a drunk little dork.

Now I have a plan, albeit not a great one, I open the backpack and find several sets of clothes inside along with a letter. My hands shake as I open the yellow envelope and pull the parchment out. I run my fingers over my name, written in my mum's beautiful, classy handwriting. A small bracelet falls out of the envelope onto my lap, and I lift it to see it's made of silver with a red stone attached in the middle of it. I put the bracelet down and open the letter to read it.

To Lilith,

I'm so sorry that I had to write this, that I couldn't tell you everything, that you're in this position. I knew if you took this backpack that everything I feared would happen has happened. I know I'm not with you because I'd never let you read this letter if I was.

First thing's first.

The bracelet is spelled. I used all of my money over my short lifetime to pay for it, and it's blessed by demons of incredible power. It will hide you from him. The Stormfire alpha can never find or track you so long as you wear it. Neither will anybody else who will look for you and have been since you were born. The Caeli pack hid you until now, but now you have to find your place in the world alone. I'm so sorry.

Wear it and never take it off, promise me this.

There's so much I wish to tell you, so much that I can't fit into a small letter. But I'm going to sum up most of the terrible things that happened right before you were born. I was born in the Caeli pack, but I gave my heart to Stormfire. To your father. Know that I created you in pure love, no matter what anyone says.

Many people died to keep you safe, to get me out of Hell, but it all went wrong. And at the very last second, I had to make a deal to leave Hell with you. The alpha of Stormfire wanted you as his mate. I think he always did because of what happened when you were born. Many want you as theirs, Lilith, and you must trust no one.

I can never write the truth in this letter because if someone else found this, it could mean the death of you. I wish I could have told you, but your dad bound me to the secrecy, so it could never leave my lips.

I'm sorry.

The secrets will come out eventually, and you'll realise what I did for you was the right thing, but for now the secret will die with me.

Be brave.

We both know that hiding in Hell is the best for you if you can get there. You'll fit in there as it is massive, full of millions and millions of wolves, the biggest population of wolves in the world. You'll be able to hide and disappear.

I will love you forever and I will protect you in the afterlife. Always know dying for you was my plan right from the beginning. I regret none of my life or my choices.

Tell your brother that. Let him know there is a letter for him in our secret place.

Love,

Mum

By the end of the letter I'm in sobs as I pick up the small bracelet my mum said she spent so much money on. No wonder we barely had anything and Dad hated me so much. It looks expensive, and it radiates with magic. The sort of magic that doesn't come cheap anymore. The only things in this world that have magic are demons. Demons don't sell their magic easily or cheaply or to anybody in Caeli. I clip the bracelet onto my wrist, feeling my mum's love and protection in it like she is here at my side. The stone rests right in the centre of my wrist, fitting me perfectly.

What secret would my mum die to protect about me? What could be so bad but desirable to the Stormfire alpha?

What the hell happened when I was born?

Of course, no one answers me, and I bet the secret is with the Crescent Goddess now.

I need to get to Caspian and somewhere safe because I can't die or get caught now. My mum needs me to be strong, to fight this and live my life. Rizor will tell his people to look for me, no doubt. I need to get into the city and disappear. Soon he will have the entire pack searching for a new wolf.

Quickly, I drag on the leggings, boots, and the large hoodie that's in the backpack, one of my favourite hoodies that I thought I'd lost over a year ago. *I know exactly where it went now.* I smile for a brief second at the idea of my mum stealing it.

Then my smile falls when I remember she isn't here anymore. She is likely dead.

I pull my wet hair into a ponytail with a hairband I find in the bag and drink the small bottle of water that's at the bottom before putting everything back and standing. Strapping the backpack onto my back, I glance up at the enormous city. A city big enough for any wolf to get lost in.

Time to go into the city of Hell and pretend I'm from here.

I don't know if that's even possible because I have no idea what I'm walking into. The river will have hidden my scent and washed away all traces of any Caeli wolf on me. That's one good thing. I walk towards the city walls, and when I get to them, I realise there's no door anywhere I can see. I search up and down the wall, realising I have to go through the main gates of the city.

Unless…

I look up and grimace. Maybe I can climb the wall and get into the city, even if my climbing skills might not be great. It's worth a try. Using the roots, I climb as quickly as I can despite that every few steps I almost slip. My heart pounds faster each time.

I keep climbing until I get to the top and pull myself onto my back, breathlessly staring at the roots above me. Sweat coats my forehead, and I wipe it away. Falling, burning leaves drift down from the tree above and around me. They seem so beautiful in the many lights around me, the smell of smoke and fire is relaxing even as the noise of the city drowns out the idea of silence. The wall must have blocked some sounds as it's much louder up here and reflects the noise a city of millions in it would have. The red glow is bright on my face, followed by a mixture of white light coming from the city. It almost appears like a sunset here, a sunset of so many shades of oranges, reds, and pinks. I always wanted to travel the world, but I always wanted to do it and then come back to tell my parents about the world outside of Caeli.

Now that can't happen.

With strength I didn't know I had, I slide myself over the other side of the wall and climb down the roots until I can jump to the floor. I quickly glance around me to make sure I'm safe. No one is close to me, nothing but rubbish and a dumpster that blocks anyone from seeing me. Two buildings are to my left, and I walk down the space between them and hide by the wall to peek around the corner. One massive pathway that leads right into the city is near me, and hundreds of wolves in human form stroll down them, some with small demon creatures on chains walking at their sides. So many people, and not one of them turn my way. I sneak out from behind the building, joining the crowd but keep my eyes down on the floor, and pulling my hood up to cover my hair. It doesn't take long to get closer to the middle of the city. The noise of people talking, music playing, bangs, and wolves howling fills my ears and senses when I try to break out of the crowd.

I search the buildings, reaching out with my senses for any trace of Caspian, but there are too many scents, too many wolves for me to search for him alone. It's all too much here, and a part of me likes it. The energy of the city is amazing. I come past a poster clipped to a building side and pause, seeing an advertisement for the bounty hunting trials in big bold letters.

Someone there might know where Caspian is, and it isn't a place the alpha would look for me, I don't think. At the bottom of the advertisement is a small map of Hell with a star over where the bounty hunting trials are. I rip it off and take a deep breath before setting off to find the only wolf in Hell who can help me.

Lilith Thornblood

CHAPTER FIVE

Lilith Thornblood

"Derek, if that's you back without my fucking demon—" Caspian pauses mid-sentence, slowly dropping his deep caramel eyes down onto me.

I didn't think the tip I got from a man outside the large fenced-off area for the demon-hunting trials was right when he said Caspian lived here. Mostly because the man appeared drunk, and it was too lucky that the first person I asked actually knew Caspian at all.

Turns out the long shot was bang on.

Caspian's six-foot, built-as-hell frame towers over me. I forgot how intimidating his stare is.

"Who the fuck are you and what do you want?"

I'm speechless for a second too long. With unseeable speed, he whips a silver dagger out from his back and places the tip under my chin. Fury burns in his eyes, and two black marks that run down from his forehead and around his eyes to his cheeks glow a vibrant red. "You might be fucking drop-dead beautiful but you won't trick me into whatever you're selling. Get the fuck out of here before you regret it."

He lowers the dagger and walks back into his house.

"I'm Leo's sister!" I shout seconds before the door shuts in my face.

But then it swiftly swings open again, and Caspian rests his shoulder against the doorframe. This time, he pauses to look at me from head to toe, and I do the same to him.

Caspian Hardling has changed since he was eighteen.

He's still as breathtakingly handsome as he was then but he is more now. So much more.

Beefy shoulders fill out his white button-down shirt, which is tucked into black leather trousers with laces at the front of his narrow but toned waist. The trousers showcase his thick thighs and other areas. His soft, silky blond hair is tipped white and falls to just below his ears. His ears are spiked at the top, a reminder of his demon blood, and I've always thought they suit him. All demons have tipped ears in human form, but it's more complicated for half-demon, half-wolves like Caspian.

He is rare. Few half-borns survive childhood.

"You grew up, songbird."

I narrow my eyes at his stupid nickname for me. The memory of it comes back like a hammer. How did I have a crush on this guy? Oh, right. Wine, teenage hormones, and one sexy-ass half-wolf.

Apparently, I sing as well as demon songbirds, which for the record, screech all night and can make human men go deaf. They are popular for torture.

"Clearly you haven't," I say, crossing my arms.

"Did you come all the way to Hell to insult me? Or did you miss my pretty face?"

Swallowing my pride, what is left of it, I tell him the truth. "Neither. I need your help because I'm in danger."

Something changes in his eyes, the playfulness disappearing as he straightens. "I can't help you. You need to go."

"Wait!" I stop his door closing in my face this time.

He sighs.

"My brother said you owed him. A life debt, if I'm not mistaken."

He arches a pierced brow. "And?"

"This will make you even. Help me, for my brother, for the debt if nothing else," I reply, hoping this will work. I'm sure Leo will go along with the plan if I had any way to safely get in touch with him.

Caspian stares down at me once more, and slowly he steps back, waving me into his house. "Get the fuck in, songbird."

"My name is Lilith, in case you've forgotten," I respond. I walk into the spacious yet empty room. There is a generic kitchen with four counters, a fridge, and a small bathroom behind a screen on the other side. A double bed is in the middle, with a couch at the end and a big orange rug in front of it. A wardrobe is near the bed, with two hooks on either side and countless weapons hanging off the large hook.

Other than that, there is nothing else here. Nothing personal to be seen.

Caspian slams the door shut behind me and walks around me to the fridge. "Do you drink yet? How old are you again?"

I drop down onto his leather sofa. "Old enough."

"Good, because we need vodka for this conversation where you blackmail me into saving you from whatever the fuck you have done."

Caspian brings over a half-drunk bottle of vodka and two shot glasses, chucking one at me. I hold it up, and he pours me a shot. I down it, keeping my eyes on him, and he raises an eyebrow at me before taking his own shot.

He downs another one and then pours himself a third. "Talk."

"My mum and dad were killed by the Stormfire alpha. He wants me dead, and I need to hide," I blurt out in one long rush.

Caspian coughs on the shot and smacks his fist against his chest a few times, staring at me with wide eyes.

"Then you're dead already. I can't help you fight him," he replies, still looking shell-shocked.

I get the impression not much surprises this guy.

Rolling my eyes, I glance away. "I know that and I need somewhere to hide in the city. Permanently."

"Does the alpha know you're here?"

"Maybe," I respond, clasping my hands together. "I don't know for sure. So can I hide here?"

"Minor problem, I'm leaving here tomorrow." He rubs the back of his neck and tilts his head at me. "The demon hunter trials begin tomorrow, and I'm joining them."

"Shit," I mutter. "Do you know anyone who could hide me? Someone you trust?"

He scoffs. "I don't trust anyone in Hell, and you shouldn't either, songbird."

He sits on the sofa next to me, only a few inches between us, and I try not to look at the gorgeous fucker who is clearly going to ditch me.

"I'm sorry about your parents. Really, I am," he eventually says. "More your mum though. Your dad was a dick."

"Technically, he wasn't my dad," I counter, trying to make light of it with some dark humour.

Caspian chuckles low. "Lucky you."

We drift into silence once more before Caspian lets out a long sigh. "I'm going fucking mad because I have an idea. It's crazy, but it just might work if you don't fuck it up."

My heart thrashes. "I'm willing to go for crazy right now."

Caspian's gaze trails over me, the marks on his cheeks almost glowing red for a second, and I wonder what that means. When he was in Caeli, his marks never glowed, and I overheard him telling Leo that they were from his father's demon side, not his wolf's.

"I could get you into the demon hunter trials under a fake name," he says slowly, "and I doubt the alpha would search for you there. The faces of all contestants are kept a secret, so they can move around the city freely. The alpha gives his protection to each of the ten winners. If you could win, which I highly doubt, by the way, you could gain the alpha's protection. Then he won't be able to kill you without breaking his vow."

"Which means death for an alpha," I whisper, filled with hope. "You're right… That is a crazy plan."

"Told you. Now the question is, can you fight? Do you know fuck all about demons?"

"Well, I know you."

He smirks and rests back, picking the vodka bottle up and taking a long drink. "That you do, songbird. That you do."

I just manage to resist snorting at him. "I don't think your plan will work, but it might buy me more time to find a safe place to escape. Somewhere the Stormfire alpha can't reach," I say and stand off the sofa. I snatch the vodka bottle from his hands and take a sip.

He grins when I scrunch my face up at the taste. "There are no demons on the moon."

Rolling my eyes, I shove the bottle back his way. "I've always wanted to be a demon hunter."

Caspian slowly moves his attention up my body, and I feel his gaze like fire against my skin until he clashes with my eyes.

"You're going to make an interesting partner, songbird."

"Thank you for helping me," I reply shakily.

He stands, stretching his long, thick arms. "Don't thank me yet. There is every chance the leader of the trials is going to take one look at you and say fuck no."

"Then I'll have to be charming," I say with a wink.

Caspian flashes me a devilish smirk. "If you can charm the alpha's only son, then I'm a fucking virgin."

He laughs, walking away from me. My cheeks burn as red as my hair. I have to get into these trials; alpha's son or not, I'm going to get in.

"By the way, we need to dye that white streak of hair. It makes you stand out," he calls back, walking to his door. "Don't go anywhere, songbird."

"Like I can!" I shout as he leaves me alone in his apartment.

What the hell, pun intended, have I gotten myself into?

DESCRIPTION

The alpha of hell is my fated mate and he rejected me.

I'm an outcast in my pack and have been since the day I was born. Shunned by most of the wolves around me, I've managed to stay out of trouble... until now.
Now The Alpha of Stormfire is hunting me, but he doesn't want to claim me as his mate.

He wants me dead.

Forced to leave my old life behind, I have no choice but to go on the run. Luckily, The Demon Hunting Trials is the perfect place to hide, even if it comes with a few obstacles.

Such as their leader is a total jerk, a wolf is blackmailing me to be his friend, and I swear my new, sexy as sin partner is trying to get us killed.

With demons running amok and the alpha of hell searching for me, I hope I can live long enough to get my revenge.

Description

18+ Dark reverse harem romance full with a sassy and sarcastic heroine who finds her match.

1

Bonus Read of Alpha Hell...
LILITH THORNBLOOD

There isn't enough booze in the shifter world to deal with alpha egos.

I take a deep drink of the red wine I stole from the teacher's lounge at Caeli Pack Academy before passing it to my best friend. The only person in the whole world (okay, just the academy) who I like. She's also the sole reason the alpha's sons are walking right over to us at this lame excuse for a party to celebrate the rare blood moon. Who throws a party for eighteen-year-olds without booze?

Aurelia Winters coughs as she takes a long drink and rolls her eyes at me when I chuckle. Although she tends to think otherwise, Aurelia is ridiculously stunning, and it's mostly down to her bloodline. She looks just like her mum, but her father's genes are strong and make her the perfect example of a Caeli wolf. Taking another sip from the bottle, Aurelia tucks her curly blonde hair behind her ears and looks past me at the alpha's sons with her big blue eyes. She is the perfect wolf at the Caeli Pack Academy, whereas me, on the other hand, I stand out as the outcast they put up with. I'm a red in a world of white with my dark-red hair and red-furred wolf. Other than the streak of white hair that falls down the side of my cheek, there isn't much about me that lets me mix in with the pack I have always lived in.

The Caeli Pack is hidden deep in the snowy Mountains of Alaska, where no one ever comes because it's too high up and the humans are afraid of us. Mostly because we're supernatural beings who don't mix well with them since they only see us as a means to protect them from the bad things in the world. Every pack in the world has its mission, its purpose, and Caeli's is learning and recording every event in the world of shifters. Basically, librarians with a bite.

"I stand out everywhere," I mutter to Aurelia.

"So? You're pretty and unusual here. That's not a bad thing," she replies. "Don't worry so much."

Says the girl who fits into our pack better than my ass fits into these skinny jeans. I don't hide or blend in very well. Aurelia is the opposite. At least, she is until we're at a party like this where she stands out far more than I do in some sense. It's all because of the mating season. In a year's time, most females will have chosen a mate, and the males all want the prettiest wolf in the pack which is Aurelia.

Finding a mate is definitely not on my to-do list. At least not with any of these wolves.

I take the bottle from Aurelia. "I think I should just leave at the end of the academy year in two weeks. Maybe join the demon-hunting trials in the Stormfire pack or something." Throwing back a deep mouthful, I wipe my lips with the back of my hand. "Hell, maybe I could look for my father and actually fit in there."

Aurelia gawks at me, then snatches the bottle. "Are you freaking crazy? You could also die in the trials. That's it. No more booze for you."

I glare at her jokingly. "Hey, I'm not even tipsy!"

"You're speaking like my aunt on New Year's Eve! Have you forgotten that you could get killed trying to capture those disgusting demons? They eat wolves for fun. Why would you even want that?" She shakes her head. "You're safe here. You shouldn't leave."

"My brother left."

With a sigh, she rests her head on my shoulder for a few seconds. "But he's a male and strong. There are like three female demon hunters in the whole of the Stormfire pack, and each of them are totally badass."

"So you're saying I'm not a badass?" I question with a raised eyebrow.

She laughs. "If you were brought up in Stormfire, taught to fight from a kid instead of how to read a book and study like our pack taught, we might be having a different conversation. But your circumstances are totally different. You were brought up a Caeli, and we both don't have a clue about fighting demons or capturing them. Come on, Lilith. You know this. Please tell me you weren't being serious?"

I don't answer her because I know she's right. But the thought of studying wolf history and doing nothing more than studying for the rest of my life makes me feel sick. It's like my pack is squeezing the life out of me with each passing day, and the only way to stop is to find an escape.

"We can talk about it later," I say, shrugging my shoulder. "They are nearly here."

Aurelia raises her head and straightens her tight, sparkling yellow dress that shows off her long legs. I cross my own covered legs, the movement straining my jeans and knocking mud off my heavy boots. Aurelia decided that we both needed to dress up and come to this party at one of her friend's houses, something that I would never attend before now because honestly, parties are not my thing. I'd much rather be drinking this bottle of red wine on my own back in my room, but I can't always be unsociable when my best friend is a big extrovert. I need to compromise sometimes, even if that means leaving my bedroom. C'est la vie, right?

The alpha sons stomp over from the dance floor that we can see at the end of the corridor we are sitting in. The blasting music vibrates through the room, shaking the floor almost from the noise of it, and pop song comes on that sings about humans shaking their asses. Another reason I tend to avoid these things. Why does the music always suck? I'd much rather they played some rock. Hell, if they put on some Guns N' Roses, I might even bust some real moves. None of this swaying, grinding nonsense.

Beside me, a dancing Aurelia knocks my shoulder as she sings the song word for word. I can't help but smile at her. I thought I could hide back here with her, but now the alpha's twin sons' shadows hang over us, I'm thinking my hiding skills need work.

This was a really bad idea.

They're both looking at her like she's the answer to their prayers, the very air to their lungs, while their mating scent invades my own lungs so much that I nearly gag. They never stop staring at Aurelia even as they finally come to a stop, and I know why. Everyone knows she's going to be an alpha female at some point because her wolf is strong, a born leader, and her human incomparably beautiful.

All the things you need to be on the alpha's sons' radar.

As for me? Everyone knows I'm only ever going to be the outcast. It's because I really, really don't belong in this pack. Caeli is all about reputation and utmost control, of unrivalled intellect and centuries-old knowledge that are the very bones of our existence. Each pack in our world has its own unique purpose. Caeli's is record-keeping and the continuous search for better, more proficient pack medicine; something that has been installed into me since I was a pup.

Learn for the Pack—the motto every wolf here lives by.

Every wolf except for me.

As my mum puts it, I've always been too wild, too uncontrollable, and in general too nosy for my own good. I'm sure that's the sole reason most of the teachers at this academy absolutely hate me and most likely the reason that my adopted brother sometimes pretends I'm not really his sister. Being an embarrassment to the shifter world is weirdly something I can live with. But being an embarrassment to my own family is the only thing that's kept me from running away.

Damn, I need more wine if I'm going to think about my family.

The alpha's sons, Dumb and Dumber as I've nicknamed them, just gaze with wide eyes at Aurelia. Their expressions are almost panicked. Aurelia watches back and sighs. It always makes me laugh how the simple fact she stares down future alphas who will no doubt one day fight for the chance to be pack leader, and subsequently, choose her as the alpha female if she chooses them, too. But I don't know if she will. Aurelia is picky about her guys, a lot like me. Not that many have been interested in the girl who doesn't belong here. Beyond their curiosity, I'm usually too different for them to look at twice.

The alpha sons may be handsome and muscular, both of them built like dump trucks, but for as strong as they are, there's not a lot going on upstairs under their thick, white-blond hair. My point is proven when they both stumble for a second on what to say to Aurelia. They scratch their heads, no doubt in search of a cheesy, overthought chat-up line, and then one of them says something that surprises even me a little.

"Would you like to come and dance to the song that is playing? I heard you say it was your favourite once."

And for whatever reason in the world, Aurelia appears almost happy that one of them noticed she likes the song that's playing.

She looks at me, and I nod. "Go. I'm going back to my room with the wine."

"Okay, see you back there later," she replies with a big smile.

The two of them quickly wander off down the corridor, and I hear her laugh a while later as I take another long drink of the bottle. A warm buzz floats down my body, the wine finally kicking in, but then I notice I'm left alone with the other alpha's son who I can never remember the name of. Every girl at this academy, other than me and Aurelia, has got their names memorised and written down in their diaries with love hearts. I know she doesn't do silly stuff like that just because we share a room and have done since we both came here when we were eight, like every young pack member. Their names come back to me now I gaze at them; Mathi and… Dammit, I can't remember what the other one's name is.

I stand and fake a big yawn before trying to walk away. But Mathi reaches out and grabs my arm, stopping me. I knew it was never going to be that easy. These alpha-holes rarely ever take a hint.

I narrow my eyes on his brown ones, a big contrast to my light grey. "Let. Go."

A smirk slides over his lips. "No. Why should I?"

He moves closer to me, lining up our bodies, and the disgusting thoughts circling in his head are written on his face as clear as day. This asshole better back off. He can't touch me; his father himself accepted me into the pack, which means I have the alpha's protection until he isn't alpha anymore. Of course, I worry about what will happen to me if the next alpha, AKA Dumb or his brother, Dumber, become alpha. But that won't be for some time yet. Right now, my focus is to get this unwanted paw off my body.

At the sight of me trying to wiggle my arm free, his smirk deepens into a malicious smile. He tightens his grip and pulls me closer, bringing his lips to my ear.

"You and I both know no one would notice if you went missing. You are just the outcast, the red wolf in a pack of white purebreds." He jolts me harder against him, his hands leaving bruises on my arm, but I refuse to turn away, to even wince at the pain. "Actually, that begs the question as to why you are still here. I'm surprised my father let you into the academy at all, half-breed."

Searing rage slams into me at the insult. Half-breed is the delightful nickname purebreds use for wolves like me; a subtle reminder of our so-called inferiority. Well, that's what they like to think. Anyone who's called me a half-breed usually walks away with a black eye.

I ball my hands into fists. "Maybe your dear father likes my mum a little too much. He does always seem to be admiring her."

The wolf's smile fades, and I inwardly chuckle at his stupid expression. So easily provoked, these young alphas. However, my satisfaction is short-lived. With a growl, he slams me into the wall, and I gasp from the impact. He presses his thick forearm against my neck, holding me in place, and the air dies in my lungs.

"Is that... any way... to treat a lady?" I choke out, unsure why I'm using my last breaths to anger him further. Then again, the fury burning on his gaze does make my sacrifice worth it. Besides, it's not like I'm unused to assholes like this one asserting their authority over me. Alphas love putting unruly wolves like me in their place.

Too bad I've never quite learned how to stay in mine.

Despite the black spots seeping into my vision, I stare up at him, wondering what exactly he's going to do. One thing is for sure—this dickwad has solidified my desire to leave his pack as soon as possible. I'll never follow an alpha who treats their packmates this way.

"Do you want to die, half-breed?" he growls.

I resist the urge to give him a sarcastic reply. I may be brave, but as my brother puts it, I can be pretty stupidly brave.

And I know that challenging an alpha son is really not a good idea.

I might be able to fight well, thanks to all the training the Academy has taught me. But even I know that you can't beat a guy twice your size in a small corridor like this, with no weapons on me, and his forearm pressed on my windpipe.

He gazes down at me and raises an eyebrow, but something burns on my arm.

In the corner of my eye, my wolf mark in the middle of my arm burns vividly. The swirls that form a wolf shape glow a deep, vibrant red, at first burning painfully but they quickly fade into a dull ache that fills my entire body.

Mathi follows my gaze to the mark and smiles.

"Seems like your parents are calling you home," he snarls, loosening the pressure on my throat. "Did your mum's mate ever realise that you weren't his?"

This asshole knows damn well my dad knows I'm not his. I was conceived and born before my mum ever mated. Everyone in the pack knows it. It was a big scandal, and to this day I still hear the boring wolves talking about it. Caeli wolves love to gossip because they have nothing better to do.

I grit my teeth at the jab. "Fuck. Off."

He raises his free hand as if to strike me. I don't flinch,

and that seems to piss him off. He grabs me by the scruff of the neck and slams me against the wall again, drawing everyone's attention.

"Go back to your little family, half-breed. But just remember that when I'm alpha, your kind will never be welcome here." He releases me with a derisive scoff. "Off you go now, run back home."

I don't reply despite the tinge of fear that his threat elicits in me. My wolf, however, bares her teeth and snaps her jaw at him in retaliation. I need to get out of here before I shift and try to take on an alpha twice my size. The fading burn from my family's mark sears in my mind, screaming down to my soul for me to move.

Biting back my spiteful retort, I jog down the corridor and take a left out of the noisy house, dodging students who whistle and tease me. The cool night air lifts my hair over my shoulders when I step onto the porch. I take a deep breath and jog into the snowy outskirts that surround the house. Snow-capped trees line the distance, and I make a break for them. The cold doesn't bother me, even when I duck behind a tree and strip off. Once I'm fully naked, I bundle my clothes into a ball and shove them into the small bag I always carry with me.

I rest my head against the tree and gaze up at the moon cutting through the frozen leaves. My breath comes out in puffs of smoke, and for a moment I stay there, thinking about how much I'd have liked to punch that alpha-hole in the throat.

But my family needs me.

I dig my feet into the earth and arch forward, spreading

my fingers through the snow. Shifting is an effortless, painless task for me, almost like breathing. I transform into my wolf easily, letting my body change until my red paws sink into the ground. Picking the bag up with my fangs, I run through the forest back towards the towering academy hidden in a clearing shrouded in blankets of untouched snow. It's eerily silent at this time of night. Most people are sleeping, and those who find themselves awake under the light of the moon, venture into the woods to hunt.

The side door of the academy is always left open, and I slip through it. The wood corridors echo every hit of my wolf's claws on them as we dodge around corridors of lockers. We keep running until we get to the main stairs and head straight up to our room and pause. My wolf drops my bag on the floor, and we use our advanced hearing to make sure no one is around before shifting back. Most wolves don't care about nudity, but I'm not one of them.

I unlock my door and head inside with my bag, quickly getting back into my jeans, plain black tee-shirt and boots. I search the messy floor for my phone next. I push a few items of clothing around before I find it and try ringing my parents, but it goes straight to voicemail. I ring my adopted elder brother, but again, straight to voicemail. My family are bloody useless with phones. Instead of trying to keep ringing them, I decide I might as well just go and see them since it's not too far to walk. It's a weird thing for them to use a wolf call with my mark, but I'm sure everything is fine, even if something in the back of my mind doesn't think so. My mum never uses the mark to summon me, and my dad definitely hasn't done it. He likes to pretend I don't exist. That only leaves my brother, but Leo's too busy working as a new demon hunter to bother summoning me. I guess there's only one way to get to the bottom of this.

Time to go home and see what the hell is going on.

ALPHA HELL (THE REJECTED MATE SERIES #1)…

CHAPTER TWO

Lilith Thornblood

Burning leaves.

It's all I can smell when I emerge from the trees surrounding my childhood home. The scent clings to my snow-covered fur and permeates the night air like a sceptic perfume. I pause on the outskirts of the forest and lift my head towards the sky. A stiff breeze sweeps over me and carries the scent downwind, meaning it's coming from the direction of my house.

The scent can only belong to a Stormfire wolf, but why would one of them trespass into our territory? Unless my parents invited them. Could that be why I've been summoned?

I slip out of the trees and run across the field towards my home. The three-storey, red-brick building has been in my family for generations. The slanted roof is covered in a thick blanket of snow, and icicles dangle from the gutters to overshadow the wooden porch. My dad's car is parked in the driveway, and the shed, which we use for shifting, has been left open.

Slowing my gait, I scan the ground. Fresh paw prints. They're triple the size of my own when I step into them. I take a cautious sniff, and sure enough, burning leaves cling to the indentations.

I hurry into the shed and shift back. Rummaging through my bag, I dress quickly, lock the door behind me, and climb the porch steps. Only the kitchen light is on. Mum must be cooking dinner. My stomach clenches, and a feeling of dread washes over me when I touch the door.

Someone with magic has been there. The only creatures who can use magic nowadays are demons. Not even the headmaster at the academy is able to cast spells; he has to summon a demon to do it for him.

I take a deep breath and open the front door. One step, two steps over the threshold, and my heart clenches at what I see inside our little kitchen. My mother, held by the throat by the largest man I've ever seen, and my father standing beside her as pale as a ghost. The unfamiliar male towers several feet above the both of them, and his grasp on my mum's throat.

"Welcome home, Lilith Thornblood."

His deep, powerful voice sends a shiver running down the length of my spine. He's completely naked from the waist up. His torso is covered in symbolic tattoos the same black colour as his hair. Thick gold bands encircle his arms, and a black medallion with a ruby centre hands around his neck. The jewel glows just like his crimson eyes, all of them cutting into me like molten shards.

"I believe introductions are in order," he says, flashing the tip of his fangs in a smile that doesn't reach his eyes.

My mother's wide, terrified ones never leave my face. It kills me to see her so afraid. Even my dad has cowered a little in size; a gesture meant to convey submission in the presence of an alpha.

"I know who you are."

He lifts a scarred brow. "Oh?"

I peel my gaze from the hand on my mother's throat to glare at him. "You're the alpha of Stormfire. You guard the Gates of Hell. Apparently, you have quite the temper and once wiped out an entire pack just because their alpha stole from you."

The alpha inclines his head. "The very one."

He regards me through the barest slits of his eyes. A minute shake of his head threatens disappointment as he looks at me. Look isn't quite the right word. The Stormfire alpha is dissecting me into pieces, stripping me naked with his gaze until I'm only flesh and blood. From his stony expression, I appeal less to him than a mildly interesting object, and for some insane reason it raises my hackles.

Despite everything my parents and pack have taught me, I make a point of holding the alpha's gaze as boldly and firmly as he holds mine. "What do you want?" I practically spit out at him.

My dad crosses the length of the kitchen and slaps me so quickly I stumble back in surprise, my body thudding into the back of the door. I'm used to his temper, and his fists, but still, I didn't expect this hit.

"Show the alpha some goddamn respect!"

The impact forces me to break eye contact, but not before I catch sight of the alpha's eyes glowing a deep shade of black.

"Touch her again and you'll lose more than a hand." He adds just the slightest bit of pressure to my mum's throat, and the tips of his claws dent her skin.

She doesn't so much as draw a single breath. Dad takes a big step back from me in fear for my mum, his mate's, life.

The alpha cuts his gaze to me. "Come."

He drags my mum from the kitchen, and my dad slowly takes up the rear, his expression a little grimmer than before. My heart thrashes so violently I can scarcely make out their footsteps as they head into the dining room. For a moment I just stand there in the kitchen, and then I follow suit, each step laced with a growing, burning hatred for this alpha. And my dad. Why is he letting this alpha treat my mum this way? It's almost like he couldn't care less about her. While he's always been like that towards me, he's never disrespected my mum. I don't even care if he's only doing it because there's an alpha in our home. It's unacceptable.

If my mum didn't appear so terrified in the alpha's presence, I'd grab a knife from the kitchen and swing at the alpha, then I'd take my mum away where my dad can never find her again. She's always deserved better than him.

We both deserve better.

Once I reach our open-plan living room, everyone is seated at the dining table; the alpha where my dad would usually sit, my mum beside him. I sweep my gaze over the surface, unsurprised to find it set for only one. Of course the alpha would eat before any of us. It's customary in packs that alphas should eat first and, usually, alone. With a wave of his tattooed hand, a thin chain slithers around my mum's wrist. It wraps around the table leg, binding her to the alpha's side. She glances at me standing in the doorway, her eyes wide and stark with fear, and more searing-hot fury consumes me.

The alpha pulls out a chair and gestures to it dismissively. "By all means, have a seat."

Everything about this male pisses me off. From the arrogant way he struts around my home like he owns it, to the manner in which he curls the edge of his lips and looks at me like I'm a piece of meat… So typical of every other alpha out there, and yet so, so much worse.

He doesn't even wait to see if I'll obey his command. With not a care in the world, he claims the seat at the other end of the table and reaches for the bottle of red wine. My dad sits across from my mum, leaving only the pulled-out chair at the end for me. My every instinct screams to shift and challenge this alpha, but I'm not an idiot. Not only does he hold my mother prisoner, but I'm willing to bet his wolf is three times the size of mine. I'd be dead before I could so much as sink my teeth into his throat.

There's really nothing for it. If I'm to figure out what the hell is going on and get my parents out of this alive, I need to play nicely; something I've failed to do so far in my eighteen years.

I settle down on the opposite side. The silence is so tense I could cut it with the alpha's butterknife. Instead, I lift my eyes from the polished surface of the table and look at him.

"Why are you here?" I repeat, ensuring my voice is firm. "And what do you want?"

My dad slams his fist on the table and prepares to stand. "Dammit, child! How many times have I told you? Do not speak unless spoken—"

The alpha's voice stops him. Dad freezes in his half-crouched position, and his worried eyes flick to the other end of the table.

"You'd do well to follow your own advice, Valerio." The alpha narrows his eyes on me. "At any rate, I see no problem in answering her questions. She is my mate, is she not?"

CHAPTER THREE

Lilith Thornblood

It's clearly a rhetorical question, one that sends my heart shooting to the pit of my stomach. Did he just say what I think he did? My pulse skyrockets, and I clench my hands underneath the table. For the first time since entering the dining room, my mother isn't looking at me. It's as if she can't bring herself to. I've never seen my mum as anything but the beautiful and graceful wolf with long white hair I wish I had. I can't ever remember seeing my mum scared or weak. I know her expression scares me far more than the alpha behind her and calling me his mate could ever do.

"I'm here to collect what's mine." The alpha pours himself a glass of wine and sniffs the contents before taking a sip. His eyes cut over the glass to me. "That would be you."

A nervous laugh bubbles in my chest and quickly escapes my lips. "W-what? You can't be serious?" I glance at my mum, my chest rising unevenly. "Mum, what the hell is going on?"

But she doesn't say a word. The colour has completely drained from her face. She seems like she's about to be sick.

"One thing you should know about me, little mate," the alpha says in a dangerously low voice, dragging my attention back to him, "is that I am only ever serious. You belong to me and you are my fated mate. The Crescent Mother wills it."

The glimmer of anxiety that had gripped me a moment ago vanishes, replaced with more searing-hot anger.

"I don't belong to anyone," I spit back at him. "Especially not a wolf who came here uninvited and raised his own hands to my mother!"

He picks up my mum's favourite cutlery and begins cutting his meat. "Who says I came here uninvited?"

My dad shifts nervously, and my mum's face turns a violent shade of red. This doesn't make any sense. If they invited him, why would he threaten to hurt my mum? There's no way my mum would invite the alpha of another pack to our home. It's unheard of unless it's to the house of another alpha. And as much as my dad likes to pretend he's an alpha behind closed doors, he's nothing of the sort.

I straighten. "I don't know how things work in your pack, *Alpha*, but shackling your host to a table isn't something we do in Caeli."

He chuckles and shoves a slice of meat into his mouth. "You've got fire in you, little mate. Good. You'll need it when I take you home."

"*This* is my home," I snarl at him.

The alpha dismisses my retort and continues eating. "I see your mother failed to inform you of your situation. Allow me to explain." He wipes his mouth with a silk handkerchief and then tosses it on his near empty plate. "Eighteen years ago, your mother and I came to an agreement. In exchange for helping her flee a rather complicated situation, your mother promised me a mate worthy of the Stormfire alpha. I've come to see just how worthy of a mate you truly are."

The air clamps in my chest. It's like the alpha has thrust a paw into my chest and is squeezing my heart with his razor-sharp claws. Through the tears blurring my vision, I glare venomously at my dad. He used to say there would come a day when my past would catch up with me. Until this very moment, I never understood what he meant. But it was that I'd been promised to an alpha who would one day come to collect me. And he knew.

My *mum* knew.

I wonder if my brother and Aurelia were aware, too.

The thought twists my stomach into a pile of knots, and a rush of anxiety trickles down my spine. This can't really be happening. It's like I've fallen through a portal to an alternative universe where my own family would betray me. I glance at my mum, searching for something, anything, that will tell me the alpha is lying. But she only looks away as her lower lip trembles. She really did do it.

My mum promised me to an alpha when I was just a baby.

I snap my head to the alpha in question and glare at him. He just fucking smirks at me like this is an amusing game to him. But then something changes. His lips thin, and he sniffs the air. His prior amusement melts from his countenance like wet snow, and he rises from the table. Slowly, he comes towards me, and I struggle to hold his gaze this time. There's something darker about it, something primal and deadly. Power radiates off him like an all-encompassing shadow. His presence alone swallows up everything in the room, and despite my best efforts, I shrink a little in my chair.

He stops beside me and picks up a strand of my long, auburn hair. A muscle ticks in his jaw, and a crease forms between his brows when he lifts the strand to smell it. His eyes darken into a deeper onyx. Faster than I can blink, he leans forward and brushes his fangs along my neck. I grip my thighs and close my eyes. I know what he's doing. He's taking in my scent to see whether or not I'm 'worthy' of him. From the way my palms turn sweaty and my heart convulses, he can no doubt smell the whirlwind of emotions wreaking havoc within me.

"You smell of weakness," he breathes, the tip of his fangs sweeping over the pulse in the side of my throat. "Weak wolves do not belong in my pack."

"My daughter is a lot of things, Rizer. A half-breed and nuisance, sure, but no wolf of my line has ever been weak," my dad says.

In my shock, I open my eyes to gawk at him. I've never heard him defend me like this before. Even when our own pack ridiculed me, he said nothing.

Did nothing.

A foolish part of me actually hopes to find compassion when I face him, but there's only that same old, familiar coldness. I wish I knew what I did to make him despise me so much. The fact that he just said I'm part of 'his' line means he does see me as part of the Valerio family, so it can't be that I'm not his biological kid.

"Your line is also descended from cowards and liars," Rizer growls, moving behind me.

Again he sniffs my hair, and I dig my fingernails into my jeans. My mother holds my gaze, but ever so quickly, she glances at the front door.

"That I could ignore. But weakness? That is disgusting and cannot be tolerated. You should not be allowed to exist."

I swallow the nervous lump in my throat and watch my mother drape her free hand over the alpha's knife. Her glancing at the front door was a signal for me to run. But I can't just run while she's chained to the table. However, before I can so much as protest, she throws the wine glass onto the table. The glass smashing against the wooden floor rouses the alpha's attention, if just for a second. That's all I need to jump up from the table and out of the way, moments before the knife whistles through the air towards the alpha.

The blade pierces him in the chest, and for a second, he just stands next to me, his eyes wide.

"*What have you done?*" My dad's chair falls over and he shoots up from his chair. He rushes over to the alpha and stumbles to his knees beside him. Shaking hands hover over the dead body, but they can't quite bring themselves to touch the bloodstains on his chest. Unfortunately, the alpha won't remain dead for long; alphas always regenerate, usually once the source of their death has been removed from their body, but there's rumours that alphas don't require that.

I doubt a knife to the heart will keep Rizer dead for long.

"He'll kill us," my dad chokes out, his hands trembling so violently his whole upper body shakes. "He'll kill us all!"

My mum doesn't even glance at him. "Lilith, go. We don't have long."

Blood pounds in my head and I shake it in disbelief. "The chain—"

"Go without me!"

I flinch at the volume of her tone but keep shaking my head. "N-no, I can't. I'm not leaving you here, Mum!"

As I rush over to her side, my dad continues muttering about how the alpha will kill us—him—once he wakes up. He really is a coward. I'm glad he's not my real dad. Once I reach my mum and look down at the chain cutting into her skin, the tears I've been struggling to hold back finally fall from my lashes. She follows my gaze, and instead of being scared or upset, she just smiles at me. Slowly, she tucks my hair behind my ear and pats my head like she's done since I was a kid.

"Don't worry, sweetie, I'll be right behind you." And with that, she pushes me towards the front door, her chain scraping the table. "Take the backpack hanging by the door and go. Don't turn back. I love you, baby."

A sob bursts from my trembling lips. "I love you, too, Mum."

I quickly hug her, grab the bag, and then I'm taking off through the front door without so much as a glance at my dad.

My boots barely hit the ground when I shift into my wolf, take the bag into my mouth, and run. I never feel the cold, but right now I'm as cold as the snow crunching beneath my paws. My breath streams out in harsh, rapid puffs but I head into the trees as fast I've ever ran in my life, not even bothering to bring my clothes. I keep going until a deafening howl cuts through the air in the distance and my fur instantly stands on end.

Rizer.

His burning-leaves scent carries on the downwind, and my stomach roils with a mixture of fear and anger. I pause by a frozen creek and stare down at my reflection on the icy surface. My wolf looks as dejected as I feel. Did my mum even make it like she said she would? A small part of me hopes she did and that I'll see her soon, that she will catch up with me. But the rest of me, no matter how much I want to refute it, shatters as if I knew all along: my mum was never getting out of that house alive.

A sick, twisted piece of me hopes my dad never made it out. He'd been perfectly willing to hand me over to the alpha like a bit of discarded meat. My mum had been nothing but terrified from the moment I entered the kitchen. My eyes water at the thought of her, but I quickly push them aside and continue. There will be time to mourn for her later. I need to get out of here before the alpha catches up with me.

With this shadowing over me, I run faster through the forest. It's a little ironic that I've spent my childhood exploring these woods. I know every tree, every creek and clearing, and yet I don't know where to go. I could go back to the party and get Aurelia, then come up with a plan. But I don't want to drag her into this. My best option would be to seek refuge in the academy. That means going east.

Another howl echoes in the near distance, followed by

another. Their cadence is so different to what I'm used to hearing amongst Caeli wolves, which means these ones aren't part of my pack. They must be from Stormfire. Damn it! They've blocked out the academy. West will just take me to Aurelia, and I don't want to endanger her. All I can do is head north in hopes that I find a place good enough to hide.

After hours of running, my limbs ache from exertion, and I have no choice but to stop to rest. The Stormfire howls stopped about a mile back. I'm not stupid enough to think they've given up hunting me. Leaning against a tree, I glance up at the bloodstained moon, and a powerful urge to howl at her fullness consumes me. My mum used to say that the Crescent Mother was more likely to bless her wolves on the night of a full moon. It's a slim chance, but right now, I'll do anything to get out of here.

I need your help. Please tell me where I should go. Give me a sign. Please. Something. Crescent Mother, help me.

In answer to my prayer is the cloying smell of more burning leaves, and the low grumble of a howl rumbling in the back of a wolf's throat. I whip my head around in search of the wolf. Through the shadowy trees, I'm able to decipher an enormous red wolf surrounded in tendrils of smoke. The medallion around its powerful neck gleams in the moonlight.

Uhh, Crescent Mother… This isn't what I quite had in mind.

Rizer snaps his bloody jaw at me and takes a step. The blood on his lips carries my mum's scent. A low whimper escapes me, and I instinctively back away from him. I lower my head and press my tail tightly between my hind legs. More howls resonate close by. There's no way I'll be able to fight off Rizer let alone the others.

In the corner of my eye, a light flickers in the darkness around me. The bright glow pulls me towards it like gravity. I turn my head ever so slightly, and relief washes over me. A huge staircase stands proudly on the forest floor, and right at the top is a bright orange light.

A portal.

I don't even stop to question where it might lead me.

I charge up the stairs and dive head-first into the blinding, beautiful light.

CHAPTER FOUR

Lilith Thornblood

I really hate portals.

I stumble through the light, my stomach feeling like a thousand bees are bouncing around in it, and smack hard into the stairs on the other side. I stand, my wolf shaking our head, just as the edge of the old, cracked steps to the portal gives way under my feet.

My wolf whines as we fall down the steps, right off a damn cliff of all things. My body smacks across the rock side, sharp pebbles digging into my calves. My wolf tries to dig its claws into the cliffside to stop us. Roots and branches snag in my fur and against my legs as I keep falling, unable to find anything to stop us. I briefly see everything is red and burning right before I crash into something that instantly burns my back.

Standing quickly, I move off the tiny pool of lava under me, letting my wolf heal the brief burns. Breathlessly, I take a second to glance around me and I freeze. My blood runs cold when I realise exactly where I am.

The Stormfire pack.

Also known as—Hell itself.

What the hell? I'm not even on Earth anymore.

In my horror, I look up at the portal on top of the mountain, wondering why the alpha isn't right on my heels. He should be able to follow me.

This is his frigging pack, after all.

Shit. Shit. Shit.

My brother once told me Hell was a really beautiful place, but I never quite believed him. How could a place where demons and wolves live be beautiful? Until this second when I'm staring at all of Hell right in front of me, I never once imagined it was like this. A giant tree has grown from below the city and its entangled roots stretched everywhere they could. I remember the tree being called The Tree of Ignis. The tree has made winding paths that swirl around the main trunk, lit up with red fire on its edges. Pack homes are also woven into the branches and roots, almost like they are part of the tree. Sharp and steep rocky mountain walls make a circle around the outskirts of the city, one of them I've just fallen down, which must have one of many portals to Hell on it.

No wonder that hurt like a bitch. The fall must be about thirty feet.

I didn't even know there was a portal to Stormfire near my home. In fact, it should be impossible for that portal to even exist. *Problem for another time.* The Stormfire city surrounds the major part of the ancient and wondrous tree.

The looping roots and gnarled vines hold much of the city together. There are tall towers of apartments wrapped in vines and red flowers, that are like flames, on the edges of the city. Closer to the middle are large stone buildings that seem untouched by the tree themselves, and perhaps newer.

The tree isn't the most beautiful and fascinating part of the city.

No, it's the leaves.

Burning leaves constantly fall off the branches at the top of the tree. They flutter down and then disappear into nothing but embers before they hit the ground. I stare around in awe at the place I've always wanted to come to see.

Terrified awe.

What the hell am I going to do? I bite my backpack in my mouth a little tighter, wondering what Mum packed inside it for me and if she is still alive. My wolf whines softly, our pain shared between us, threatening to take over the fear we need to focus on. It isn't safe here. I glance back up at the portal at the top of the massive hill that I've just fallen down. Rizer is going to follow me here soon. He is too powerful for me to fight head-on, and there's no way I'm going to get away from him in his pack's territory if he spots me now. I glance back at the tree and Stormfire city resting around it.

There's only really one thing I can do to survive: hide in Rizer's pack of millions of Stormfire wolves and make sure he doesn't find me.

He won't think I'm brave enough to hide in his own pack. *Hopefully.*

At least I won't stand out in Stormfire, not with my red

fur wolf, as they all appear the same as me, something I've always wanted. Just not like this. Except for the white streak of hair, but I can disguise that with a hat or something in human form. Not so much as a wolf. I lean back on my heels and tighten my grip on the backpack before I break out into a run. My wolf bolts across the rocky terrain that seems like it's on fire, but it does nothing but heat my paws. In fact, I feel warm but not on fire like I should do.

"Outside the gates of Hell's city burn all those who flee and do not belong."

My academy teachers' words come back to haunt me as I keep running and come to a large river made of clear, crimson water. Sharp rocks sit at the bottom, and a few strange fish swim around them. *Let's hope none of them bite.* The current of the river flows fast, and I don't see a bridge in sight or anywhere I can cross.

We'll have to swim.

Feeling my wolf's reluctance to go into it, and I'm completely in agreement with her, I figure we don't have a choice. We're not great at swimming. It was never one of our bonus points at the academy, but there's no way around it. I pull the backpack tightly into my mouth, knowing I need to hold on firmly to it in the river.

We can do this!

I dive into the water, and my wolf uses all our strength to swim to the other side. We try not to get pushed too far down by the current, but the river is deeper and bigger than we thought. The water is warm, almost painfully warm, but I try not to focus on it as we swim as fast as we can to the other side. Soon we realise the current is much wilder than we predicted, and suddenly we are being pushed harshly around. My wolf dives underwater, and we bare our teeth, holding the backpack to push through the current. It directs our path. I know I need to let the current take me and not fight it, even as I can't see or hear anything but red water.

It's official. Hell sucks, and they even ruined water.

My wolf pulls free of the current eventually, and we break out of the top of the river, gasping for air around the backpack. We end up just being pulled and pulled farther down the river, not able to get out of the current to either side. My legs ache, and tiredness takes over with every brush of a wave of water against us. The only good thing is that Rizor is unlikely to find me now. The dreadful thing is that rivers like this can only end in two ways. One could be a pretty lake and the other a deadly waterfall.

With my luck, it is definitely going to be a waterfall.

No sooner do I think that than the rushing of a waterfall in the distance carries to my ears, and pure panic makes me struggle around in the water. I want to shift back, but I know it's not a good idea. My wolf is stronger than I am. She goes back underwater with the current, and we try swimming tougher when we come back up, but it doesn't get us anywhere. I glance around as quickly as possible, looking for anything to help us get out of this damn river. That's when I see it, a big rock ledge on the left side, next to the edge of the waterfall cliff. If I could just land on to that, I can climb out and be on the right side for the city.

I swim as hard as I can towards it, pushing my wolf to her limits, begging our body not to give our tiredness.

We really need to work on our cardio and swimming skills if we survive this.

We just about slam our body into it, my lungs gasping from the impact, and I nearly drop the backpack out of my mouth. Pulling myself up onto the ledge, I reel my weak legs across to the side of the rocky pathway and finding a hidden space between a few roots of a stray tree that will hide me for a bit.

Fucking hell, I think to myself, letting out a small, frustrated whine.

I shift back, needing to be human for a moment, and take a deep breath before breaking down in sobs as the pain of everything that has happened catches up with me. Wrapping my arms around my knees, I don't know how long I cry for. Knowing that my mum's gone, knowing my dad is most likely gone, too, and I'm the alpha's intended mate.

And he rejected me.

Being rejected by someone who you're meant to mate with is unheard of in the pack world. At least I've never heard of it. But then it's also unheard of for the Stormfire alpha to take a mate. I know he has one son whose mother he murdered, but she was never his mate. Just his breeder.

How he ever thought I could be his mate is insane to think about. I'm no alpha female and I never want to take a mate. I don't want to love someone because magic forces me to. Too many times I saw my mum resist her mating bond because her mate was an asshole.

Sorry, Dad, but you were one. RIP. Hopefully.

I grit my teeth, and my wolf lets out a growl that echoes in my chest when I think of Rizor calling me weak. *I am not weak.* Taking a deep breath, I try to control my emotions, try to push down my urge to shift back. To run and run until we get out of this world, to somewhere safe from him. But I know we need to be smarter than that right now. I don't have anywhere to go back to. The alpha of Caeli won't fight the Stormfire pack for me, which he would have to do if he protected me. Rizor will never stop until he kills me…even I don't understand what he wants with my death. I can't go straight to my brother because that's exactly where he'd think I'd go. Watching my brother is going to be his first move, no doubt. I search my brain for an answer for a long time before I come up with the perfect (ish) idea.

I look up at the falling embers that drift down around me, matching the same colour as my hair. I think of my brother's best friend who lives here in Stormfire. The boy who always smelt of burning leaves and bad decisions.

Caspian Hardling.

I met him a few times as a young teenager and I fixated on him because he was Stormfire, new, interesting, and most importantly, gorgeous. His parents let him spend two years training in Caeli Academy as part of a student exchange programme to help with peace between the four packs. Caspian is a good guy, and I can trust him. My brother said he trusted Caspian with his life, and I really have no one else to turn to here. I doubt Caspian is even going to remember me; I haven't seen him since I was thirteen and blurted out I had a big crush on his handsome eighteen-year-old ass.

I was a dork who had just discovered wine. *A bad combo.*

I have to ask him to hide me until I can come up with a plan. He's a bounty hunter, or at least I heard that he was in the bounty hunter trials last year. My brother never said if Caspian passed them, like he did, but I doubt Caspian failed. When he sets his mind on something, he always gets it in the end. He told me that himself when I was a drunk little dork.

Now I have a plan, albeit not a great one, I open the backpack and find several sets of clothes inside along with a letter. My hands shake as I open the yellow envelope and pull the parchment out. I run my fingers over my name, written in my mum's beautiful, classy handwriting. A small bracelet falls out of the envelope onto my lap, and I lift it to see it's made of silver with a red stone attached in the middle of it. I put the bracelet down and open the letter to read it.

TO LILITH,

I'm so sorry that I had to write this, that I couldn't tell you everything, that you're in this position. I knew if you took this backpack that everything I feared would happen has happened. I know I'm not with you because I'd never let you read this letter if I was.

First thing's first.

The bracelet is spelled. I used all of my money over my short lifetime to pay for it, and it's blessed by demons of incredible power. It will hide you from him. The Stormfire alpha can never find or track you so long as you wear it. Neither will anybody else who will look for you and have been since you were born. The Caeli pack hid you until now, but now you have to find your place in the world alone. I'm so sorry.

Wear it and never take it off, promise me this.

There's so much I wish to tell you, so much that I can't fit into a small letter. But I'm going to sum up most of the terrible things that happened right before you were born. I was born in the Caeli pack, but I gave my heart to Stormfire. To your father. Know that I created you in pure love, no matter what anyone says.

Many people died to keep you safe, to get me out of Hell, but it all went wrong. And at the very last second, I had to make a deal to leave Hell with you. The alpha of Stormfire wanted you as his mate. I think he always did because of what happened when you were born. Many want you as theirs, Lilith, and you must trust no one.

I can never write the truth in this letter because if someone else found this, it could mean the death of you. I wish I could have told you, but your dad bound me to the secrecy, so it could never leave my lips.

I'm sorry.

The secrets will come out eventually, and you'll realise what I did for you was the right thing, but for now the secret will die with me.

Be brave.

We both know that hiding in Hell is the best for you if you can get there. You'll fit in there as it is massive, full of millions and millions of wolves, the biggest population of wolves in the world. You'll be able to hide and disappear.

I will love you forever and I will protect you in the afterlife. Always know dying for you was my plan right from the beginning. I regret none of my life or my choices.

Tell your brother that. Let him know there is a letter for him in our secret place.

Love,

Mum

BY THE END of the letter I'm in sobs as I pick up the small bracelet my mum said she spent so much money on. No wonder we barely had anything and Dad hated me so much.

It looks expensive, and it radiates with magic. The sort of magic that doesn't come cheap anymore. The only things in this world that have magic are demons. Demons don't sell their magic easily or cheaply or to anybody in Caeli. I clip the bracelet onto my wrist, feeling my mum's love and protection in it like she is here at my side. The stone rests right in the centre of my wrist, fitting me perfectly.

What secret would my mum die to protect about me? What could be so bad but desirable to the Stormfire alpha?

What the hell happened when I was born?

Of course, no one answers me, and I bet the secret is with the Crescent Goddess now.

I need to get to Caspian and somewhere safe because I can't die or get caught now. My mum needs me to be strong, to fight this and live my life. Rizor will tell his people to look for me, no doubt. I need to get into the city and disappear. Soon he will have the entire pack searching for a new wolf.

Quickly, I drag on the leggings, boots, and the large hoodie that's in the backpack, one of my favourite hoodies that I thought I'd lost over a year ago. *I know exactly where it went now.* I smile for a brief second at the idea of my mum stealing it.

Then my smile falls when I remember she isn't here anymore. She is likely dead.

I pull my wet hair into a ponytail with a hairband I find in the bag and drink the small bottle of water that's at the bottom before putting everything back and standing. Strapping the backpack onto my back, I glance up at the enormous city. A city big enough for any wolf to get lost in.

Time to go into the city of Hell and pretend I'm from here.

I don't know if that's even possible because I have no idea what I'm walking into. The river will have hidden my scent and washed away all traces of any Caeli wolf on me. That's one good thing. I walk towards the city walls, and when I get to them, I realise there's no door anywhere I can see. I search up and down the wall, realising I have to go through the main gates of the city.

Unless…

I look up and grimace. Maybe I can climb the wall and get into the city, even if my climbing skills might not be great. It's worth a try. Using the roots, I climb as quickly as I can despite that every few steps I almost slip. My heart pounds faster each time.

I keep climbing until I get to the top and pull myself onto my back, breathlessly staring at the roots above me. Sweat coats my forehead, and I wipe it away. Falling, burning leaves drift down from the tree above and around me. They seem so beautiful in the many lights around me, the smell of smoke and fire is relaxing even as the noise of the city drowns out the idea of silence. The wall must have blocked some sounds as it's much louder up here and reflects the noise a city of millions in it would have. The red glow is bright on my face, followed by a mixture of white light coming from the city. It almost appears like a sunset here, a sunset of so many shades of oranges, reds, and pinks. I always wanted to travel the world, but I always wanted to do it and then come back to tell my parents about the world outside of Caeli.

Now that can't happen.

With strength I didn't know I had, I slide myself over the

other side of the wall and climb down the roots until I can jump to the floor. I quickly glance around me to make sure I'm safe. No one is close to me, nothing but rubbish and a dumpster that blocks anyone from seeing me. Two buildings are to my left, and I walk down the space between them and hide by the wall to peek around the corner. One massive pathway that leads right into the city is near me, and hundreds of wolves in human form stroll down them, some with small demon creatures on chains walking at their sides. So many people, and not one of them turn my way. I sneak out from behind the building, joining the crowd but keep my eyes down on the floor, and pulling my hood up to cover my hair. It doesn't take long to get closer to the middle of the city. The noise of people talking, music playing, bangs, and wolves howling fills my ears and senses when I try to break out of the crowd.

I search the buildings, reaching out with my senses for any trace of Caspian, but there are too many scents, too many wolves for me to search for him alone. It's all too much here, and a part of me likes it. The energy of the city is amazing. I come past a poster clipped to a building side and pause, seeing an advertisement for the bounty hunting trials in big bold letters.

Someone there might know where Caspian is, and it isn't a place the alpha would look for me, I don't think. At the bottom of the advertisement is a small map of Hell with a star over where the bounty hunting trials are. I rip it off and take a deep breath before setting off to find the only wolf in Hell who can help me.

CHAPTER FIVE

Lilith Thornblood

"Derek, if that's you back without my fucking demon—" Caspian pauses mid-sentence, slowly dropping his deep caramel eyes down onto me.

I didn't think the tip I got from a man outside the large fenced-off area for the demon-hunting trials was right when he said Caspian lived here. Mostly because the man appeared drunk, and it was too lucky that the first person I asked actually knew Caspian at all.

Turns out the long shot was bang on.

Caspian's six-foot, built-as-hell frame towers over me. I forgot how intimidating his stare is.

"Who the fuck are you and what do you want?"

I'm speechless for a second too long. With unseeable speed, he whips a silver dagger out from his back and places the tip under my chin. Fury burns in his eyes, and two black marks that run down from his forehead and around his eyes to his cheeks glow a vibrant red. "You might be fucking drop-dead beautiful but you won't trick me into whatever you're selling. Get the fuck out of here before you regret it."

He lowers the dagger and walks back into his house.

"I'm Leo's sister!" I shout seconds before the door shuts in my face.

But then it swiftly swings open again, and Caspian rests his shoulder against the doorframe. This time, he pauses to look at me from head to toe, and I do the same to him.

Caspian Hardling has changed since he was eighteen.

He's still as breathtakingly handsome as he was then but he is more now. So much more.

Beefy shoulders fill out his white button-down shirt, which is tucked into black leather trousers with laces at the front of his narrow but toned waist. The trousers showcase his thick thighs and other areas. His soft, silky blond hair is tipped white and falls to just below his ears. His ears are spiked at the top, a reminder of his demon blood, and I've always thought they suit him. All demons have tipped ears in human form, but it's more complicated for half-demon, half-wolves like Caspian.

He is rare. Few half-borns survive childhood.

"You grew up, songbird."

I narrow my eyes at his stupid nickname for me. The memory of it comes back like a hammer. How did I have a crush on this guy? Oh, right. Wine, teenage hormones, and one sexy-ass half-wolf.

Apparently, I sing as well as demon songbirds, which for the record, screech all night and can make human men go deaf. They are popular for torture.

"Clearly you haven't," I say, crossing my arms.

"Did you come all the way to Hell to insult me? Or did you miss my pretty face?"

Swallowing my pride, what is left of it, I tell him the truth. "Neither. I need your help because I'm in danger."

Something changes in his eyes, the playfulness disappearing as he straightens. "I can't help you. You need to go."

"Wait!" I stop his door closing in my face this time.

He sighs.

"My brother said you owed him. A life debt, if I'm not mistaken."

He arches a pierced brow. "And?"

"This will make you even. Help me, for my brother, for the debt if nothing else," I reply, hoping this will work. I'm sure Leo will go along with the plan if I had any way to safely get in touch with him.

Caspian stares down at me once more, and slowly he steps back, waving me into his house. "Get the fuck in, songbird."

"My name is Lilith, in case you've forgotten," I respond. I walk into the spacious yet empty room. There is a generic kitchen with four counters, a fridge, and a small bathroom behind a screen on the other side. A double bed is in the middle, with a couch at the end and a big orange rug in front of it. A wardrobe is near the bed, with two hooks on either side and countless weapons hanging off the large hook.

Other than that, there is nothing else here. Nothing personal to be seen.

Caspian slams the door shut behind me and walks around me to the fridge. "Do you drink yet? How old are you again?"

I drop down onto his leather sofa. "Old enough."

"Good, because we need vodka for this conversation where you blackmail me into saving you from whatever the fuck you have done."

Caspian brings over a half-drunk bottle of vodka and two shot glasses, chucking one at me. I hold it up, and he pours me a shot. I down it, keeping my eyes on him, and he raises an eyebrow at me before taking his own shot.

He downs another one and then pours himself a third. "Talk."

"My mum and dad were killed by the Stormfire alpha. He wants me dead, and I need to hide," I blurt out in one long rush.

Caspian coughs on the shot and smacks his fist against his chest a few times, staring at me with wide eyes.

"Then you're dead already. I can't help you fight him," he replies, still looking shell-shocked.

I get the impression not much surprises this guy.

Rolling my eyes, I glance away. "I know that and I need somewhere to hide in the city. Permanently."

"Does the alpha know you're here?"

"Maybe," I respond, clasping my hands together. "I don't know for sure. So can I hide here?"

"Minor problem, I'm leaving here tomorrow." He rubs the back of his neck and tilts his head at me. "The demon hunter trials begin tomorrow, and I'm joining them."

"Shit," I mutter. "Do you know anyone who could hide me? Someone you trust?"

He scoffs. "I don't trust anyone in Hell, and you shouldn't either, songbird."

He sits on the sofa next to me, only a few inches between us, and I try not to look at the gorgeous fucker who is clearly going to ditch me.

"I'm sorry about your parents. Really, I am," he eventually says. "More your mum though. Your dad was a dick."

"Technically, he wasn't my dad," I counter, trying to make light of it with some dark humour.

Caspian chuckles low. "Lucky you."

We drift into silence once more before Caspian lets out a long sigh. "I'm going fucking mad because I have an idea. It's crazy, but it just might work if you don't fuck it up."

My heart thrashes. "I'm willing to go for crazy right now."

Caspian's gaze trails over me, the marks on his cheeks almost glowing red for a second, and I wonder what that means. When he was in Caeli, his marks never glowed, and I overheard him telling Leo that they were from his father's demon side, not his wolf's.

"I could get you into the demon hunter trials under a fake name," he says slowly, "and I doubt the alpha would search for you there. The faces of all contestants are kept a secret, so they can move around the city freely. The alpha gives his protection to each of the ten winners. If you could win, which I highly doubt, by the way, you could gain the alpha's protection. Then he won't be able to kill you without breaking his vow."

"Which means death for an alpha," I whisper, filled with hope. "You're right… That is a crazy plan."

"Told you. Now the question is, can you fight? Do you know fuck all about demons?"

"Well, I know you."

He smirks and rests back, picking the vodka bottle up and taking a long drink. "That you do, songbird. That you do."

I just manage to resist snorting at him. "I don't think your plan will work, but it might buy me more time to find a safe place to escape. Somewhere the Stormfire alpha can't reach," I say and stand off the sofa. I snatch the vodka bottle from his hands and take a sip.

He grins when I scrunch my face up at the taste. "There are no demons on the moon."

Rolling my eyes, I shove the bottle back his way. "I've always wanted to be a demon hunter."

Caspian slowly moves his attention up my body, and I feel his gaze like fire against my skin until he clashes with my eyes.

"You're going to make an interesting partner, songbird."

"Thank you for helping me," I reply shakily.

He stands, stretching his long, thick arms. "Don't thank me yet. There is every chance the leader of the trials is going to take one look at you and say fuck no."

"Then I'll have to be charming," I say with a wink.

Caspian flashes me a devilish smirk. "If you can charm the alpha's only son, then I'm a fucking virgin."

He laughs, walking away from me. My cheeks burn as red as my hair. I have to get into these trials; alpha's son or not, I'm going to get in.

"By the way, we need to dye that white streak of hair. It makes you stand out," he calls back, walking to his door. "Don't go anywhere, songbird."

"Like I can!" I shout as he leaves me alone in his apartment.

What the hell, pun intended, have I gotten myself into?

Description

When Winter started university with her best friend Alex, she didn't expect to find herself in the middle of a supernatural war. Who knew saving a stray wolf could earn you the alliance of the pack.

To make things more complicated, the broody and very attractive Jaxson is tasked with keeping her safe from the growing vampire threat in town. It's a shame he can't stand her and enjoys irritating the hell out of her.

When she finds out her new boyfriend has his own secrets, can she trust anyone anymore?

What happens when you get yourself stuck in the middle of a war?
This is a reverse harem book series.

Description

The blue-sided human will choose a side.
When four princes are born on the same day, they will rule true.
Her saviour will die when the choice is made.
If she chooses wrong, she will fall.
If she chooses right, then she will rule.
Only her mates can stop her from the destruction of all.
If the fates allow, no one need fall.
For only the true kings hold her fate, and they will be her mates.

"The prophecy has come true. I found out that the vampire, angel, and witches' royal sons were born yesterday," my sister says to me, a look of worry on her faultless face as I hold my little baby closer to me.

I look down at the sweet, little boy in my arms. The new shifter prince, my son and the last royal male wolf. His green eyes are glowing as he looks up at me like he holds the entire earth in his sweet eyes. I know the goddess will protect him.

"Then it's true. The goddess planned this all," I whisper.

"We must make sure they are close. Despite our wars and

disagreements, the children should grow up together," she tells me and I know she is right.

"We have a lot of planning to do, sister." I stare down at my little boy as I speak to her, "You are right, if they have any chance of winning the human's heart, they must be united."

"Yes, my queen." My sister bows her head at me and leaves the room. If only I could protect my child from the responsibility he now has on his tiny shoulders.

The responsibility of saving the whole world.

Winter

Why did I take this class?

"Everyone, please start by reading page thirty-two in your textbooks," the professor goes on, as my class starts after he walks in. The professor looks as ancient as the old room we are all sat in, with his brown hair and beard, and very dated clothes that look like he hasn't washed them in a while.

Description

I push my own out-of-control, wavy brown hair over my shoulder, wishing I had tied it up this morning. It's a hot day, and the room is stuffy because of the lack of opened windows, making my hair stick the back of my head. I glance over at my best friend, Alex, who has her head on her desk, lightly snoring. I chuckle before kicking her leg and waking her up. She moves her waist-length, straight, red hair off her face to glare at me.

"I was resting, Win," she mutters, hiding her eyes with her arm and huffing at me.

"The professor is here," I giggle, trying to whisper to her as she nearly falls off the side of the desk, while still half asleep.

"Oh, what page?" She yawns, looking like she is going to drop back off to sleep already. I sigh, remembering how she actually has a boyfriend to keep her up all night. I, on the other hand, can't find a good one. The last time I had a boyfriend was over a year ago, and I found out he had a bad habit of sleeping around at parties. The unfortunate way I found this out was when I walked into his bedroom at his party, to find him in bed with two other girls. Let's just say he has put me off men for life, or at least for a while.

"Thirty-two," I reply, rolling my eyes at her grin.

"I might nap instead, I had a long night," she says with a wink.

"Don't rub it in," I groan.

"Well, you're coming to Drake's party this weekend, and no, you don't have a choice. I bought you a dress, and I found you a date."

I don't know which one was worse about that sentence.

Description

The fact she has bought me a dress, which I know will be way too slutty for my style, or the unlucky guy she has found for me. I decide to go with the second problem first.

"A date? You know I don't date," I hiss, while she continues to grin.

"Hey, you can't judge every man because of one. This guy is nice, a friend of Drake's." She makes that annoying face she knows I haven't ever been able to say no to since we were eight. I will never forget when I first met Alex. My mum had taken me to get an ice cream from the local ice cream van. Alex had just gotten hers in front of me, and I decided to get the same because her ice cream looked good. When the truck left, Alex tripped and dropped hers. My mum and I rushed over as she cried her eyes out over her ice cream. I offered to share mine and then, when I saw her at school the next day, we were inseparable.

"Fine, but if this doesn't go well I'm blaming you," I laugh.

"Winter Masters, is there something wrong?" My professor asks, causing the whole class to look at me. I can hear Alex's quiet snort as I answer.

"No, sir. We were just discussing the work," I answer with red cheeks. The professor raises his bushy eyebrows at me. I know he doesn't believe me. Damn, I wouldn't believe me, either.

I'm a terrible liar.

"Well, discuss it more quietly next time, I'm sure the whole class doesn't want to know about your dating life," he replies. I hold in the urge to hide under the table at his blunt reply. A guy about my age puts his hand up at the front, drawing the whole room's attention to him. The boy has messy, brown hair that's covered up with a backwards cap. He is quite muscular under his top and shorts from what I can see. I've heard a few comments about how attractive he is, which he definitely is, but I can't remember his name.

"I would like to know, sir," he says loudly before winking at me over his shoulder. I know I'm redder than a tomato now, and one glance at Alex shows how funny she thinks this is. I'm leaving her to sleep through the class next time.

"That's enough, Harris. All of you get back to work. I am running tests on this next week." He picks up a large pile of papers, most likely the tests he made us do last week, and hasn't bothered to mark yet. I watch as he goes to his desk and pulls out his phone. I'm sure he is playing some game by the way he is typing, but he definitely isn't marking the tests.

"Also, while I remember, you need to find work experience in the next week or you'll be helping me sort out the university lost and found…for four weeks." I swear the old professor even smirked but I didn't see him do it. I bet they would be getting him more coffees than they would be doing anything else.

"Have you heard back from the local vets yet?" Alex asks, opening her book as everyone else starts reading quietly.

"Yes, they called yesterday, and I'm all sorted." I grin, remembering jumping up and down in happiness after the call. I had applied months ago, and no one from our course was accepted, but I held out hope as I hadn't been rejected. My back-up was to work at a local farm, with half our class. Studying to become a vet is hard work, and there isn't much work experience available. This is an English class, and we have to pass it to stay at the university. That's why Alex, who is a music student, is taking this class with me.

"That's great," she smiles widely, making a few guys next to us turn to look at her. Alex is that very pretty girl you always wanted to be. She is tall with boobs and hips that are perfect no matter what she eats. I look at a McDonald's meal, and my ass gets bigger. I've been told I'm pretty, but I like my food too much. So I have curves, unlike my skinny-ass best friend. My best qualities are my shiny, brown hair and blue eyes, which I have to admit, suit my golden complexion. We don't say any more and get on with our work. At the end of class, I hand in my permission forms for the work experience, before finding Alex with her boyfriend, Drake, outside class.

"Hey, do you still need a lift?" I ask when I get close to them.

"Nope, thanks, honey. I'm going to Drake's, but I will see you tomorrow to get ready for the party." She winks, leaning against Drake. Drake is a good-looking guy, but is kind of strange-looking, and I can't put my finger on why. Honestly, he looks like a typical, scary-ass man all the time. I don't think he has a non-serious expression. He has dark, nearly black eyes and black hair that's cut in a buzz cut, but he makes it work. It's the eyes that give him the strangeness, they are too dark, darker than I have ever seen anyone's. I always thought that he must spend a lot of time in a gym or something because he is all muscles, wearing expensive clothes. Alex has told me he is well off, but I knew that anyway from the car he drives and the designer clothes he wears. It's not just the looks and money, it's more how much older he acts, when he must be around twenty, like us. Alex doesn't answer many questions about him, but they have dated a while, so I'm guessing she really likes him.

"My friend is looking forward to your date," Drake says coldly in a slight Russian accent. Alex says he is not actually from there, but his parents were, apparently.

"Me, too," I lie and frown at Alex's chuckle.

"I love you, Win, never change," she says to me, as she gives me a hug before we wave goodbye. Drake doesn't say anything else but that's normal.

I click my old, red Rover open before sliding in. My mum bought it for me as a going away present, and I love the old car, though maybe not the unusual stain on the driver seat I can't seem to get rid of; I think it's red pen. *Well, I'm hoping it is anyway.* We never had a lot of money growing up as it was just me and mum. As I drive home, I try to think about ways to get out of this date, but eventually come to the conclusion that it couldn't go that badly. *Right?*

Winter

"You're joking, right? I can't wear this." I gesture to the tight, red dress I'm wearing. My hair is up in a messy bun with a few wavy strands around my face. My makeup is perfectly done, thanks to Alex, but I have to admit I don't look anything like myself.

"You look hot, Win," she says, pretending to cool herself down by waving her hand at her face. I look back to the mirror and glance down at the dress. It stops around mid-thigh and has a slit down the middle at the front, stopping just before my underwear, and making it impossible to wear a bra. Not that I'm worried, I'm not big chested enough to really have an issue.

"He is going to think I'm easy if I'm wearing this," I say, sighing and turning around with my arms around my waist.

"No, he is going to think he is a lucky fucker," she laughs before straightening her own dress. Alex is wearing her little, black dress, which is a little too little but looks nice.

Description

"Alright. But again, I'm blaming you if anything goes wrong." I laugh to myself, knowing this could only go wrong. I shut the door to my bedroom before leaving our apartment. Alex and I have a two-bedroom apartment near the university, which we rent together. It's cheap enough, and the area isn't too bad, but we still make sure we lock up.

"So, what's my date's name?" I ask as we wait outside for Drake to turn up. We are lucky the weather has been so good recently. Welsh weather is known for its constant rain, and our town is right in the middle of the mountains. Calroh is a small town but has a great university, and that's why we chose it, also the cheap apartments to rent helped. It's right in the middle of two large mountains and surrounded by a large forest. There's only one road out of town, but the town is well-stocked enough to look after itself with many large superstores.

"Wyatt. I haven't met him, but Drake speaks highly of him," she winks at me.

I think of his name for a second trying to imagine the guy. "So, is it getting serious between you and Drake?" I ask gently, knowing Alex doesn't like to speak about relationships. Not her own at least.

"I don't know. He is so secretive that I–" she stops talking as Drake's car pulls in front us. I glance at her, and I am wondering what the end of that sentence was, but she shakes her head, smiling before opening her door. I do the same sliding into the back.

"Hey, Drake," I say as I get in, and Alex pulls back from kissing Drake hello.

"I thought Wyatt was coming with us?" Alex asks,

Description

noticing the empty seat by me. I smile widely, hoping he is ill or isn't coming.

"He is meeting us there," Drake says bluntly before driving off.

There goes my dream of taking off this dress and changing into my PJ's, with a bottle of wine.

I don't say anything, growing a little more nervous the nearer we get to Drake's apartment.

As we pull into the expensive apartment building, we can see the party has started. The music is loud, and there are cars everywhere. I mentally tell myself that going to a party at twenty years old is normal, and I should smile before getting out of the car. I walk next to Alex as Drake puts his arm around her shoulders. Just as we walk in, and the loud music fills my ears, I see a blond man leaning against the wall next to the door of Drake's apartment. I can't help but stare a little at his muscular frame and his strong-looking face that I have to admit is a little scary. He seems to notice me staring and looks right at me. I first notice his eyes are that nearly black in colour or maybe just a dark-brown like Drake's. I look around quickly noticing that nearly every girl nearby is watching the breath-taking guy like I am. My eyes draw back to his, noticing how powerful he looks. He can't be more than twenty-five but looks like he owns the very street he is standing on. The guy's eyes never leave mine as I look him over, and I shiver from the anger I feel in his eyes. *How can someone look so serious and cold at our age?* I continue walking with Alex until we stop in front of the guy, and I want to get to know him or hear him speak. My mind and body feel drawn to him, and I don't like it.

"Drake, this must be my date," the man says in a dark, underwear-dropping voice, nodding at Drake before looking back at me. I feel myself blush as his gaze takes in all of me slowly. I do the same, noticing for the first time that he is wearing a black jumper with black jeans, which look like they were custom-made for him; they possibly were.

"Wyatt. It's nice to meet you, Winter," he offers his hand. I take his cold hand, and he shocks me by bringing it up to his mouth and placing a kiss on the back. His lips feel cold on my hand, but I feel a strange shock when his lips meet my skin. It takes everything in me not to pull my hand away and run in the other direction like my body is screaming for me to do. For some reason, I don't feel safe with him.

"Nice to meet you, too," I mutter a slight lie, pulling back my hand.

Wyatt just flashes me a knowing look before saying to Drake, "There was a problem tonight, they are getting braver," his deep voice gets stronger about whatever they are discussing. It's almost like his voice draws you in and demands that you listen.

"Just a few newbies chasing a pup, it's being dealt with," Drake smiles with a cold look in my direction.

"Good. Now, can I get you a drink?" Wyatt asks looking back at me. It's strange to see how Wyatt spoke to Drake then. It was like a boss ordering around an employee, and worse, I had no idea what they were speaking about. *What's a pup?* Maybe it's a kind of business talk, I doubt they mean a puppy.

"Sure," I say taking his open arm and letting him guide me through the house. I can feel how cold he is even through his jacket. I look back to see Alex, who has disappeared with Drake. Knowing Alex, they might have already left, thinking Wyatt seems nice. While I don't feel that he is at all; he seems too haunted to be described as nice. Seeing how he spoke to Drake just then, makes me more distrusting of him.

"Are you cold?" I ask noticing that's it's a hot summer day in May. I'm even warm, in a little dress, and he is cold in a jumper.

"Just cold-blooded," he winks at me. I can't help but blush a little, but who wouldn't when a very hot guy flirts with you. I know I need to act normal for a bit, before making an excuse and leaving. We weave through the hallways of the building and up two floors in the elevator, which is filled with couples making out. I watch as they stop and stare at Wyatt like he is a god and ignore me completely. It's all very odd.

"So, tell me, what do you study?" he asks as we enter the kitchen. It's a modern kitchen with many cabinets that don't look used, and there's even a bar on the one side next to an impressive window. There are a few people around, but it's quiet enough in here to not have to talk too loudly. Wherever the loud music is coming from, it's not nearby.

"I'm studying to become a vet. What about you?" I look over the view of the nearby forest and mountains as he hands me an opened beer. I don't like beer, but I'm not telling him that, so I pretend to drink it.

"The family business," he says still looking at me. He moves closer, so I have to lift my head up to look at him.

Being so short can be really an annoying at times, I think to myself. This guy has at least a foot on me, and I feel small

Description

around him. Now that he is closer, I can see that his eyes are definitely black with little silver sparks in them. I've never seen eyes like his, and they are really stunning. I clear my throat before asking, "Have you known Drake long?"

"Yes, it feels like I've known Drake forever, sometimes," he grins at me like I'm missing a joke.

"I feel like that with Alex, sometimes," I say, looking away because his eyes are so stunning that they draw you in. The other door in the room opens as a drunken man stumbles in, he quickly leaves again when he sees Wyatt but leaves the door open. I can see the living room, well it's more a dance room. The dancing bodies are pushed so closely together that you can't see their faces. The music is beating hard and fast compared to the slow-moving young people swaying around. I turn back to see Wyatt watching me closely.

"Dance with me? You seem like you need to relax," he asks. I lift my head to stare into his eyes, and I feel the need to dance with him, to do anything he wants. I stare at his eyes as he smirks, moving closer to me. I could have sworn his eyes had silver sparks, nothing like the empty, black pits I'm staring into now.

I shake my head, stepping back. "No thanks, I don't dance," I say to Wyatt's cold gaze. This time, his face converts into confusion, and he steps closer to me than before. We are almost touching with how close he is.

"Dance with me, Winter," he says looking into my eyes again, his eyes glowing far brighter than they should. I yelp when he grabs my arm roughly. I take a step away. His grip is strong, but I realise he isn't trying to hurt me. I don't dare

Description

look away from him as the black, glowing eyes stare into me, like he is looking into my soul.

"No, let go, Wyatt," I say firmly, challenging his grip by struggling away. I don't know what changes, but he lets me go with an utterly confused and shocked look marking his handsome face.

"How is that possible?" he mutters to himself, running his hands through his hair, and stepping away from me. I take the chance he gives me to run out the door, not caring who is looking. I have a feeling challenging a scary man like that is not a good idea. I don't think running from him is a good idea either, but, hey, it's all I have right now. *I couldn't have seen glowing eyes, right?* I mean that doesn't even make sense to me, it must have been a trick of the light or something. I eventually make my way outside. I can't believe my luck when I spot the guy from class, Harris, opening his car door for a young girl to get in. I'm glad I remembered his name now.

"Wait, Harris!" I shout from the door, and he turns to me, looking a little shocked, but more worried than anything else.

"Are you alright?" he asks none too gently as he grabs my shoulders, pulling me closer, and looking me up and down.

"Yes, but I could use a lift home," I say gently as I pull away from him a little, enough that he drops his warm hands.

"Sure, I was just taking my sister home. My parents are going to kill her for sneaking out tonight. So, I'm sure she needs some extra time to come up with a decent excuse," he laughs, opening the back door for me.

As I get in, I look behind me to see Wyatt watching me

Description

from the door. I swear I'll never forget the look he has on his face as watches me get into the car. He is looking at me like he is a starving man, and I am his meal. I gasp before slamming the door shut and closing my eyes for a second, resting my head against the cold leather.

"So, what's your name?" the girl in the front asks the minute I get in. I smile as I hear her draw out the sentence. I open my eyes to see a pair of light-blue ones sparkling at me.

"I'm Winter, and you are?" I put on my seat belt as Harris gets in.

"I'm Katy. How do you know my brother?" she smiles, but it looks cheeky.

"You should be thinking of excuses to help yourself, and not asking questions," Harris answers her question as he looks at me in the rear-view mirror. I smirk at him when I see he is trying not to laugh, and he winks at me.

"They are going to ground me for life, anyway," she says to Harris with a huff and looks back at me, "so, do you have a boyfriend?" she asks, clearly not concerned about her parents, and I look her over now. She has the same light-brown hair as Harris and matching blue eyes, that are lighter than most. I would guess she is around sixteen, making her way too young to be here. She is wearing a purple dress that is as short as mine but makes her look a hell of a lot older than she is. I can see why Harris' parents are going to be mad. I'm guessing the amount of makeup she has on isn't going to help her case. She doesn't need it, though, I can see under it all that she is very pretty.

"No. I'm escaping a bad date, actually," I mutter as she laughs.

"Harris should ask you out, he wouldn't be a bad date," she winks, and I see Harris blush.

"I'm not dating anymore, but if I was, Harris would be a good choice," I say gently, letting them both down easily.

"You should change your mind. You're really pretty." She sighs, finally turning around. Harris asks for the address, so I give it to him before opening my phone. I'm surprised not to see any messages from Alex, I send her a quick one:

Date was awful, shame the hot ones are always crazy. I got a lift home. I will see you tomorrow. Love you xx

I missed out on the start of the argument, as I was texting, but from Harris's angry face he isn't happy.

"There are loads of them around right now, Katy. I don't want to find you sneaking out again." He shouts leaving me to wonder what he is talking about. Katy is looking tense in her seat at whatever it is.

"I know. But, I never get to leave the pack," she says looking out the window with a long sigh. I'm sure that I see tears in her eyes as she picks her nails, looking worried.

"It won't always be like this, but please, for me, don't leave again without one of us." He stares at her through the mirror, and I see her lower her gaze quickly.

"I promise," Katy says with a frown, and Harris nods, looking back at the empty road. I watch as he turns to look at me, and a grin lights up his face when he sees what I'm wearing. Typical guy, but at least he has the common sense to look back at the road after a second, not voicing his opinion.

"What's a pack?" I ask clearing my throat and hopefully

my red cheeks from Harris's stare. I remember reading about packs of wolves in class, but I don't think they are talking about that. Maybe it's some kind of gang or a name of a house, I don't want to guess because I'm sure I'm going to come up with something worse than what it actually is. I glance at Harris who isn't answering my question, so I repeat myself.

"Oh, it's nothing important," Harris says quickly, all the while he is glaring at Katy like a parent whose kid just told someone a big secret of theirs. I glance back at Katy, who looks very guilty, as she shrugs at me, and avoids looking at Harris at all. This night is proving to be all kinds of confusing, and I'm pretty sure forgetting it is the easier way. No one says anything else while we drive home, and a tense silence descends on the car.

"Are you going to be okay to walk in? I don't think I can get in the car park with the gate down," Harris looks at me, as he stops on the road outside my building. The whole building is close to the university, so it has to be on lock down after a certain time, and you can only walk in, past a locked gate. I'm lucky the gate's broken, so you don't need a key to get in. Well, unlucky in certain ways because it means anyone can get in.

"Yeah, I'll walk in. The gate is open," I say to Harris, and he nods, watching me closely like he wants to say something, but I get out of the car before he can.

"Bye Katy, and good luck with your parents," I say through the open window, and I laugh, hearing her grumble before I move away from the car. I wave them both off before opening the broken gate to the locked car park, the

Description

door is slightly open anyway from our neighbours. The car park is almost as big as the building in length, and you have to walk across the whole thing to get to my building. My building has three flats, on three levels, and we have the bottom one. The car park is empty, besides my car and one other. I walk slowly; only the dim lights of the street lamps near the building are lighting my path, showing me where I'm going. In the distance, I notice a big, dark shape lying next to my car, near the door to my building. I run over quickly, my footsteps being the only noise in the dark night. I'm hoping the person is okay and pull my phone out of my bag as I run, to call an ambulance, but as I get closer I see it's a wolf.

Could my night get any more weird?

Winter

I slowly move forward to get a closer look, slipping my phone back in my bag. I'm a little relieved to see it's not a big

Description

wolf. The wolf is the size of a small child and has light-brown fur or it could be black, but I can't tell in the dim light. The light catches against the large dagger, stuck in its back leg. I hear him whine as he looks up at me with dark eyes, I don't feel like he could attack me if he tried, so I carefully move closer. I know how dangerous it is, and Alex would kill me for this, but there's a reason I wanted to be a vet. I love helping animals, I've been helping injured animals since I was a little girl, and I brought home a cat that had been run over. So, there's no way I can leave this wolf now, no matter how foolish it might seem.

"Hey you, look I'm a vet," I say in a calm, soothing voice and then think to myself that I should leave out the in-training part.

"I can help you, but you can't hurt me, or I will have to leave you alone, alright?" I say gently, hoping my calming tone of my voice soothes him enough that he will trust me. The wolf must be smart because I swear he is listening to every word and hasn't growled at me once yet. He might be someone's pet, as he doesn't seem to be scared of me like most wild animals are of humans. I don't know why I'm suddenly calling this wolf he, it might be a girl for all I know.

The wolf whines at me, so I take that as a yes. I know I can't take him to a vet, or they might put him down. Even if he is tame, most vets won't help him. The wolf is a wild animal that is usually hunted in other countries, but I can't just do nothing. My mum would be going mad right now; like the time I brought home another injured cat, that was a local stray, and it chased me around the house when it woke up, trying to bite me. That cat was not thankful for my help.

I crouch down on my knees, carefully turning my phone light on to look closer. The wolf is nearly all black, as I run a hand over his fur and pull it back because he is mostly covered in blood. I know I need to pull this dagger out and then get him inside to stitch it up. I'm lucky I have some stuff in my emergency medical box that I can use.

"Alright, handsome wolf, I'm going to pull this out and then get you inside to my apartment. I can stitch this up for you," I say to him. I swear that he actually blinks at me as an answer.

"Please don't hurt me for this," I mutter and quickly pull it out with a shaky hand, and he yelps loudly. I'm surprised when he doesn't growl at me, and I could swear little tears are coming out of his eyes as he crashes to the ground.

"Shush, I'm so sorry, little wolf," I say gently as I stroke his neck. He passes out after a few minutes, which is likely from all the blood loss. I'm hoping he is strong enough to make it through this because I have no idea how much blood he could have lost just getting here. I stand up, looking down at the wolf and think through my options quickly. I know with him unconscious, I can get him back to my flat without making too much noise, or distressing the poor creature. I look at the knife in my hand, it's heavy, and I think it's real silver as it shines in the moonlight, the blood dripping off it looking unnatural and scary. It has unusual drawings all over it, that I don't recognise, but they look very much like crowns. I put it in my handbag with my phone, shutting off the light. I'm lucky I'm kind of strong because half carrying the large wolf the short walk to my ground floor apartment is almost killing me. I eventually get to my door, opening it before carrying the wolf into my lounge. I lean against the wall, getting my breath back and look down at my red dress, now covered in blood and stuck to me with sweat. I put the lights on and walk out to grab the first aid box out in the kitchen. When I come back in, I scream.

I must be going crazy because where I left the wolf, there is now a young boy around eight or so, curled up in a ball, with a mop of black hair with blond tips covering his face, and he's naked. I rush over to him, seeing how pale he is and looking around for the wolf in my small lounge. The front door is shut, so I know he didn't get out, but as soon as I'm close to the boy, his body shakes before he shifts back into the black wolf.

I scream again, dropping the box on the floor and just stare at the passed- out little wolf.

What the hell? I know I'm having a really bad night, but I really didn't think I had gone completely mad. I slide to the floor staring at the wolf, and I remember some weird things. Like all the books I read as a teenager about werewolves, and now there is a real one in my living room. Who knew they were actually real? *Should I be running out of the room screaming?* The image of the small boy appears in my mind as I look at the wolf, and I realise that I don't care what he is, he needs my help.

I eventually calm myself down, knowing that the wolf is only a child and needs help, no matter what he is, helps me do that. I go closer to see the stab wound, and I'm surprised it is looking better, as it's nearly all sealed up. I decide to grab a blanket from my room and cover the wolf up to the neck, just in case he turns again. I'm guessing the fast healing must be a wolf thing. I do eventually think of the downside of having a supernatural creature in my house, what if others that are like him, come looking for the child and think I hurt him? I should run, but I don't because I can't leave a child, without knowing for certain he is okay.

I've always been the type to do a massive cleaning when I'm stressed. Alex is the kind that cooks everything, like my mum does, but Alex doesn't make anything edible or without a high risk of food poisoning. I get some bleach and water then start scrubbing the floor up to the door, where there is blood and outside my door too, before locking it.

I check on the wolf, and I'm not that surprised to see it's the boy again but it still looks like he is sleeping. I go to my room, taking off the now blood- covered dress and putting on some casual clothes. I avoid looking at myself in the mirror because that would make this night way too real for me, and I want some answers from the boy before I do that.

I get a wash cloth out of my bathroom, getting it a little wet before going to the boy.

"Hey, I'm just going to clean you up a little," I say to him, even if he isn't awake, I'm hoping he can hear me. I can still hear his yelp when I pulled that dagger out, who would hurt a little child like that?

I clean his face and then his shoulders. I lift the blanket to look at the dagger wound on his lower leg. It's nearly all healed, so I clean it up carefully and put a bandage on it before covering his leg up again.

I sit down on the couch, looking at the boy, wondering what the hell to do now. It's not like I can call a doctor to explain I have a boy that changes into a wolf sometimes. Or would I call a vet? I eventually lie down on my couch and drift off to sleep.

Wyatt

"Atti, I know it's her for fuck's sake," I mutter down the phone. Atti is a witch and general pain in the ass, but I need him to know about this.

"Hold on a sec," he says to someone else and puts the phone down on me. I'm the prince of the fucking vampires, and he puts the phone down on me like he couldn't give two shits. *Typical.*

"I've cleared the apartment, now tell me what's going on?" Drake says, coming into the living room.

"It's Winter, the girl we have all been waiting for. She's been your mate's best friend all this time," I tell him harshly, and he tries to hide his shock.

"I can't believe it," he eventually mutters. Drake paces by the door, and I just watch him as he tries to process this.

Drake has been my protector since I was born. I think he is around a hundred years old and never took a mate. When he told me he was mating with a human girl he had met, I was a little taken back. Drake basically brought me up and yet is never nice to anyone other than me.

"Baby, are you in here?" Alex's voice comes from the other side of the door. Drake opens the door and takes her hand gently.

"We will discuss this another time," he tells me, and I nod at him.

"Wait. How did your date go?" Alex asks pushing around Drake. Alex has known about us for over a year. She met him in a local pub, and she let Drake feed on her. From the first time he saw her, he told me he didn't want to leave her and had to get to know her. I have no idea why she thought setting her best friend up on a date with a vampire was a good idea, but she did.

"I may have messed it up a little," I say to her.

"If you upset her, I swear I'll find a way to stake your ass," she says with a glare, trying to move towards me, but Drake lifts her over his shoulder.

"Winter may have left the date after an argument," I say.

"Drake put me down and help me find a stake!" she tells him, loudly.

"Stakes don't work Alex, and I didn't upset her too much," I tell her, as Drake whispers something to her, I could listen in, but I don't.

"Fine, we can talk about this in the morning, and I know stakes don't work. But, I bet it would hurt." She grins at me, and I hear Drake's chuckle as he walks her out.

Description

A few minutes later, as I walk aimlessly around my apartment, Atti appears in the room. Witches can travel anywhere they have been before. Atti is their soon-to-be leader, their prince, and is the most powerful witch around.

"You're sure? Like completely, not fucking around with me right now?" he asks in my mind. Another annoying habit of his, forgetting to actually talk out loud, when he knows it gives me a headache.

"Yes, I tried to make her dance with me, and she resisted like it was nothing. No one has ever been able to stop me, other than my father and some witches. It's also how drawn I was to her; like she was all I could see," I tell him out loud. I sit in my chair by my fireplace, thinking about Winter.

"Don't forget me, D, and Jax. Your powers never work on us, it does make me laugh, though," He laughs out loud, and I fold in my fists. I know how much Atti likes to fuck with me.

"Tell me about her?" Atti asks, thankfully out loud, as he takes the seat opposite me.

"She has long, brown hair, light-blue eyes, a body that could outdo an angel's, and from the little I spoke to her, she seemed good," I tell him.

"Of course, she is good. Man, I love brunettes." Atti sighs, rubbing his tired face.

"I have to tell Dabriel," I tell him.

"And Jax," Atti tells me with a stern look on his face.

"No, he made it clear that he didn't want anything to do with us after what happened. We haven't seen him in seven years," I remind Atti. It's difficult to even talk about him, he was like a brother to me.

"That was in the past and nothing to do with Winter," Atti says. A sad look crosses his face, as I know he feels sorry for me. I have to remind myself not to punch him. He, too, is like a brother to me; plus I don't want to destroy my apartment by fighting with him.

"Doesn't matter. He would kill her first and ask questions later," I tell him.

"Fine. Just for now, until we tell Winter who she is, but you know D likely knows about her by now," Atti says. Dabriel is an angel and a prince. Angels have the power to tell the future, among other things.

"He doesn't see everything, and his council won't let him go near her, anyway," I remind Atti again about all the stupid, fucking rules.

"The prophecy says–" Atti starts, but I cut him off.

"It says a hell of a lot, but no one believes it anymore. Our births were deemed as miracles and not the work of the goddess. We are on our own, and it's best we keep this a secret. I don't want my father finding out about Winter," I tell him and he nods.

"It's best my coven doesn't find out yet, they are still planning this stupid marriage between me and the leader of the dark witches," Atti says, his face looking like he is sucking lemons.

"Then we are in agreement. I'll get to know her and eventually introduce you," I tell him. I may have to get Alex to help me. I think I was a bit rude and maybe scary tonight. It just took me by surprise to see her there. I expected a pretty girl for the night, and instead, this stunning girl walks up to me, looking perfect and smelling like sin. I just wanted to taste her right then. I had to drink four bags of blood tonight to stop myself from chasing after her.

"I can't see her for a few weeks, there's a meeting between our kind, and I have to be there constantly. The amount of stupid fights I'll have to break up in the next two weeks is bloody stupid," Atti grumbles.

"That's what happens when all your council are women, and you're the only male allowed in." I tell him. I don't want to swap places with him when he has to deal with their cat fights. Atti once told me that he had to put ten women to sleep when a fight broke out over him. Every woman in his coven would die for a chance to mate with him. He is lucky his mother still protects him, and as Queen, most of them are terrified of her. They should be.

"I had to be the first royal, male witch born in thousands of years," Atti grumbles.

"Yes, you unlucky fucker, hordes of hot witches throwing themselves at you," I smirk at him.

"Well, I'm going to be without a bed mate for a long time, now that we have found her," he tells me.

"Aren't we all? Honestly, after seeing her, I couldn't touch anyone else," I look away as I speak.

"She must be something." Atti stands. I don't want to admit how much of a something she is. She is the first girl I've felt anything for since I lost Demi. Demi was my childhood friend, and we only had a year together, romantically, before she was killed. I thought I'd never get over her, but I always knew she wasn't meant to be my mate. I knew since I was a child that another was destined for me, but I was young and stubborn. I never tried to mate with her, and she never asked me to. She knew I was meant for another, but she said she wanted what little time she could have. I try to ignore the sharp pain of guilt in my heart at the fact I'm moving on.

"I can't stay. A word of warning for a friend, your father has met with my mother, he wants her help for something, but she won't tell me what it is. Do you think he knows where the pack is?" Atti asks.

"No, I keep them safe. That's why I still stay around this small town," I don't mean it to sound as hostile as it comes out. Atti ignores it or is used to my curt tone, because he doesn't show any response.

"Something is changing. The witches are feeling it, be careful, brother." Atti pats my shoulder as he passes.

"I will," I reply, watching the fireplace.

"Keep her safe and no sleeping with her. Not yet," Atti tells me.

I try to keep the grin from my face, "No promises. She is going to be my mate, after all."

"Mine, too." Atti says before he disappears.

Milton Keynes UK
Ingram Content Group UK Ltd.
UKHW041822171123
432777UK00005B/73/J